What Was Written

By Troy Harwood-Jones

2026

978-1-997984-03-0

www.harwoodjones.com

Cypress Hills

1870

Table of Contents

One

The man came out of the south on foot.

He had been walking since before the light came. The country here was open grassland, wide and pale, the hills rising in long quiet folds that gave nothing back but more sky. The Cypress Hills. He had heard the name before. They did not look like hills.

Battle Creek ran below him in its shallow cut. He had been following it north for two days, or three. The ground was softer near the water. His right boot had worn through at the heel and the earth came up through the gap with every step, warm and gritty, and he could feel the blister there had long since opened and gone past pain into something duller and more permanent.

The sun was up now and already hard on the back of his neck.

Sweat had dried to salt along his collar. His clerical collar, though it had gone grey with the days and one side of it had darkened with something that was not dust, something that had seeped and dried and seeped again from the bullet wound beneath his arm where the cloth stuck and pulled with every breath. He had stopped thinking about the wound. Nothing helped it. The best he could do was keep it from his attention the way you keep a frightened animal from a fire — with patience, with deliberate misdirection, one slow step at a time.

His right leg moved the way an argument moves.

Reluctantly.

By degrees.

After being asked more than once.

He asked it again.

It answered.

He kept his eyes on the line of the creek. The grass on either side of it was taller than elsewhere, greener, moving slowly in whatever passed for wind this morning. Somewhere in that grass a bird called once and did not call again. A hawk hung above the western ridge, impossibly still, the whole turning world beneath it of no apparent concern.

He walked.

The wound spoke when he breathed too deep. He had learned to breathe shallow, to keep his left arm close, to move from the hip in a way that did not ask the damaged side for anything. The body will negotiate, if you let it. He had learned that too, though he could not have said where.

Forty steps.

Fifty.

The creek bent east.

Across the water, inside the bend, lodges stood against the treeline. Cook fires burned low in the morning. A dog sat at the far bank and watched him pass and did not bark.

He kept walking north.

The path carved away west into a copse of birch. The ground rose.

He climbed it.

Dust filled his steps and his mouth.

He reached the crest.

There, below him, where the land opened into a rough flat between two low rises, the fort sat. A dozen buildings, maybe fewer. Rough log walls gone pale in the sun. A low timber boundary that suggested more than it enforced. Beyond the nearest structure, a scatter of canvas and horses, the faint grey rise of smoke.

He stood at the top of the rise and looked at it.

His vision swam once, briefly, like something passing under water.

He blinked. The fort steadied.

His body asked him to lie down.

He refused.

Step.

Step.

Step.

The descent off the rise was worse than the flat ground had been. His leg wanted to buckle on the downslope and he put his weight back and negotiated with it, quietly, the way you negotiate with something that has the power to end the conversation entirely. Not yet. The wound had begun seeping again. He could feel it. Warmth at his side, slow and insistent, and the cloth pulling differently now.

He did not look down.

He reached the flat and the ground levelled and he walked.

The fort resolved itself slowly as he came near. A gate, standing open, or what served as one. The buildings were rougher up close than they had appeared from the rise. Gaps in the log walls plugged with mud and straw. A window with no glass, a piece of sacking hung inside it, lifting and falling in the draft. The smell reached him — smoke, horses, the ferment of things left in the heat — and underneath all of it the smell of people, ordinary life, wood and grease and the stale warmth of habitation.

He had been braced a long time. It almost gave.

He did not give.

At the gate he straightened. The movement cost him. He did it anyway.

The street — what passed for one — was beaten earth between two facing rows of buildings. A woman outside the dry goods store. Another beside her. A man at a gate post somewhere to his left, a tool in his hand.

They were watching him.

He knew this the way you know weather is changing — not by looking at it, but by the stillness around it.

He walked toward the centre of the street.

His vision moved again at the edges, a slow brownish softening, as though the light had thickened. The buildings went slightly uncertain at their corners. He fixed his eyes on a dark doorway ahead and kept them there.

A boy stood in it.

Watching.

How far is the boy.

Twenty feet. Fifteen.

His leg asked its question.

He had no answer.

The ground came up and he was on one knee in the dirt. The pain arrived fully then for the first time.

His hand found his collar.

He held it there — between his fingers, facing out toward the watching faces — as though the cloth itself might speak for him.

The boy in the doorway had not moved.

The man looked at him.

"Get someone," he said.

His own voice came to him from far away, as though it had traveled the same distance his feet had.

The boy was gone.

The man put his other hand in the dirt and held himself there. The earth was warm against his palms. Around him the fort had resumed itself in small sounds — a horse somewhere, a door, the wind in the grass beyond the boundary moving through it as it had always moved through it, indifferently.

He had not died on the road.

He noted that.

Then the dark came.

Two

He woke once in the dark.

Hands were holding him upright. Someone was cutting at his boot with a knife. The pain in his foot arrived fully then and he made a sound he did not recognize as his own.

* * *

He woke to the taste of iron.

A tin cup against his mouth. Something warm and thick that he swallowed because his body required it.

"Again," the same voice said.

He did.

* * *

The days passed in pieces.

Light through the window.

The woman's hands changing the dressing beneath his arm.

A cup pressed into his hand each morning.

* * *

On the fourth morning the woman who had been tending him said he could sit up.

She was a narrow woman with iron-grey hair braided tight behind her head, brown skin and high cheekbones weathered smooth by years of wind and smoke. Small beaded earrings moved when she bent over the wound. Her hands moved with the certainty of someone accustomed to injury. She had been in the room each morning since he woke, changing the dressing beneath his arm and saying little beyond what the work required.

"Try," she said.

He did. The world tilted. Then steadied.

"That will do," she said.

A moment later the door opened and a larger man stepped in. Broad through the shoulders, beard gone mostly silver, the sort of face that had spent more time in wind than indoors. He carried a leather bag darkened along the lower seam with old water.

He set it on the end of the bed.

"Yours," he said. "We waited till you could see to it yourself."

The man on the bed looked at it.

"Thank you."

He drew it toward him and opened the buckle. His hands were steadier now. The woman had been feeding him horse blood for three days — warm in a tin cup each morning — and the trembling had gone out of his fingers.

The Bible lay on top.

He lifted it carefully.

The leather was worn pale at the corners and the spine had been glued twice. He opened the front board.

On the flyleaf a careful hand had written:

Elias Jonathan Wilson

John 1:5

He closed the book again and set it beside him.

"Good," the big man said.

The vial came next. Stoppered glass on a thin leather cord.

Then a small brass communion case — plate and cup nested together on velvet gone brown with age.

Last came the gun.

A Colt revolver. Navy pattern. The bluing worn thin where a thumb had turned the cylinder many times.

The big man studied it without surprise.

"Practical country," Elias said.

"It is," the man said. "Though most clergy I've known carry a testament and a flask. Not always in that order."

"I was told the country north of the line was unsettled."

"You were told correctly."

The man nodded toward the gun.

"The bishop in Rupert's Land outfit you with that as well?"

"No," Elias said. "That was my own arrangement."

The man watched him another moment.

"Solomon will want to hear that," he said.

"Abel Farwell," Mary said, nodding toward the man. "This is his post."

She set a cup beside the bed and moved to leave.

"And you?" Elias asked.

She stopped.

"Mary."

* * *

He read the Bible every day.

Partly devotion.

Partly necessity.

The margins were crowded in places and untouched in others. The psalms worked through in a small slanted hand. The gospels marked twice in different inks as though returned to years later. Romans circled and revisited.

Elias read slowly.

Not as a preacher reads.

When the door stood open he kept his posture easy with it.

A priest with a book.

* * *

His foot was another matter.

Mary had cut the boot from him on the second day. The blister he had felt on the road had been the least of it. The bone beneath the heel had shifted.

"It will knit," she said. Then: "It will knit wrong."

He believed her.

He had been walking on it wrong for days before reaching the fort.

The bullet wound was cleaner.

In and out beneath the left arm, high on the ribs. Missing anything that would have ended him outright.

The kind of wound that required explanation.

Or silence.

* * *

Evening light came through the sacking at the window.

He read the same line often.

The light shines in the darkness, and the darkness has not overcome it.

He read it again.

* * *

Mary came before anyone else in the mornings.

She checked the dressing beneath his ribs and then the foot. Her hands moved with quiet certainty.

She had not asked him anything.

On the sixth morning she set the tin cup on the table and stood looking out toward the creek.

"You hold that book like a man learning something," she said.

Elias looked at her.

"Most priests hold it like a man remembering."

She handed him the cup.

"Drink."

He did.

She watched him the way she watched the wound.

"The bishop of Rupert's Land," she said. "What is his name."

"Machray," Elias said. "Robert Machray."

She nodded.

"My father knew Anderson."

"The one before him."

"He was a serious man."

She took the cup and went out.

Elias lay back and stared at the ceiling.

* * *

Solomon came on the eighth day.

A narrow man. Pale eyes. Coat buttoned despite the heat.

He entered with Farwell.

They pulled chairs beside the bed with the ease of men accustomed to bedside conversations that were not always voluntary.

Farwell leaned back.

Solomon leaned forward.

"Feeling stronger," Farwell said.

"Some."

"We've been patient."

"You have."

Solomon said nothing.

"The bishop sent you," Farwell said.

"The bishop approved the mission," Elias said. "There's a difference. I came on my own initiative. The territory west of Rupert's Land has no ministry."

"And you volunteered," Solomon said.

"Yes."

"Why you?"

"I had no parish. No encumbrances."

Solomon watched him.

"You came through Fort Benton," Farwell said.

"I did."

"Fort Benton," Solomon said. "That's south."

"A trader out of Fort Garry gave me passage," Elias said. "I meant to stay a week. I stayed longer than was wise."

"Why?"

"There were men in Benton running whiskey north of the line," he said. "I thought it wise to understand the trade before coming here."

Farwell said nothing.

"And then you became afraid," Solomon said.

"Yes."

"Of what?"

"A man named Crews."

"That the one who shot you?"

"Yes."

"And where is he now?" Farwell asked.

"Dead."

"He caught me at a creek crossing south of here. I killed him."

He paused.

"In self-defence."

The room held the words.

"A priest," Solomon said, "who carries a gun and has killed a man."

"A man," Elias said, "who was ordained before he came to this country and has since learned what this country requires."

Farwell stood and picked up his hat.

"Well," he said. "A man followed you from Benton and you put him in the ground."

He turned the hat once.

"That tends to simplify things."

"Does it?"

"Means whatever trouble you brought with you, you brought the end of it too."

He studied Elias a moment.

"You have plans," he said, "beyond getting vertical?"

"Fort Whoop-Up."

"I'd heard they are in desperate need of God there."

"Long way to go on a bad foot."

"I've already taken enough of your kindness."

"Well, about that," Farwell began, "there are women here who haven't heard a word of scripture in two years, and at least one man I know of who'd like to make his confession before he dies. So if you're inclined to minister, you could work off the debt."

Elias considered him.

"I'd be glad to."

Farwell put on his hat.

"Well, then that's decided."

He moved toward the door. Turned.

"Reverend, this here is a trading post, not a parish. The men here work hard and drink what they like and don't generally want to be told about it." He paused. "Just so we understand each other."

"We do," Elias said.

Farwell went out.

* * *

Solomon remained.

His eyes had not moved.

"Fort Garry," he said.

"Yes."

"Your family there."

"My mother. And a sister."

Solomon stood. Buttoned his coat.

"A man ought to have people who know where he is."

He went out.

Elias picked up the Bible.

Lay still.

Three

He had been lying still long enough.

The foot was wrong and would remain wrong. Mary had said so and he believed her. Bone knits the way it is asked to knit when time and tools are lacking — not perfectly, but well enough for a man who intends to keep moving.

He intended to keep moving.

The clerical collar had been washed and pressed by someone who had not asked his permission. It sat slightly off-centre and he adjusted it once without improving it. He left it.

Fort Farwell was not much of a town. A trading post with ambitions it had not yet fulfilled — twelve buildings if a man counted generously, log construction mostly, the walls gone pale under the prairie sun, the chinking between them a mixture of mud and straw that had been repaired in some places and forgotten in others. A blacksmith shed, the dry goods store, Farwell's office which was also the trading post and whatever else the country required it to be. And the saloon, broader than the others, plank-fronted, the wood already beginning to warp with seasons it had not expected to endure. Smoke lifted from three chimneys in thin straight lines. The creek moved through the grass behind the buildings the way creeks always moved — quietly and without regard for the concerns of the people beside them.

People watched him as he passed. Not openly. The way people watch something that does not belong yet to the ordinary pattern of the place. A woman paused in the doorway of the store. A boy stared until someone behind him pulled him inside.

Elias walked. His foot negotiated the ground carefully, each step placed with the attention of a man who had learned that the body could betray him if he assumed too much of it.

Outside the saloon a Cree man lay in the dust, curled on his side with one arm beneath his head in the particular stillness of whiskey sleep.

Elias had seen that sleep before. In Benton a trader had stepped over a man lying the same way and said something about the cost of doing business. Elias had not answered him then.

He did not answer now.

He kept walking.

The Hawthorne house sat at the edge of the settlement where the ground sloped toward the creek. The place had been built quickly but kept alive with intention. The roof patched twice with sod that had since gone brown. A garden ran along the south wall, the soil worked but thin, something green attempting to become useful if the summer cooperated. Behind the house stood a chicken coop. No chickens.

He stepped up onto the porch and knocked.

The woman who opened the door studied him without speaking. The bones of her face suggested a younger beauty that life had used hard. Her hands rested against the door frame — working hands, the hands of someone who had kept a house standing without assistance.

"Mrs. Hawthorne," he said. "My name is Elias Wilson. Mr. Farwell asked me to come."

He saw it in the way her shoulders settled slightly, as though something long expected had finally arrived. She stepped back.

The room smelled of hay and sweat and the long patience of sickness. A single window admitted a column of light that illuminated dust and little else. A child stood behind the stove, watching. She did not come forward.

Anderson Hawthorne lay on a settle pushed against the far wall, a hay mattress beneath him and a blanket across his legs though the room was warm. The frame of the man suggested former strength. The flesh had left it slowly. His chest worked hard for each breath. He turned his head as Elias entered.

"Reverend," he said.

Elias pulled a chair near and sat.

"Mr. Hawthorne."

The man studied him. "You're young."

"Some."

Anderson coughed. The cough took him for several seconds before releasing him. When it finished there was blood at the corner of his mouth. He wiped it away with the back of his hand.

"How long?" Elias asked.

"Bad since Christmas," Anderson said. "Before that — some."

Bella Hawthorne remained standing near the stove. Her eyes moved between the two men but she said nothing.

"I want my rights," Anderson said. "Last rites."

Elias nodded once. "I'd like you to fight," he said.

Anderson blinked.

"Your wife," Elias said. "Your daughter."

The man followed Elias's gaze toward the child.

"She'll be seen to."

"You don't know that."

Anderson looked back at him. "A man knows when he's dying."

"A man knows when he's tired," Elias said. "That's not always the same thing."

"We don't know what's coming," Elias said. "What God has planned for us."

Anderson looked at him. Then he shook his head slightly.

"Don't tell me to live," he said. "Not when God's calling me. I shouldn't have to tell you that."

Another breath.

"Give me my rights."

Elias opened the Bible. His hands moved across the page and found nothing. He turned one page. Then another. He could feel the man watching his hands and he kept his eyes down as though the right passage were simply a matter of looking, as though he had not been a man with a gun in his bag longer than a man with an answer.

Anderson turned his head toward his wife.

"The book," he said.

Bella Hawthorne crossed to the shelf and brought back a small dark volume. She placed it in Elias's hands.

The Book of Common Prayer. A ribbon lay across the page. Elias opened it there and began to read.

I am the resurrection and the life, saith the Lord…

Anderson closed his eyes. The child did not move. Bella stood with her hands at her sides, her lips pressed together in a line that was neither prayer nor its absence.

Elias read until the room grew quiet.

Elias stepped down from the Hawthorne porch. Voices carried from the direction of Farwell's yard — not loud, the measured sound of men conducting business. He walked that way.

The wagon stood near the rail fence with its canvas rolled back. Two traders stood beside it with horses tied to the rail. Opposite them stood a Cree man holding the lead rope of a fourth horse — a good animal, strong through the shoulders, uneasy among strangers.

One of the traders lifted a crate from the wagon bed and set it in the dust. Wood, iron-banded, the lid already loose. Elias slowed. He had seen it plenty in Fort Benton. Robes. Horses. Sometimes rifles. Often whiskey. The trader pushed the lid back and glass caught the sun inside the box. The Cree man's eyes followed the movement.

Elias took another step forward.

A man turned. Saw the collar. The trader's hand stopped halfway into the crate. The yard fell quiet. Farwell looked up. The trader straightened slowly, the neck of a bottle visible now above the crate but not yet lifted free.

No one spoke. The men were no longer looking at the Cree man. They were looking at Elias.

Four

Elias stood on the broken porch of the Hawthornes' place and let out a long breath. The sky above sat huge, pale blue, and unconcerned.

The town had settled into the quiet of afternoon chores. A woman beating dust from a rug. The sound of a bucket striking the side of a well.

He walked slowly. The foot had stiffened again. It always did after sitting too long. He moved carefully until it remembered how to carry him.

He might say his goodbyes first. Farwell had been direct with him. Directness deserved the courtesy of reply.

The yard behind the trading house came into view as he approached. He heard the sounds of commerce before he saw them.

He slowed at the gate.

Five men. Trading. Or were until they saw the collar arriving.

The trader stood by a wagon with the lid of a crate open beside him. Across from him a man held the lead rope of a horse.

Assiniboine.

The animal stood quiet. Good shoulders. Clean legs. Dark bay. It shifted its weight once and settled again.

The buyer stood opposite the man with the patient expression of someone explaining arithmetic to a child.

The trader pushed the lid back and glass caught the sun inside the box. The smell reached him a moment later. Not whiskey. Something underneath it, sharper.

The horse was worth more than the crate. The men at the fence were Farwell's. In case the arithmetic went badly.

The trade remained stilled.

All eyes on him.

Elias stepped into the yard.

He moved past the wagon and the open crate and stopped at the fence rail beside the animal.

The horse turned its head.

One dark eye regarded him with the indifferent patience of a creature accustomed to men circling it and deciding its future.

He ran his hand along the neck. The muscle under the hide shifted once beneath his palm. Sound animal.

He stepped back.

After a breath, the business continued.

"Pastern's soft," the buyer said.

He said it to Farwell.

Not to the man.

Farwell turned his hat once in his hands.

"Animal walked here under its own direction this morning."

"I'm thinking about what it walks like two winters from now."

Elias wasn't watching the trade. He was watching the man.

He had not spoken.

His eyes had gone past the buyer now, past the yard, toward the shallow line of the creek cutting through the grass beyond the fence.

His body was still. Too still.

The eyes of a man who did not warn.

A man still bargaining keeps his eyes on the thing he is bargaining over.

The buyer went on talking.

Farwell listened.

The two men at the rail did not move.

Then the man said something in Assiniboine. Low. A single sentence. Elias caught the word for horse and thought he caught the word for worth, though he was not certain of either.

Flatly spoken.

Farwell's expression did not change.

The buyer ignored it.

The horse flicked an ear.

Elias felt the moment turn. He had felt it before. At crossings and in the long grass back east near Fort Garry and in rooms where a language was being ignored by a man who could have understood it if he had wanted to. The laugh was always the same. The careless kind. The kind that did not hear itself.

The buyer said something else.

The man spoke again, shorter this time.

The buyer laughed.

Not loudly.

Carelessly.

The man's hand shifted on the rope.

Elias was already moving.

He did not decide to. His feet had made the decision and his body had followed and the thought arrived only after he had placed himself between the two men with his hand on the horse's neck.

"Fourteen hands," he said.

"Clean legs. Teeth put him at six, maybe seven."

The yard went quiet.

"You won't find another like him this side of the Qu'Appelle for what's in that crate."

The buyer looked at him.

"I didn't ask you."

"No," Elias said.

He kept his eyes on the horse.

"You didn't."

The buyer looked at Farwell.

Farwell said nothing.

One of the men at the rail shifted his weight slightly, the movement small but visible.

The buyer considered the horse again. Considered Elias. Considered the yard.

"Fine," he said.

The man handed over the rope.

The trader slid the crate across.

The man lifted it without looking inside and walked out through the gate.

The buyer led the horse away.

The yard resumed its breathing.

Farwell remained where he stood. Elias stepped back. His foot complained.

Farwell watched him with the particular stillness of a man who has just finished counting something.

"You've looked at many horses, Reverend."

"Some."

"And you've heard Assiniboine spoken."

"Some."

"And you saw what was coming before any man in this yard did."

Elias said nothing.

Farwell turned his hat in his hands.

"You did not say a word about the whiskey."

"I did not come into the yard for the whiskey."

Farwell looked at him the way a man looks at a tool he did not know he needed and has since picked up and weighed.

"You carry a revolver, Reverend?"

Elias opened one side of his jacket. The Colt's worn handle stuck out from the vest pocket.

Farwell looked at it. Looked at the collar. Looked at Elias.

He set the hat on his head.

"I have a small matter needs doing," he said.

He turned toward the street.

"You may be the man for it."

Five

Farwell did not explain the matter in the yard.

He put on his hat and walked toward the street and Elias followed because the alternative was to stand in the yard alone and that would have required a reason.

His foot complained with each step. He kept pace.

The saloon was the broadest building in the settlement and also the most honest about what it was. Plank floor worn smooth at the threshold and rough everywhere else. Daylight coming through the warped boards in thin lines that shifted when the wind moved. The smell of whiskey and tobacco and wet wool and underneath all of it the older smell of wood that had been asked to hold everything and had complied without complaint. Two men sat near the window with glasses in front of them. A third leaned against the far wall studying a hand of cards with more attention than they merited.

Farwell sat where he could see the door.

A girl appeared before Elias had taken three steps inside. She set a glass on the nearest table and poured without asking. He looked at the glass. Then at her back as she moved away.

He sat down.

Farwell came over carrying his own glass and pulled out a chair. He sat with the ease of a man in a room he had arranged to his satisfaction.

"Foot giving you trouble."

"Some."

"Mary said it would."

Elias said nothing.

Farwell turned his glass once on the table.

"You handled yourself well in the yard."

"It wasn't much."

"No. But it was the right thing at the right moment."

"Where'd you pick up the Assiniboine."

The question arrived the way Farwell's questions always arrived. Conversational. Unhurried. With the weight of something more deliberate behind it.

"Around Garry," Elias said. "Before I went south."

"Garry's a long way from here."

"It is."

"And then Benton."

"Yes."

"You were there a while."

"Longer than I intended."

"Men go to Benton to do business," Farwell said.

Elias looked at the whiskey in his glass. A thin line of light crossed it from one of the gaps in the wall.

"I knew someone going that way who didn't mind the company," he said. "As I said."

Farwell nodded. Said nothing. He had the patience of a man who had conducted enough transactions to know that silence was its own kind of pressure.

"The territory west of Rupert's Land had no ministry," Elias said. "I meant to come straight up from Fort Garry. Benton was a detour."

"Long detour."

"It was."

"Men in Benton running whiskey north," Farwell said. "You told Solomon you wanted to understand the trade before coming here."

"I did."

"Learn what you needed to learn?"

"Enough."

Farwell drank. His eyes had not moved from Elias.

The girl moved past them carrying a bottle. She stopped at the table near the window and poured for the two men there. One of them said something low and she answered it without laughing. She went back behind the bar.

Outside, a horse moved against a rail. The wind pressed briefly at the warped boards and released them.

"You were fixing to leave," Farwell said.

"Whoop-Up," Elias said.

"Whoop-Up." Farwell set his glass down. "Long way to go to preach to men who'll shoot at you for the interruption."

"Ministry goes where it's needed."

"I expect it does."

Farwell turned his hat in his hands, which he had set on the table. He was not wearing it. He had set it there the way some men set a tool they intend to pick up again shortly.

"I have a small problem."

Elias waited.

"One of the girls hasn't come in. Two nights." He said it the way he might mention a horse that had wandered. "She pours a good drink and keeps the place from getting quiet. Customers notice when a girl stops coming in."

The serving girl had gone still behind the bar. Not obviously. Just still.

"What do you know?" Elias asked.

"She was seen heading south two evenings back. Before dark."

Farwell paused.

"Toward Little Soldier's camp."

Elias knew the name. An Assiniboine camp in the creek bend south of the settlement. Lodges on the far bank, inside the trees. They came and went with the trade.

"She go on her own?"

"Far as anyone saw."

"Then she may want to be there."

"She may." Farwell turned the hat once more. "She's Métis. Her mother's people have a connection to that camp."

Elias looked at him.

"Men from this post going down there after her would cause a different kind of trouble than the kind I need. Little Soldier's people don't answer to the fort. The whiskey's already made things tender between us." He said it the way a man explains the weather. Something real and unmovable and not his fault. "Misunderstandings down there tend to settle in ways that are difficult to undo."

The two men near the window had begun talking about something else. The man with the cards laid them down and looked at them without pleasure.

Farwell looked at the collar.

"A man wearing that," he said, "might walk in there easier."

He did not rush it.

"Talk to her. See if she intends to come back."

Not bring her back.

Elias understood the distinction.

His foot throbbed beneath the table.

He drank the whiskey.

Set the glass down.

"Her name," he said.

"Nora. Dark hair. She speaks English and Michif."

"The camp."

"South of the fort. Cross the creek and follow the near bank into the bend. You'll smell the fires before you see it."

The girl behind the bar began moving again. Whatever she had been listening for, she had heard it or decided she wouldn't.

Farwell watched him with the particular attention of a man who has just placed something on a scale.

"If she walks back in with you," he said, "we'll call the matter between us settled."

Outside, the afternoon had gone long and yellow. Shadows of the buildings lay across the beaten ground in dark bands. Horses at the rail stood with their heads down in the particular patience of animals that had learned to outlast whatever men were deciding about them.

He walked toward the creek.

He was walking out with a task he had not asked for and a conversation he had not won. Farwell had not raised his voice. He had not made a threat. He had simply kept talking.

The road north was still open. Whoop-Up was still two days' ride.

He would go to the camp.

Talk to the girl.

Come back.

And then he would leave.

He told himself that.

Six

The smell reached him before the camp did.

Woodsmoke. Hide. The fat smell of meat over fire. He followed the trail where it bent around a stand of willows and the camp opened ahead of him across a rough flat in the creek bottom — lodges in a loose circle, most of them facing the same direction, east, toward the morning. A few of the hides had been patched with canvas, pale squares against the darkened skins, the repairs careful but visible. Horses picketed beyond the nearest edge. Not many for the size of the camp. A frame of poles with a hide stretched pale across it. Meat drying on a rack, dark strips in the wind. Not much of it.

He slowed without deciding to.

Dogs came out from between the lodges at a low angle. Three of them. The first circled left. The second and third stopped ten feet away and considered him. Not barking. Deciding.

A child called out from somewhere. Sharp. Once.

The dogs sat.

He walked forward.

The camp continued its business. A woman tending a fire. A man crouched over a saddle laid flat across a log, his hands working a strap. A younger man near the far edge sat with his back against a lodge, a dark bay horse picketed behind him. He did not look up. Two older men seated to the south with something between their hands that Elias could not make out. No one looked at him directly. The motion of the place did not stop or hurry. It simply attended to him sideways, the way a horse attends to something it has not yet decided about. There were more lodges than people. He noticed that the way you notice a table set for more than have arrived.

He came to the edge of the lodges and stopped.

A woman was scraping a hide on a frame beside the nearest one. Her back was to him. The knife moved in long strokes.

He said the name in Assiniboine. The sounds went wrong as he made them. He knew it before she answered. She did not answer. He said it again, adjusting what he could. She kept working.

The knife continued.

A man came from behind the next lodge. Younger than Elias. Compact, unhurried, dressed in a mixture of cloth and hide. He said something in Assiniboine.

Elias understood the word for *why* and thought he understood the word for *here*.

He answered in what Assiniboine he had. He had come to speak to Little Soldier. He was from Fort Farwell. He was a priest.

The young man listened without expression. Then said something shorter. The word Elias caught was the word for *enough*.

The man looked at him. Said nothing. Turned and walked between the lodges.

Elias followed.

* * *

He was seated near a small fire outside a lodge, working a length of leather with a piece of bone. Perhaps fifty. The shirt he wore was fringed hide gone soft with years, the shoulders crossed with beadwork in blue and white — a careful pattern, the kind that takes winter evenings and belongs to a man his people have decided is worth the work. Two long braids. Trade beads worn close at the throat. His hands moved without hurry. His face had the quality of ground that has been under weather long enough to stop reacting to it.

He did not look up when they arrived.

The younger man spoke quietly. Little Soldier listened. He set the bone tool down and turned the leather once in his hands, studying it.

Then he looked at Elias.

Elias greeted him in Assiniboine. He could hear the words go wrong as he spoke them.

Little Soldier heard it too. He answered at length and Elias caught one word in four.

He said as much.

Little Soldier looked at him. Then looked toward the lodges and said something Elias didn't catch.

A Métis man came out from between two lodges and crossed toward them. Middle-aged, dark-complexioned, a coat that had weathered more than it had been tailored. He spoke with Little Soldier in Assiniboine for a moment and then turned to Elias.

"He asks why you have come," the interpreter said.

"I have come about a woman. Nora. From the fort."

The interpreter translated.

Little Soldier did not respond.

The silence held. Near the hide frame the woman had not resumed her work. The older men to the south were still. People moved at the edges of his vision but nothing came closer and nothing departed.

Little Soldier spoke.

"He asks where you learned Assiniboine," the interpreter said.

"Along the trade routes. Around Garry."

Translation. A pause. Another question.

"He asks why a priest walks alone."

"I have business north of the creek."

Translation. Little Soldier received this without expression. He looked at the fire between them and then at Elias.

"He asks why a priest comes from a whiskey fort."

"I was injured on the road. The fort had medicine."

Translation. A longer silence. A child appeared from somewhere behind the lodges and stood a short distance off, watching Elias with the unguarded attention that the adults had declined to give him. Three years old. Maybe four. A piece of dried meat in her small hand. She did not come closer and did not look away.

No one called her back.

Little Soldier spoke again. Shorter this time.

The interpreter looked at the fire before he translated. "He says there is a name for men who travel to whiskey forts to learn the country. That name is not priest."

Elias held still.

"What does your God say," the interpreter continued, "about a man who is not what he appears to be."

The question arrived in him the way cold water arrives — all at once and everywhere.

He considered it.

"That such men are common," he said. "And that God is patient."

The interpreter translated. Little Soldier studied him. The silence was not hostile. It was the silence of a man measuring something against a standard the other person could not see.

Then he spoke briefly to the younger man who had brought Elias there.

Food arrived. Pemmican. A piece of bannock. A woman set it in front of Elias on a piece of bark without being asked or at least without Elias seeing anyone ask. He ate. Conversation moved around him in Assiniboine. The older men spoke occasionally. Little Soldier answered. No one addressed Elias.

The child had drifted two feet closer and was still watching him. He met her eyes. She did not look away.

* * *

When the food was finished Little Soldier looked at him. He spoke to the interpreter.

"He says the woman came here two nights ago," the interpreter said. "She came on her own."

Elias waited.

"She hid money. Her partner found it. He beat her."

He said this without emphasis. The way you say the creek is high.

"She came to her mother's people here. Métis. Not Assiniboine." A pause. "Her partner followed."

"She's free to come back," Elias said.

Translation. Little Soldier's response was longer.

"He says the man does not agree with that."

"Then Nora and I can leave before the man has an opinion about it."

The interpreter translated this carefully. Little Soldier listened. Then spoke.

"He says the man is not Assiniboine." The interpreter paused. "He rides from Fort Solomon."

The afternoon light lay long across the camp. Somewhere beyond the lodges a horse moved against its picket.

"He says this is not an Assiniboine matter," the interpreter continued. "The woman is not Assiniboine. The man is not Assiniboine. But it has become a camp matter."

Another pause.

"He sent men to speak to the man."

"What did he say."

"He laughed." The interpreter's face was still. "He said Little Soldier has no authority over a white man and his woman."

People had drifted within earshot in the way the camp had been doing since Elias arrived — without appearing to move toward anything, attending to work that happened to have migrated nearer. A man mending harness fifteen feet off. The woman from the hide frame now carrying water somewhere behind him. The child with the dried meat had sat down in the dirt at the edge of it and watched with the patience of someone not yet old enough to pretend otherwise.

Little Soldier spoke.

"He says you came from Farwell," the interpreter said. "The man came from Solomon." A breath. "You are a priest." Another. "A priest speaks when something is wrong."

He did not frame it as a request. He said it and let it stand.

Elias looked at the interpreter. "Where is he?"

The interpreter spoke to Little Soldier. Little Soldier gestured toward the north edge of the camp. A lodge standing slightly apart, its door flap drawn.

"He is there," the interpreter said.

"He has been drinking since before midday."

This last he offered himself, without translation. His eyes went back to the fire.

Little Soldier picked up the bone tool and the length of leather. His hands found the place they had left off. He did not look up.

He was finished.

Not with the camp. With Elias.

The weight had passed and he had set it down and returned to his work, and that was the whole of what his face said.

Elias stood.

His foot said what it always said.

He let it.

He walked north through the camp.

The dogs watched him pass.

The child with the dried meat watched him go, still chewing, her eyes following him all the way to the edge of the lodges.

The hide frame stood empty now. The woman was gone.

The lodge was at the far end, set apart a little from the others, a thing the camp had been organizing itself around without naming. The door flap was down.

From inside, a man's voice. Low, careless, English.

Then a woman's voice. Very quiet. Then nothing.

He reminded himself that he was a priest.

That was worth something.

He hoped.

He loosened his coat. Not for the weather.

He lifted it and went in.

Seven

The man was sitting against the near wall with a knife in one hand and a piece of dried meat in the other. He looked up when Elias entered.

The fire had burned to coals. What light came through the door flap lay in a strip across the dirt floor and faded before it reached the walls. The smell was whiskey and grease and the particular close heat of a space sealed too long against the weather.

Nora sat in the far corner with her back against the hide wall, her knees drawn up. She had positioned herself there the way a person positions themselves in a room where something may come from any direction.

Her face. The bruising had gone yellow and purple at the edges. Three days old. Maybe four. Her left eye was swollen at the corner. She did not look at Elias. She was watching Jacob.

Jacob was looking at the collar.

He was a thick man gone soft through the middle, the kind of body that had once done hard work and had since found other arrangements. Dark stubble on a broad jaw. His eyes moved from the collar to Elias's face and back. He took another bite of the meat and chewed slowly.

"You're the priest," he said.

"Yes."

"From Farwell's."

"I came from the fort."

Jacob turned the knife in his hand. The way a man turns something he is deciding whether to put down.

"The hell do you want."

Elias stepped inside. He moved to where the coals gave what light there was and stopped. He did not look at Nora.

"I came to speak with the woman," he said. "Farwell sent me."

Something moved across Jacob's face. Not fear. Something closer to recognition.

"That right," he said.

"She works at the saloon. Her absence is noticed."

"Her absence." Jacob said the words flat, as though testing their weight. "She's right here. I notice her just fine." He glanced toward the corner and back. "Sit down, Reverend. You're making the place feel small."

Elias did not sit.

"The woman is free to go if she wants," he said. "That's all I came to say."

Jacob looked at him. The whiskey was in his eyes — not the vacancy of a man gone under, but the bright flat quality of a man still in the middle of it. Moving. Deciding.

"Is she," he said.

"I believe so."

"You believe a lot." He set the meat down but kept the knife. "Man of faith and all." He looked past Elias toward the door flap, then back. "What I believe is she's mine. And she took something of mine. And here she sits." The knife lifted slightly toward the corner. "Right there."

Elias said nothing.

The coals shifted and settled.

"I'm not here to cause trouble for you," Elias said.

"That's good to hear."

"But I'd like to understand your situation. If you want to tell it."

Jacob studied him. Something shifted in his expression that wasn't quite suspicion and wasn't quite surprise. He hadn't expected that.

"Why."

"A man's situation deserves to be understood."

Jacob looked at the knife in his hand. He looked at the collar. He seemed to be working through something the whiskey had made slow.

"Solomon had me beat," he said. "You know that?"

"I didn't."

"One of his men. In front of men I work with." His jaw tightened. "Over a misunderstanding. And then he says he's thinking about letting me go." He looked at Nora for a moment. "Her money could've settled things. What I owed. She hid it from me."

Nora said nothing. She was still watching Jacob. Reading him the way she had been reading him since before Elias arrived.

"And your job," Elias said. "At Solomon's. Is it still yours?"

"He said he'd think on it."

"He hasn't given you an answer."

"No."

Elias looked at the coals.

Then Jacob stood.

He came up from the blanket in stages, the way a man moves when his body has been still too long and the whiskey has settled into his joints. The knife stayed in his hand. Standing, he filled the space between the fire and the door flap. He was not a small man.

He was not steady.

"Now you heard it."

He took one step.

Elias did not move.

He measured the distance without deciding to. Six feet. Maybe five. His coat hung open at his right side. If the man took two more steps the coat would come open further and the revolver would come out. And if the revolver came out the thing would be decided.

The knowledge arrived in him quietly, the way cold arrives — before you've named it.

He had not come here for this.

"You're going to leave," Jacob said. "And she stays."

"That doesn't help you," Elias said.

His own voice reached him as though from a short distance away.

"She works, she earns. She stays here, you drink your way through what's left and Solomon makes up his mind without you." He let that sit. "You said he hasn't given you an answer yet. That means the door is still open."

Jacob stopped. The knife turned once in his hand.

"Speak plain."

"You go to him. You tell him you want your position back. You tell him you'll repay what you owe — with interest. That you're a useful man and you intend to prove it." Elias kept his voice even. "That's what a man does when a door is still open. That's what Solomon understands."

"He don't work that way."

Elias could smell the whiskey on him now. Sweet and close.

If he turned his back on this man the knife might follow him out of the lodge.

And if the coat opened and the revolver came out the matter would belong to the gun.

He thought briefly of walking back into Farwell's yard and saying the collar had not been enough.

The thought did not travel far.

"Farwell told me otherwise," Elias said, straightening. "Said Solomon told him himself. Said he respects a man who comes back and offers terms. Said you walking away without a word was the thing that disappointed him."

The name landed the way Elias had needed it to. Jacob went still.

"You're lying," he said.

"I have no reason to."

"I don't know you. I don't know what your reasons are."

"No."

A long silence. The coals breathed.

"Swear it," Jacob said.

"I swear it."

"Swear to God."

The lodge was very quiet. The smell of the whiskey and the old grease and the closed heat.

"I swear it," Elias said.

Jacob looked at him. The flat bright eyes moving over his face, looking for the place where the lie was kept. Finding nothing he could name.

He looked at Nora.

"Get back to work," he said. "You cheat me again—"

He didn't finish it.

Nora did not move immediately. She looked at Jacob. Then at the knife still loose in his hand. Then at the ground between herself and the door.

Then she stood.

She did not look at Elias. She went past him and lifted the flap and was outside.

Elias followed.

* * *

The air came at him all at once. Wide and cold and full of distance. The camp went on with its evening. Smoke from the fires. Somewhere a dog had started and then gone quiet.

He was three steps from the lodge before he realized his right hand had been inside his coat the entire time.

He did not remember putting it there.

He let it fall.

Nora had stopped a short distance away. Standing with her back to the lodge, waiting.

He came up beside her and they walked. Past the horses on their pickets. Past the woman at the hide frame who did not look up. The dogs watched them pass. They reached the trail south and followed it into the grass.

The camp fell behind them.

After a while Nora said:

"You lied to him."

"Some."

She walked. The grass moved along both sides of the trail in the last of the light.

"He'll go to Solomon now."

"Maybe."

"Moses doesn't forgive."

Elias said nothing.

He was thinking about six feet and two steps and the thing that had settled in him beside those coals. The arithmetic of it. The way it had arrived without asking permission.

He was not thinking about Jacob walking toward the fort in the dark.

He put that away.

"You want to go back," he said.

"Yes."

"Then let's go."

They walked.

The trail ran south through the grass and the grass moved as it had always moved, without concern for the people passing through it or the things they were not thinking about.

Eight

The night had brought rain. The street was soft underfoot and the sky had gone the particular white of a morning that intends to stay grey.

Farwell looked at Nora the way a man looks at goods returned in poorer condition than they had left.

Not cruelly.

Practically.

His eyes moved across her face — the bruising gone yellow at the edges, the eye still swollen where it had closed once and reopened badly — and he noted what he saw the way he noted the condition of anything that passed through his hands.

"Jacob Burr," he said.

It was not a question.

Nora said nothing.

Farwell turned his hat once in his hands.

"What are you doing getting mixed up with Jacob Burr for."

He studied her with a kind of puzzled disappointment.

"Thought you were smart."

Nora looked past his shoulder toward the bar. Her hands were folded in front of her. Very still. The stillness of a person who has learned that motion draws notice and notice rarely helps.

Farwell watched her another moment.

Then he nodded toward the room behind him.

"Get the reverend a drink."

She went.

Farwell looked at Elias.

"Come along."

* * *

Farwell's office was a small room partitioned off from the saloon floor with rough planks that stopped the eye better than the sound. Voices came through in softened shapes. A laugh. The scrape of a chair. Glass set down harder than needed.

A desk stood by the window. Ledger open. Ink bottle beside it. Afternoon light came through the wavering glass and lay across the pages in a broad pale band. The column nearest him showed two entries in Farwell's hand: *whiskey — bar stock* and below it *trade spirits — post.* The second figure was larger.

Farwell sat and set his hat on the desk. He did it with the ease of a man occupying ground he had paid for twice — once with money and once with the continuing effort required to keep it his.

"You did well," he said.

"I spoke to a man."

"You spoke the right way."

Farwell leaned back slightly in the chair.

"That is not the same thing."

Nora came in with two glasses and set them on the desk. She did not look at Elias. Did not look at Farwell. She left at once.

Farwell watched her go, then picked up his whiskey.

"A place like this," he said, "doesn't often see a man of your sort."

Elias looked at the glass.

"There are things a collar does that a gun won't."

Farwell turned the whiskey once between his fingers.

"Rooms it opens. Tempers it cools. Business it lets proceed without anyone deciding afterward they were insulted."

Elias said nothing.

Farwell drank.

"This settlement has gone without a service two years now. Maybe more. Long enough for people to begin thinking they can do without one."

"I am only passing through."

"So is everybody."

Farwell smiled faintly and set the glass down.

"I could use a man like you here."

"I appreciate the kindness."

"It is not kindness."

"No."

Farwell nodded as though pleased to have that much settled.

"I have reason to keep moving," Elias said.

"North."

"Yes."

"Whoop-Up."

Elias did not answer.

Farwell regarded him a moment.

"Long way on that foot."

"It will carry me."

"Somewhere."

The sounds outside the room rose and fell. A door opened. Closed. Someone called for another bottle.

Farwell tapped one finger lightly against the desk beside the ledger.

"I could outfit you."

Elias looked at him.

"A horse. Provisions. Maybe a better start than limping off like a man trying not to lose an argument with his own body."

"You said the debt was settled."

"It is."

Farwell lifted the glass again.

"This would be a different arrangement."

Elias let that sit.

Farwell drank and went on.

"I am not certain I have a horse to spare."

"You have horses."

"I have horses I rely on. A man has to be careful what he parts with out here. Some things are easier lent than replaced."

Elias looked toward the window. The light had begun its turn toward evening.

"One service," Farwell said.

Elias did not move.

"Sunday," Farwell continued. "The people here could use it. Solomon's people too, perhaps, though whether they'd admit it is another matter."

At that Elias looked back at him.

Farwell saw it.

"Even Little Soldier's camp comes near the forts some Sundays."

He lifted one shoulder.

"Trade day tends to gather souls whether they came for salvation or not."

Elias said nothing.

The shape of the thing was plain now.

Farwell had been building toward it since the yard. Since before that, perhaps. A room offered. A debt settled and then reopened in another form. An obligation small enough to accept without admitting what accepting it meant.

The sort of arrangement a man walked into thinking his could leave.

"One service," Elias said.

Farwell nodded once.

"And I'll see what can be done about a horse."

* * *

Farwell arranged a room for him above the saloon.

"Just until Sunday," he said.

The room was small and low-ceilinged.

It was above the saloon, which meant it was also made of the saloon. The sounds came up through the floorboards at intervals — a chair dragged back, a voice lifted too high, the blunt knock of a bottle set down on wood.

A rope bed stood against one wall. A basin on a washstand. One chair. A window looking out over the back of the settlement toward the creek. The glass was old and uneven. The world beyond it seemed to shift slightly even when nothing moved.

The light was failing.

Elias sat on the edge of the bed and pulled off his boot.

His foot objected in several places at once.

He looked at it a moment, then set the boot down on the floor and lay back without undressing further.

Below him the saloon worked through its evening in the ordinary sounds of men spending what they had earned or stolen or convinced themselves they were owed.

Farwell had given him a room.

A room had weight.

A room was the sort of thing a man accepted when he was not ready to admit he had stopped travelling.

He reached for his bag.

The Bible came out in his hands the way it always did — worn pale at the corners, spine repaired, pages softened by years of use not all of them devotional.

He held it a moment without opening it.

Three days.

Three days until Sunday.

Three more days in Fort Farwell.

He had been in this country weeks and had accomplished little beyond continuing to live. He had come north with a purpose clear enough to himself at the time and that purpose had since been delayed by injury, weather, necessity, other men's needs, and now the practical designs of Abel Farwell.

Below him someone laughed. Another voice answered. A moment later glass broke and no one seemed especially concerned.

He opened the Bible.

Read in the half-light.

Below him the saloon went on without reference to Scripture.

* * *

He did not need to go back to the Hawthorne place.

He went anyway.

The afternoon had cooled by then. Cloud was coming in from the northwest in the slow certain manner that promised rain by morning. He walked along the softer edges of the settlement where the ground gave more kindly beneath his bad foot.

He had no reason he wished to name.

A dying man was a dying man. He had read what was required. Said what had been asked of him. There was no office of the church that demanded return.

He knocked.

Bella Hawthorne opened the door.

She did not look surprised to see him, which suggested that surprise had not been of much use to her for some time. She stepped aside and let him in.

The room had changed.

Not in its objects. In its arrangement of silence.

The quiet now was the quiet of a place beginning to organize itself around an absence not yet complete.

Anderson lay where Elias had left him. The blanket had been pulled higher on his chest. His face had thinned further in the few hours since. Or perhaps the light was less forgiving. His breathing had changed. Each breath arrived with a pause after it, as though the body had to be convinced each time to continue.

The girl stood near the stove again.

Watching.

Bella moved to the settle and adjusted the blanket with careful hands. Then she rested one hand against her husband's shoulder until a catch in his breathing passed.

Elias watched her hands.

Working hands.

The hands of a woman who had been keeping things from falling apart for longer than anyone had thought to thank her.

He drew the chair closer and sat.

After a time Anderson opened his eyes.

The effort showed.

He looked at Elias with the careful concentration of a man for whom concentration had become expensive.

Neither man spoke.

Bella shifted slightly and looked at Elias then.

Not for comfort.

For confirmation.

He understood the question, though she had not asked it.

He inclined his head once.

Nothing more.

Bella looked at him a moment longer, then back at her husband.

The girl came out from behind the stove. She crossed the room slowly and stopped near Elias, close enough that he could have touched her shoulder had there been any reason to. She looked at her father. Then at Elias.

Children that age look at things the way they look at weather — not expecting an answer, only confirming that someone else sees what they see.

He stayed.

The room darkened by degrees.

At one point Bella lit the lamp. At another Anderson slept or passed into some shallower state that resembled sleep enough not to disturb. The girl sat on the floor by the stove with her hands in her lap. No one suggested she should go elsewhere.

Twice Bella moved to do some small necessary thing — pour water, fold a cloth, place the chair more squarely near the settle — and each time Elias rose to help and found she had done it already.

She did not hurry.

She did not collapse into usefulness either.

She simply continued.

Once, when she turned from the table, the failing light caught her face fully and Elias saw more clearly what hardship had not yet taken from it. The structure of it. The dark hair drawn back without thought for appearance. A face that would have been called handsome anywhere and perhaps had been, though not often lately.

He looked away.

Anderson woke again near dusk.

His eyes found Bella first. Then the girl. Then Elias.

His mouth moved.

Bella bent near to hear him.

"Cold," he whispered.

She drew the blanket higher and placed her hand against his cheek. Whether to warm him or steady herself Elias could not tell.

Anderson turned his head slightly toward Elias.

"Tomorrow," he said.

The word was little more than breath.

Elias leaned closer.

"Yes," he said.

Anderson closed his eyes again.

Whether he had heard, Elias did not know.

When at last Elias stood to leave, Bella rose with him and followed him to the door.

The girl remained where she was.

At the threshold Bella opened the door and stood with one hand on it. Beyond the porch the settlement had gone muted under the coming weather. The creek moved behind the buildings in its usual manner, indifferent and continuous.

For a moment Bella looked out into the middle distance as though she had already begun considering something she would rather not consider yet.

"Tomorrow," she said.

Still not quite a question.

"I'll come tomorrow," Elias said.

Bella nodded once.

Her eyes came back to him then. Not soft. Not grateful. Merely steady.

As though some conclusion had been postponed rather than reached.

Then she closed the door.

* * *

He was halfway back to the saloon when one of Farwell's men found him.

"Mr. Farwell wants you."

Not a question.

Elias followed him past the saloon and along the side street to the house he knew. The trading post attached at the east wall, the lamp burning in the front room. He had lain in a bed in that house for eight days. He had watched the ceiling of it in the dark and listened to the creek.

Farwell opened the door himself.

The front room was warm. A fire low in the grate. The table where Mary had set his meals had a lamp on it now, and a pot of tea, and two cups already poured. Nora sat in the chair near the window with her own cup held in both hands. She looked at the fire when Elias came in. She did not look at him.

Farwell gestured to the table.

Elias sat.

Farwell remained standing.

"Jacob Burr is dead," he said.

The fire shifted and settled.

"Found at the creek crossing. Knife. Twice. Face down in the water."

Nora's cup did not move.

"Creek's a place a man would be found. A place a body might be if it was meant to be found."

Farwell looked at Elias with the expression of a man who has already completed the accounting and is now simply reading it aloud.

"She told me what happened in the lodge," he said. "What you said to him."

Elias looked at the tea he had not touched.

"Did Solomon tell you he respected a man who came back and offered terms."

"No."

"Did anyone."

"No."

The lamp held its flame between them.

Farwell turned toward the window. Beyond it the settlement had gone dark and quiet under the clouds that had been coming since afternoon. When he spoke again his voice had not risen.

"Moses Solomon just put a dead man at the creek crossing between himself and me."

A pause.

"And you gave him the occasion for it."

Nora set her cup down on the sill. Carefully. The small sound of it was the only sound in the room for a moment.

She was not crying. She was not composed in the way of someone managing tears. She was simply present, in the way of a woman who has endured harder rooms than this one and knows that enduring is not the same as being unharmed.

She still did not look at Elias.

Farwell turned back from the window.

"I need to know," he said, "whether there is anything else you have decided on my behalf that I should know about."

Nine

Farwell did not sit.

He stood at the window with his back to the room. The lamp on the table threw his shadow long against the wall behind him. Outside, the settlement had gone quiet. Only the creek, somewhere behind the buildings, doing what it always did.

Nora was gone.

Elias had not heard her leave.

"He went to Solomon," Farwell said.

Not a question.

"Straight from the camp."

Elias said nothing.

"Drunk," Farwell said. "Walked into Solomon's yard and told him he wanted his position back. In front of Solomon's men."

The lamp held steady. No draft in the room.

"And Solomon put him at the crossing."

Farwell turned from the window then. His face had the quality of a man who had already done the arithmetic and was waiting to see whether anyone else in the room had kept up.

"Head in the creek. That's the line between us."

Elias looked at the table.

"That's not where a man ends up by accident," Farwell said.

"No."

"That's where a man ends up so that other men will find him and understand something."

He moved to the chair but did not sit. He rested one hand on the back of it.

"You sent him there."

Elias met his eyes.

"I told him the door was still open."

"Was it."

Elias held the look a moment.

"I believed it might be."

Farwell looked at him steadily.

"You believed it."

"I was trying to get the woman out."

"You got her out," Farwell said. "And you got him killed."

Elias drew breath to answer—

stopped.

The wrong answer had come first.

He let it go.

Farwell watched that happen.

The words remained where they had been placed.

Elias said nothing.

Farwell pulled the chair back and sat. He set his hat on the table and looked at it for a moment. Then he looked at Elias.

"There's no law here," he said.

He said it the way a man might say the ground is dry.

"Not the kind you're used to." He glanced at the collar. "Not the kind anyone is."

Elias said nothing.

"I took this side of the creek," Farwell went on. "Years back now. When there wasn't much here but grass and a few men who hadn't decided whether they were staying." He tapped the table lightly once. "Solomon took the other."

"Fort Solomon."

"Close enough," Farwell said. "Close enough to trade. Far enough we didn't have to see each other more than necessary."

Elias let that sit.

"Moses keeps his house differently," Farwell said after a moment.

"How."

Farwell considered him.

"He finishes things."

That was all.

The lamp burned between them. Outside, somewhere in the settlement, a horse shifted against a rail.

"I want to understand something," Farwell said.

Elias waited.

"A man comes to my fort. Shot. Collar. Gun in his bag. Kills a man on the road getting here." Farwell tapped one finger on the table, lightly, once. "Understands Assiniboine well enough to stop a trade from going wrong. Didn't say a word about what was in that crate." Another tap. "Walks into Little Soldier's camp alone and walks back out with my girl." Another tap. "And now there's a dead man at the crossing between me and Moses Solomon."

He left space after it.

"That's a particular kind of man," he said.

Elias said nothing.

"The question I'm asking myself," Farwell went on, "is whether that kind of man is worth what he costs."

Elias felt it arrive in his chest before he understood it. The specific cold of a room where a door has just been opened.

He looked at the lamp.

Farwell had not raised his voice. He was simply reading aloud from a ledger he had marked, but not yet tallied.

"Moses Solomon," Elias said.

Farwell waited.

"You said he finishes things."

"He does."

"The man at the crossing," Elias said. "That was a message to you."

"It was."

"Is he done."

Farwell's eyes held him. "He's down a man."

"Of his own doing," Elias said.

A small nod. "Most likely. Though he won't see it that way."

Elias looked at the table. The tea he had not touched had gone cold. The lamplight lay across the rim of the cup in a thin line.

"You're putting it on me," Elias said.

"Well you tell me."

Elias thought about the tally, and where he sat in it.

"I'll be performing a service this Sunday," he said.

Farwell said nothing. Waited.

"Perhaps Moses might be in attendance."

"Might he."

"The Lord's day might be a good occasion for a business discussion."

Farwell turned his hat on the table. Turned it back.

The fire had burned low. The sounds from the saloon came through the partition in softened shapes. A laugh. The knock of a bottle.

Elias kept his hands flat on his knees.

"He'll want something," Elias said. "For the trouble."

"Men like Moses always want something."

"What does he want that you can give him."

Farwell looked at him.

"That's the right question," he said.

"And what does he want that you can't."

Farwell was quiet for a moment.

"Also the right question."

The silence held.

Elias could feel it now—the shape of the room, the distance to the door, the way Farwell's hands had gone still on the hat.

A man like Farwell did not keep what cost more than it earned.

"There are things a collar does," Elias said.

Farwell did not move.

"Little Soldier's camp," Elias said. "I walked in. I walked out. You said it yourself."

"I did."

"That's not a thing Solomon has."

Farwell said nothing.

"He has guns," Elias said. "And men. And a creek crossing he uses when he wants to say something."

He stopped.

The next words did not come clean.

He felt them before he chose them.

"What he doesn't have…"

A beat.

"…is someone who can walk between."

The fire shifted.

Farwell watched him.

"You're telling me," Farwell said slowly, "what you're worth."

Elias met his eyes.

"I'm telling you what I can do."

Farwell considered that.

"And what happens," he said, "when the men on either side decide not to listen to you."

Elias held his gaze.

"Then I'll know it before they do," he said. "And you will too."

Farwell's eyes narrowed slightly—not in distrust, but in recognition.

That answer had cost something.

He sat back.

"Sunday," he said.

"Yes."

"You give the service."

"Yes."

"And then we'll sit down with Solomon. And we'll see what kind of understanding we can reach."

Elias said nothing.

Farwell reached for the ledger and drew it toward him. He did not open it.

"You'll stay close to the fort," he said. "Between now and then."

Elias understood what that meant.

"Understood."

Farwell nodded once.

The matter was not settled. It had only been carried forward.

Elias rose and went to the door. He put his hand on it.

"Reverend."

He turned.

Farwell was looking at the ledger.

"Jacob Burr," he said.

"Yes."

Farwell did not look up. "Made his choices." He turned one page without reading it. "And then choices were made for him."

Elias held his eyes when Farwell finally raised them.

"That is generally the shape of things."

Farwell looked at him a moment longer.

Then he looked back down at the ledger.

Elias went out.

* * *

He stood on the step.

The road south was still open. Dark, but open. A man on foot could be past the creek line before the saloon closed.

He knew how far he'd get.

He stepped down into the yard.

Two days.

A service to give. A meeting that had not yet decided him. A foot that would not carry him to the line before Farwell's men were saddled and the sun was up.

He walked.

The creek ran behind the buildings, indifferent and continuous, carrying whatever the night had put into it southward toward the line.

He did not look back.

He told himself that was a decision.

Ten

He went to the Hawthorne place in the morning.

The rain had passed in the night but left itself behind in the yard. The ground held the wet. The boards of the porch were dark with it. Beyond the house the creek moved fuller than yesterday, not fast, just carrying more of the country in it.

He knocked once.

Bella Hawthorne opened the door with her apron folded over one hand as though she had been standing with it there some time without deciding what to do next.

She stepped aside.

The room smelled of sickness and damp wool and coffee.

That surprised him.

A pot sat near the stove. Not fresh. It had been on a while. The smell of it had gone bitter.

Anderson lay where he had lain before. The blanket higher now. His face had drawn tighter against the bone in the night. A man being reduced in plain sight.

The girl stood by the window.

She was wearing the same dress as yesterday. Or one near enough the same.

Bella saw him look.

"Heather," she said.

The girl looked at him once and then back at the bed.

He inclined his head to her. "Heather."

She did not answer.

Bella took the pot from the stove and poured into a chipped cup. Then another. She set one on the table near him.

"Thank you," he said.

She nodded and sat in the chair beside the settle without drinking hers.

Anderson's breathing filled the room.

It was worse now. The body no longer trying to hide what it was doing. Each breath came rough and shallow and ended in a small failure before the next began.

Elias sat.

No one spoke.

The coffee was hot enough still. He drank. Grounds had slipped past whatever cloth Bella had used and settled dark at the bottom. He could feel them against his teeth.

Bella watched Anderson breathe.

"You're holding church," she said after a while.

"Yes."

"Farwell told me."

He set the cup down.

"Yes."

Another stretch of breathing. Wet. Thin. Stubborn.

Bella looked at the stove rather than at him.

"I don't believe."

She said it plainly. Not as a challenge. Not as an apology.

Elias waited.

He did not speak.

Bella looked at him then, perhaps expecting the words one got from men in collars. Reproof. Instruction. A softening of her own statement into some grief she did not understand properly.

He gave her none of it.

"At one time I did," she said.

Her hand rested against the arm of the chair. Strong hand. Red at the knuckles. A burn scar near the thumb.

"When we first came west. I did then." She looked toward Anderson without turning her head fully. "Then winter came. Then another. Then one child buried and one nearly. Then men said pray on it and wait on Providence and trust the Lord and all the rest of it."

Her mouth moved once. Not quite a smile.

"You can get tired of hearing that."

"Yes," Elias said.

Heather had moved to the stove. She stood with one hand on it.

Bella picked up her cup. Did not drink.

"What do you tell people," she said, "when you don't know why it happened."

He looked at Anderson. The chest lifting. Falling. Missing once. Catching again.

"The truth," he said.

She waited.

"Which is."

He looked at his hands.

"That I do not know why."

Bella studied him.

"And that satisfies them."

"No."

A small silence.

"What good is your trade then."

"Some days," he said, "none that I can prove."

Bella looked at him a long moment.

Not disappointed.

Anderson made a sound then. Not a word. Something lower. A body objecting.

Bella was out of the chair before Elias had risen halfway. She bent over him. Adjusted the blanket. Wet his lips with a cloth. Put one hand against the side of his face.

"Andy."

The name sat strangely in the room. Softer than anything else had.

Anderson's eyes opened.

Not fully.

Enough.

He looked first at Bella. Then past her. Found Elias after a moment as though the distance to him had become longer in the night.

"Reverend," he said.

The word barely made it out.

"I'm here."

Anderson swallowed. Tried again.

The effort to speak seemed larger than the speaking.

Bella bent nearer. "Do you want water."

He moved his head once. Maybe no. Maybe simply away.

His eyes shifted again, searching.

"Heather," Bella said quietly.

The girl did not move at first.

Then she came.

Slowly.

She stopped beside the settle where her father could see her if he turned his eyes enough.

Anderson did.

A strange look came into his face then. Not peace. Nothing as complete as that. Recognition with fear still in it. A man seeing what he will leave.

Bella took his hand and put it against the child's sleeve because he no longer had the strength to lift it where it needed to go.

Heather stood very still.

Anderson's fingers twitched once against the cloth.

Then fell.

No one spoke.

After a time Bella eased his hand back onto the blanket.

His eyes had closed again. His breathing went on. If anything, rougher.

The room held.

Elias drank the last of the coffee and set the cup aside before the grounds reached his mouth.

Bella sat back down.

"He was a good man," she said.

It did not sound like a plea for agreement. It sounded like a statement entered into the record because no one else would do it properly if she left it to them.

"Yes," Elias said.

"He was not much use with money."

"No."

"He trusted men too easily."

Elias said nothing.

Bella went on looking at the bed.

"But he worked. And he did not strike me. And when our first one died, he dug the ground himself because he would not have another man do it. Those things count for something with me."

"Yes," Elias said.

"They count for more than prayer."

He held still.

Then: "Perhaps they are prayer."

Bella looked at him.

She did not ask him to explain.

Anderson's breathing changed again.

Not louder.

Further away.

A man walking into weather.

Bella heard it too. She was on her feet now without seeming to have risen.

"Heather."

The girl came to her mother's side.

Bella put one hand on the back of the child's neck and kept it there.

Anderson drew one breath.

Then another.

Then waited too long for the third.

The waiting entered the room like another presence.

Bella leaned forward. "Andy."

Nothing.

Then the third breath came after all, thin and torn and insufficient. The body unwilling to surrender without making the terms ugly.

Elias stood.

Anderson's mouth opened.

The next breath did not come properly. It shuddered in him. Failed. Began again.

A smell entered the room.

Immediate. Human. Final.

The bowels giving up.

Bella's face did not change.

Heather looked toward the smell without understanding it.

Anderson drew one last breath that seemed for a moment it might continue into another.

It did not.

The body settled by degrees, the way a house settles after a door has been shut.

Bella kept her hand on the child's neck.

No one moved.

No one said anything foolish.

The creek behind the house kept going.

At length Bella reached forward and closed his mouth with two fingers. Then his eyes.

She did it carefully. The way she had done everything.

Heather looked up at her mother. Then at Elias.

"Is Daddy dead?"

The room did not answer for him.

"Yes," he said.

Heather looked at her father.

Then she walked to her mother and pressed her face against her side.

Bella's hand came down on the back of the girl's head.

The room was quiet for a long time.

* * *

He left them to it and waited on the porch.

The settlement was going about its morning. The sound of a bucket. A horse moved somewhere behind the dry goods store. The smell of smoke from three chimneys coming thin and straight in the still air. Near the saloon an Assiniboine man sat against the wall with his legs out in front of him. His eyes were open. Not watching anything. The kind of open that was not the same as awake.

After a time Bella came to the door.

She held a small dark book at her side.

He knew it before she lifted it toward him. The worn corners. The ribbon marking a page he had opened himself, days ago, when his own Bible had been insufficient.

"For Sunday," she said.

He took it.

She went back inside without waiting for him to answer.

* * *

He walked back toward the saloon.

The book was light in his hand. Lighter than it had been when Bella placed it there at her husband's side and he had read from it what a dying man required. A dead man's book now. Given by a woman who did not believe to a man she hardly knew.

Sunday was tomorrow.

He thought about what Bella had said. What she counted for something. What she counted for more.

He thought about Jacob knifed in the back and lying finished.

The words did not come.

He kept walking.

The book was in his hand and the settlement was ahead of him and somewhere behind him the creek moved south with whatever the night had put into it.

Eleven

The day did not decide itself.

The sky held low over the settlement, a pale white that had not yet committed to rain but had not ruled it out. The ground kept the memory of the night. Boots took it up and gave it back with each step. The creek ran fuller behind the buildings, not fast. Just carrying more.

Farwell stood in the doorway of the saloon and watched the street.

"You can do it in here," he said.

Elias looked past him at the room. Tables pushed back. A few men already inside, hats on, as though they had come to watch rather than attend.

"No."

Farwell turned his hat once in his hands.

"Better for the weather."

"It's not raining."

"It might."

Elias said nothing.

Farwell watched him a moment longer. Then he nodded once.

"Where."

"The crossing."

Farwell's eyes moved briefly toward the north end of the settlement where the ground sloped down toward the creek.

"That's not my side," he said.

"It's where men will come."

Farwell considered it. The calculation visible.

"All right," he said.

He stepped out into the street.

* * *

They gathered without being called.

Word had moved the way it moved in a place like this. From the bar to the yard. From the yard to the well. From one man's observation to another man's decision.

By midmorning there were people standing at the crossing.

No seats.

A few women had brought stools and then set them aside when they saw no one else had. Men stood with their hands in their coats. Hats on. A few removed them and held them uncertainly and then put them back.

The ground was soft underfoot at the bottom of the slope. The grass beyond the cutbank moved in a low steady way that did not trouble itself with the concerns of the people beside it.

Farwell stood off to one side. Not at the front. Not quite among the others either. Two of his men a little behind him, as though they had not decided where to stand and had chosen that place for lack of a better one.

Up the far bank, Moses Solomon with three of his men stood where his ground began, looking down at the crossing.

Watching.

People from both sides of the water filled the low ground between without arranging themselves.

Bella came with the girl.

She had put on a clean dress. Work had been done to it. The effort visible. Her hair drawn back. Her hands bare.

Heather stood at her side with one hand in the fabric at her mother's waist.

They took a place not near the front and not near the back. A place where a person might see without being seen.

Elias stood where the ground flattened at the water's edge.

He held the book.

He had not decided where to stand until he had stopped.

That was where he was.

The people quieted by degrees.

Not all at once. The way a room quiets when nothing more is being said that requires answering.

A man coughed. Another shifted his weight. Somewhere behind him a child made a small sound and was hushed without being turned.

Elias opened the book.

The pages moved once in the wind and settled.

He did not look up.

* * *

"Dearly beloved," he said. "The Scripture moveth us, in sundry places, to acknowledge and confess our manifold sins and wickedness; and that we should not dissemble nor cloak them before the face of Almighty God our heavenly Father."

The words went out into the open air and stayed.

"But confess them with an humble, lowly, penitent, and obedient heart."

He left space.

"To the end that we may obtain forgiveness of the same, by his infinite goodness and mercy."

He waited.

* * *

Then he read and the people followed after him, those who knew it. The words arrived in pieces from different parts of the gathering.

"Almighty and most merciful Father. We have erred, and strayed from thy ways like lost sheep."

A few voices. Then more.

"We have followed too much the devices and desires of our own hearts."

Some nodded. Some stood still.

The creek moved quiet beside them.

"We have offended against thy holy laws. We have left undone those things which we ought to have done."

The wind pressed once against the coats.

"And we have done those things which we ought not to have done."

Silence.

"And there is no health in us."

* * *

He led them through the Lord's Prayer. Voices joined without being asked. Uncertain at first. Then more certain. The words known somewhere in nearly every person there even if the knowing had gone unused for some time.

"And forgive us our trespasses, as we forgive those who trespass against us."

The creek went on.

"And lead us not into temptation; but deliver us from evil."

He paused.

"For thine is the kingdom, and the power, and the glory, for ever and ever. Amen."

* * *

He turned to the lesson.

"The Acts of the Apostles," he said. "Chapter the ninth."

"And Saul, yet breathing out threatenings and slaughter against the disciples of the Lord, went unto the high priest, and desired of him letters to Damascus to the synagogues, that if he found any of this way, whether they were men or women, he might bring them bound unto Jerusalem."

He read it plainly. No weight added. The passage had its own.

"And as he journeyed, he came near Damascus: and suddenly there shined round about him a light from heaven."

The wind had gone still.

"And he fell to the earth, and heard a voice saying unto him, Saul, Saul, why persecutest thou me?"

He looked up from the page.

"And he said, Who art thou, Lord? And the Lord said, I am Jesus whom thou persecutest."

He held there a moment.

"And he trembling and astonished said, Lord, what wilt thou have me to do?"

He closed the book.

The sound of it was small.

He lifted his eyes.

Moses Solomon stood up the far bank with his men. Hat brim low. Hands in his coat pockets. The stillness of a man accustomed to waiting for other people to finish.

He was not watching the creek.

He was watching Elias.

Elias looked out over the gathering. The gray sky above. The low ground and the water. The faces between.

Then he began.

* * *

"Saul was not a wicked man," he said.

"He was a certain man. He knew what was right."

A man removed his hat and did not put it back.

"That is what made him dangerous."

He felt their attention now. Enough of it.

"He went with authority. With purpose."

"But God's way is not a man's way."

The wind pressed once against the gathered coats.

"The Lord does not always correct a man gently."

He held there.

"Sometimes He blinds him."

A pause.

"Sometimes He takes from him the thing he trusted most."

Another.

"His own understanding."

No one moved.

"A man can be certain and still be wrong. A man can act in the name of what he believes is right, and still do harm he cannot call back."

The creek moved.

"You have seen what it looks like."

A breath.

"You have seen it this week."

"We do not always know why a thing is taken from us. We do not always know why a man is spared when another is not."

"What we are given is this."

A pause.

"The chance to see."

"To see that we are not what we thought we were. To see that the ground we stand on is not as firm as we believed."

He felt it now. Not belief. Attention.

"And the chance to choose again."

Silence.

Then, from somewhere in the middle of the crowd:

"Amen."

A second voice.

"Amen."

A third.

Not many.

Enough.

* * *

He lowered his head.

He opened the book again and read the benediction.

"The grace of our Lord Jesus Christ, and the love of God, and the fellowship of the Holy Ghost, be with us all evermore. Amen."

The gathering held a moment.

Then it broke.

Men turning. Women gathering what they had not used. Hats going back on.

Farwell's people moved back up toward the settlement. Solomon's people withdrew north along the bank, back toward Fort Solomon.

Bella stood a moment longer than the others. Then she turned, the girl with her, and followed the others up the slope.

The crossing quieted.

Then, from the south, movement.

They came up through the coulee along the creek bottom, where the willows grew thick and the ground was still soft from the spring. Little Soldier first. Two men behind him. They had not been among the crowd.

He stopped at the water's edge.

He said something in his own language.

The interpreter's voice carried in the empty space between them.

"A man who is struck blind is not yet a different man."

Little Soldier looked at Elias a moment longer.

Then he turned and went back the way he had come, south along the water, and the coulee took him.

* * *

Farwell remained.

He stood beside Elias at the water and looked up the far bank to where Solomon still waited. He had the patience of a man who had decided the morning was not finished.

Farwell turned his hat once in his hands.

"Well," he said. "We'll see what he made of it."

He put the hat on.

He turned and started back up toward the settlement.

Elias stood a moment at the crossing.

The creek moved past him, indifferent and continuous.

On the far bank Solomon began to descend. Unhurried. The careful step of a man coming down wet ground.

Elias turned and followed Farwell up the slope.

The back of his neck knew what was behind him. The sound of it. The weight Solomon and his man walking on soft ground, closing the distance at a measured pace.

He kept his eyes forward.

The book was in his hand.

The sky remained undecided.

He did not open the book again.

Twelve

The room had been cleared before Solomon arrived.

Tables pushed back. Chairs turned and set against the walls. The bar wiped down. The air held the smell of yesterday's drink and the morning's work laid over it.

Farwell sat at a table near the middle of the room. Not the head of anything. A place where a man might see the door and the bar and the stair without turning.

He turned his hat once in his hands and set it on the table beside him.

Three glasses sat there. Two with whiskey in them. One empty.

The men stood where they had chosen to stand. One near the door. One by the back wall. Another by the stair. Not arranged. Not random.

The girls moved between the tables with nothing to do. One took a cloth to a place already clean. Another lifted a bottle and set it down again. They did not look at the door.

Nora stood behind the bar with her back to the room. The rag moved under her hand in slow, even strokes. The same place. Again.

Elias stood off to the side. No one had asked him to sit. He kept his hands clear of his coat.

The door opened.

Solomon came in without hurry. His coat was buttoned. His hat low. He closed the door behind him and stood a moment as though taking the measure of the room before crossing it.

Two men followed him in and stopped near the door. Close enough.

Solomon came to the table and took the chair with the empty glass.

He did not reach for it.

Farwell did not offer.

A moment passed.

Then Solomon looked at the glass, then at Farwell.

"A man came back across the creek," he said.

Farwell nodded once.

"He did."

Solomon's eyes stayed on him.

"He did not make it back."

Farwell lifted one of the filled glasses and took a small drink. Set it down again where it had been.

"No," he said.

Silence held.

Solomon rested his hand on the table. Thick fingers. Still.

"Ground's been moving," he said.

Farwell said nothing.

"Men walking where they don't belong." Solomon's eyes shifted, briefly, toward Elias, then back. "Getting turned around."

Farwell turned the glass once under his fingers.

"That happens."

Solomon's mouth moved once. Not quite a smile.

"Not by accident."

The room held steady.

Behind the bar, the rag stopped moving.

Solomon leaned back slightly in the chair. The wood gave under him.

"Your man went into my place," he said. "Said what he had to say. Then he came out of it."

Farwell looked at him.

"He walked himself into that."

"He walked out of it too."

Farwell said nothing.

Solomon's eyes lifted again, this time settling on Elias.

"A door was left open for him."

Elias met the look.

"I told him he could leave," he said.

Solomon watched him.

"That's not the same thing."

Elias did not answer.

A longer silence.

Then Solomon looked back to Farwell.

"Things don't hold if they're not held," he said.

Farwell's hand rested on the table beside the glass.

"They've been holding."

"For a time."

"For long enough."

Solomon's fingers tapped once against the wood. Not impatient. Marking something.

"Long enough," he said.

The girl at the bar set the bottle down more carefully than she had picked it up.

No one looked at her.

Solomon's voice stayed where it had been.

"A man lies where he falls," he said. "But he does not lie there by himself."

Farwell did not move.

"Men see where he is," Solomon went on. "They take a measure from it."

Farwell's eyes narrowed a fraction.

"What measure."

Solomon looked at him.

"What can be done."

The words sat in the room.

Farwell reached for his glass and did not lift it.

"We keep our side," he said.

Solomon nodded once.

"And the rest of it."

Farwell's hand stayed on the glass.

"That depends."

"On what."

Farwell looked at him.

"What it costs."

Silence again.

Solomon considered that. His eyes moved once across the room, taking in the men at the wall, the bar, the stair. Then back.

"There's a woman," he said.

No one spoke.

"A house empty now," he said. "A child in it."

The rag behind the bar began moving again. Slower.

Farwell did not look toward the bar.

"She's on your side," Solomon said.

"For now."

Solomon's eyes rested on him.

"For now," he agreed.

The room did not move.

Elias felt the space open and narrow at the same time. The way it had at the crossing. The way it had in the yard with the horse.

He did not step forward.

"She'll need something," he said.

The words came out quieter than the room.

Both men looked at him.

Elias kept his eyes on the table.

"Work," he said.

He did not say where.

Solomon watched him a moment.

"And you'll tell her," he said.

Elias lifted his eyes.

"If she asks," he said.

Solomon held that.

Farwell's jaw tightened once. Then settled.

No one spoke.

Solomon stood.

He adjusted his coat as though it required it. Looked once more at the untouched glass in front of him, then at Farwell.

"We'll see what she does," he said.

He turned and walked to the door.

His men followed him out.

The door closed.

The room stayed as it was for a moment after.

Then the girl at the bar set the rag down and picked it up again.

Farwell remained seated.

He looked at the third glass. Still empty.

Then at Elias.

"You put yourself in that," he said.

Elias did not answer.

Farwell studied him a moment longer.

"Be careful what you stand in, Reverend."

He took his hat from the table and put it on.

He walked toward the back without looking again.

Elias stayed where he was.

No one spoke to him.

After a while he turned and went out.

Outside, the creek moved south, carrying what it was given.

Thirteen

The rain did not stop.

Not hard at first. A thin rain that seemed undecided, falling straight in the grey air and darkening the yard board by board, patch by patch, until nothing in the place looked dry or likely to be dry again.

The grave had been dug east of the house where the ground lifted a little and the water might sit less heavily. Even so, the bottom held some of it. A dark shine in the earth. A little gathering of rain and mud where no water ought to be.

The sack lay beside the hole.

Heather stood close against Bella's skirt with one hand caught in the cloth.

Bella did not look at the sack.

She looked at the grave.

Farwell had come. Mary. Nora. Two of Farwell's men with the shovels still marked from the work. A few others from the settlement. Not many. Enough that a man might be put in the ground without it seeming he had gone there alone.

Mary and Nora had taken their place near Bella. Not touching her. Not speaking. Simply there — one on either side but with space left between, as though they understood there were kinds of company a person could accept and kinds she could not.

Farwell stood a little apart, hat in his hands, coat gone dark at the shoulders with the rain. He looked at the house, the grave, the men, the child. The way he looked at any arrangement that had to be got through.

Elias came through the gate with the Book of Common Prayer under his coat. His hat brim dripped. Mud clung to the edge of the boot that held his bad leg.

He stopped beside Bella.

"Mrs. Hawthorne. Would you like me to say anything."

Mary looked at him then.

Not sharply.

Worse.

With the plain look of a person seeing a man ask the wrong question at the wrong moment and deciding there was no point in helping him out of it.

Bella kept her eyes on the grave.

"No."

He stood with that.

The rain went on.

He looked at the sack.

He did not know Anderson Hawthorne. He knew the shape of a man in sickness. The labour of his breathing. The way Bella had said his name when the body was still warm enough to hear it. He knew the daughter. The room. The coffee with the grounds in it. He knew what Bella counted for something. What she counted for more.

He did not know the man they were burying.

He did not know how to speak for him.

He did not know how to speak for Bella.

The men came forward.

Farwell nodded once and they bent to the sack. One at the shoulders. One at the feet. They lifted carefully, with the particular care men use around the dead when there is nothing more to be done for them but doing it wrong still mattered.

Rain darkened the canvas as they moved it.

Elias opened the book.

The ribbon had shifted. He put it right with his thumb and found the page.

"I am the resurrection and the life, saith the Lord: he that believeth in me, though he were dead, yet shall he live; and whosoever liveth and believeth in me, shall never die."

The words went out into the rain and were diminished by it.

The men lowered the sack. The ropes creaked once. Mud gave under their boots. Then the weight was down and the shape of the man settled at the bottom among the dark wet soil.

No one spoke.

The wind came up a little then, crossing the yard from the creek side and driving the rain slantwise. Bella blinked once against it.

He covered the book with one hand and said what else the page required.

When he was done, he looked at Bella.

"If you wish," he said, "you may come forward."

She did not move.

"The earth. You may throw it."

She looked at him then. A long moment. Not because she needed the instruction. Because she had heard it and had not decided whether to obey it.

Then she crossed the mud to the edge of the grave.

Heather stayed where she was.

Bella bent and took up a handful of dirt from the raised mound. It was wetter than earth ought to be. It clung to itself. She held it a moment, not in ceremony but because it was mud and there was no clean way to take it.

Then she let it fall.

It landed on the canvas below with a sound that was too small for what it was.

Bella straightened.

For a moment Elias thought she might say something.

She did not.

She stepped back from the grave. The rain had come in earnest now. Not hard enough to drive a person running, but hard enough that the hat brims and shoulders and skirts of those gathered all took it fully.

Farwell gestured once to his men.

They began to fill the grave.

No one watched long.

People drifted toward the house by degrees, not spoken to, not instructed. The work of burial continuing behind them in the sound of shovels entering wet earth and turning it over.

Heather went to Bella as soon as her mother came back. She took the skirt again in one fist and Bella put one hand briefly against the child's head without looking down.

Then they went inside.

* * *

The house was warmer than the yard and not warmer enough.

Someone had brought cold meat wrapped in cloth. Someone else a loaf. Mary set a pot near the stove and moved it without asking where it ought to go. Nora found cups and put them in order by the coffee as though she had always known where Bella kept them. A woman Elias did not know laid out preserves in a jar with no one remarking on it.

People do not know what to do with death. So they carry things.

That was what the room held. Not comfort. Activity. A kindness that refused to call itself that.

Bella stood near the table and accepted none of it as though it belonged to her. She did not refuse help. She did not ask for it. She stood where the room could move around her and let it.

Heather had gone to the floor by the stove. Someone had found her a straw doll. She turned it in her hands and watched the room through it.

Farwell came in last. Rain sat on him in dark patches. He removed his hat at the door and went to Bella.

"I'm sorry for your loss," he said.

No softness to it. No false note either. Simply the thing entered where it had to be entered.

Bella inclined her head.

"Thank you."

Farwell waited a moment as though there might be more to the exchange.

There was not.

He looked once toward Heather. Once toward Elias. Once toward the room and the people in it and the narrow uses to which a place could be put when a man had died in it.

Then he put his hat back on.

"If there's need," he said, "word can be sent."

Bella said nothing.

Farwell nodded once, accepting the answer he had not been given, and went out into the rain.

People stayed a little longer after that, but not long.

The room could not hold them once the principal man had left. They finished their coffee, took one last look at Bella or did not, drew coats back on over damp shoulders, slipped out by ones and twos into the weather.

Mary paused by Bella at the door.

She did not touch her.

She said only, "The child should eat."

Bella inclined her head once.

Mary looked at Elias as she passed him. Not hostile. Merely not interested in what defence he might imagine for himself.

Then she was gone.

Nora was the last of the women to leave. She bent once to Heather and said something too low for Elias to hear. The child looked up, solemnly, and gave no sign of having heard or not heard. Nora straightened and looked at Bella.

"If you need anything."

Bella's eyes met hers.

A small nod.

Nora went out into the rain.

Then there was only Bella and Heather and Elias.

The coffee sat in the pot. The bread on the table. A cup left with a thumbprint of mud near its rim. The little signs of other people having tried and failed to improve what had occurred.

Heather remained by the stove with the doll.

Bella stood by the table with one hand resting against its edge. The grave mud had dried on her palm.

Elias had not yet sat down. Now that he had the chance, he did not know whether to. He removed his hat and held it.

The silence reached its full shape.

Then he said, "Mrs. Hawthorne."

Bella looked at him.

"I am not certain how to bring this up."

"No," Bella said. "I suppose not."

He let that stand.

"I did not know your husband well," he said. "Only at the end."

"That is better than not at all."

He thought, perhaps, that there was an opening in that.

"He seemed a man," Elias said carefully, "who understood what was his to carry."

Bella looked at him.

"My husband is in the ground."

The words were not loud.

"He is not a subject."

Elias inclined his head.

"Yes."

Heather set the doll upright on the floor. It leaned and fell. She set it upright again.

"You have managed this house," Elias said. "His illness. The child. Everything that had to be done."

Bella's eyes stayed on him.

"Is that why you stayed."

"It is part of why."

A little cold entered her face then. Not anger. Something flatter.

"You need not praise my competence to me, Reverend. I have had the benefit of it."

He felt the rebuke in the clean grammar of it.

"I meant it sincerely."

"I do not doubt that."

"There may be some comfort," he said, "in knowing that Anderson believed—"

Bella moved before he finished.

Not far. Only enough that the movement itself was an answer.

"No."

He stopped.

"You had your words," she said. "Out there."

The room held still.

"I said no."

He said nothing.

"And you said them anyway."

The rain struck the roof harder for a moment and then settled back.

Elias looked at the table between them.

"They were meant for the dead."

"They were meant for you."

He lifted his eyes.

Bella's face had not changed. That was the force of it. Not an eruption of grief. Not tears. Not even heat. Merely a woman who had reached the point where accuracy mattered more than politeness.

"Andy would have wanted—"

"My husband's name was Anderson."

The line cut the room in two.

Elias stood with it.

"You do not call him that," she said. "Not now. Not after standing there with a book open and speaking over him because it was easier for you than silence."

A small sound came from the stove corner.

Heather had stopped moving the doll.

She was watching her mother.

Bella knew it. So did Elias. Neither looked at her.

"My husband never got what he wanted," Bella said. "And you do not get to change that with words."

The house went very quiet.

Then Bella drew a breath and the surface of her returned.

Not softened.

Composed.

"Thank you, Reverend," she said. "My daughter and I need to be left alone."

That should have been the end of it.

Elias knew it. Felt it. Stood in it.

Then he said, "There is another matter."

Bella looked at him and something in her stilled.

"Not now."

"Yes," he said.

The word surprised him by the firmness of it.

"Yes. It is now."

Bella did not answer.

Heather had risen and come to her mother without being called. One hand reached for Bella's skirt. Bella gathered the child in almost absently, as if her body had moved first and her mind had followed.

"There is a place for you," Elias said.

Bella's eyes remained on him.

"At Fort Solomon."

Nothing in the room moved.

Not the stove. Not the rain. Not the coffee in the pot. Not even Heather, who seemed suddenly to have understood that the world had turned and that she would best survive it by becoming still.

Bella said, "No."

It was not protest.

It was recognition.

"My place is here."

He said nothing.

"My place is here."

"It has been arranged."

The words felt ugly as he set them down.

Bella sat.

Slowly.

She drew Heather onto her lap and held her there, one arm across the child as though to shield her, or perhaps to give herself something to hold that was not the table or the edge of the world.

"Do you know what Fort Solomon is, Reverend."

He answered carefully.

"I know it is a place where there is room for you. Where there is work. Where you may earn something. Where—"

Bella looked at him.

"That is a lie."

He stopped.

"It is worse than a lie," she said. "It is a lie spoken gently."

A pause.

"It has been decided," she said.

He did not answer.

"By who."

"Abel Farwell."

The name landed.

Bella took it without visible reaction at first. Then something in her face altered. Not rage. Devastation had come too often and learned to wear quieter clothes.

"And he does not come himself."

Elias said nothing.

"He stands in this house and says words over my husband while I am being traded like a horse."

Her arm tightened slightly across Heather.

"What did he get from Moses."

"Nothing."

The answer came too quickly.

He heard it. She heard it.

A beat.

"Peace," he said.

"Which is it."

He held her gaze.

"Peace."

"What does that have to do with me."

He opened his mouth.

The first answer came.

He let it go.

Bella saw that.

"Farwell will hear from me," she said.

"You could do that."

Her eyes did not move.

The truth of his answer sat there plainly enough.

It would change nothing.

"When."

The single word entered the room like weather.

"When."

He understood now what she was asking. Not whether. Not why.

When.

"I can speak to Farwell," Elias said. "Say you need time."

Bella looked at him for a long moment.

"You have said enough."

He stood still.

"I want you to leave."

No heat in it now.

No anger left for the use of him.

Only decision.

Elias put his hat on.

Heather was watching him over her mother's arm.

He looked at her and looked away first.

He crossed to the door.

Stepped to the porch.

Behind him, the door closed with small final sound.

He stood a moment in the yard.

The rain had thinned but the yard was gone to mud and the grave beyond stood dark and fresh under the weather.

* * *

The saloon was warm and he did not want warmth.

He sat at the bar because the table in the corner where he had first taken whiskey with Farwell was occupied, and because sitting at a table alone was the kind of thing a man did when he meant to stay a while and he did not intend to stay a while.

Nora set a glass in front of him without being asked.

He looked at the glass.

She did not move away.

"You should go," she said.

"I know it."

"Tonight."

He looked at her.

Her face was steady. The bruising had faded to a yellowish shadow along her cheekbone. The cut on her lip had closed.

She was not asking him.

He drank the whiskey.

She took the glass and poured another and set it there and went to the far end of the bar.

* * *

He was considering the second glass without drinking it when they came in.

Four of them. Big men. Travel-dirty. The cold came in with them and then the door closed and the smell was all that remained.

They came to the bar loud and certain. Coins set down without counting. Orders given before coats were off.

Nora poured. She did not look at their faces.

They spoke over one another. A horse. A man. Something that made one of them laugh hard enough to set his glass down.

Elias drank.

He thought about the road north. The state of his foot. The days he had stayed past what he had said he would stay.

He thought about Bella.

You have said enough.

He set the glass down.

He rose.

The men did not see him.

He moved toward the stair.

His hand found the post.

"—Solomon's—"

The word came up out of the noise.

He stopped.

"—girls he keeps over there—"

Laughter.

His foot found the first step.

"—worth the ride—"

He did not take the second.

The men laughed again. One of them said something lower. The others answered.

Elias stood on the step.

The men laughed behind him. Easy. Certain.

"—worth the ride—"

The words sat where they had been said.

He saw the room again. The table. Solomon's hands on the glass. Farwell not looking at him.

"She'll hear it from me."

He had said it.

He saw Bella.

Do you know what Fort Solomon is, Reverend.

He stood with that.

The voices went on behind him.

He did not turn.

He went up.

Fourteen

He woke before the light.

Not from rest. From the end of it.

The room held the smell of the place below. Old liquor worked into the boards. Smoke that had nowhere else to go. Damp wool. A sourness that did not belong to any one man and so belonged to all of them.

No voices.

That was the strange part.

A saloon without sound was not empty. It was waiting.

He lay still and listened to it.

A board settled somewhere below. A faint shift. The building easing itself into morning. The rain had not stopped. It marked the ceiling above him in a dark spreading stain.

He sat up.

The foot complained. Then steadied.

His things lay where he had put them. The shirt. The coat. The collar. The gun.

He dressed without hurry. The shirt still damp at the cuffs. The coat taking its weight on his shoulders.

He held the collar in his hand.

A small pewter mirror sat on the dresser. Some old carelessness had cracked the glass. It lay inside the frame like a jagged artery. He looked at the man within.

The break ran through the face.

He set the collar in place and fastened it.

Then the gun. He checked it. Turned the cylinder once. Closed it.

He did not look again.

* * *

The rain came down steady.

The yard had gone to mud. Wagons had cut it deep and men's boots had made it worse. Water stood in the ruts and darkened the wood at the thresholds.

Farwell's house sat tight to the trading post. No space between them. A man's living and his business sharing a wall.

He went to the house door and knocked.

Mary opened. She did not move aside. Her eyes went over him once. The collar. The coat. The set of his face.

"You've decided something," she said.

"Yes."

"That's not the same as being right."

"No."

The rain filled the space between them.

"Abel's in the post," she said. "Go around."

He did not move.

"You don't need to do it," she said.

"Yes," he said. "I do."

She studied him a moment longer.

"You'll say what you came to say," she said. "And he'll listen. And then he'll do what he was going to do."

She held the door.

"You got mud on your boots," she said. "Go around."

He touched his hat.

She closed it.

* * *

The wagon stood under the overhang beside the trading post.

Four horses in the traces. Two more tied off behind. Heads low against the rain. A mounted guard sat half-turned in the saddle, hat brim dripping. Another man stood near the lead team with his coat open and one hand under it where the weather was not the reason.

The canvas had been pulled back.

Barrels. Crates. The black letters burned into the side.

T.C. Power & Bro.

The smell of whiskey came off them even through the rain.

Elias slowed.

Then stopped.

His hand rose without permission and found the collar at his throat.

Not to straighten it.

To feel whether it was still there.

Farwell emerged from the trading post with a man beside him. Broad through the shoulders. Beard gone rough with weather. A scar running from the temple down into the beard line and lost there. The kind of scar that changed the shape of a face without improving it.

The man looked at Elias once.

Stopped.

Not openly.

Not enough for anyone else to name it.

But Elias felt the look land.

The rain ran off the brim of his hat and into his collar. He did not wipe it away.

Farwell turned then and followed the man's glance.

"Reverend."

Elias straightened. Lowered his hand.

Said nothing.

Men worked the wagon. A crate came down hard. A lid pried loose. The smell lifted stronger.

The scarred man kept looking at him.

Farwell nodded once toward the open door.

"Why don't you get out of the rain."

* * *

The trading post doors stood open.

Inside, the place was already in motion.

Flour. Coffee. Cloth. Powder. Shot. Tin. Beads. Harness stacked near the rear wall. A ledger open on the high desk. The room held the mixed smell of dry goods and wet men.

Elias stepped in and kept his hat on.

The scarred man came in behind him carrying one end of a crate with another man at the opposite side. They set it down by the rear wall.

The scarred man straightened.

Looked at Elias again.

Longer this time.

Elias turned his eyes to the shelves. Needles. Thread. Salt pork. Tobacco twists in a jar. He saw none of it.

"Hoy," the man said.

Elias did not answer.

"Reverend."

Elias turned.

The man's eyes moved over his face. Not hurried. Not friendly.

"You got a name."

"Elias."

The man waited.

"Wilson."

"Where you come out of."

"East."

The scarred man's mouth moved once. Not quite a smile.

"You travel far for a collar."

"Far enough."

The man held him there another moment.

Rain beat on the roof. Someone outside swore at a mule.

Then the scarred man said, "Maybe," and turned back to the work.

The cold moved up Elias's back and stayed there.

* * *

They unloaded in a wet steady rhythm.

Barrels rolled. Crates thudded. Farwell marked entries in the ledger without seeming to hurry any of it. Elias stood among the goods and tried to take up no room.

Once the scarred man passed him close enough that Elias caught old sweat, damp wool, gun oil.

The man's shoulder brushed his coat.

Not by accident.

Still he said nothing.

When the work was done Farwell closed the ledger and looked over the room.

"Saloon's open," he said. "Tell Nora I sent you."

One of the men laughed once through his nose. The others went out without comment.

The scarred man was last to the door.

He put on his hat.

Looked back at Elias.

Only for a second.

Then he went through.

The door closed behind them.

* * *

Rain on the roof.

The room larger now.

Farwell rested both hands on the high desk and looked down at the ledger as though one more figure might yet present itself.

Elias stepped closer. Took off his hat. Waited.

Farwell closed the book.

"Say what you came to say," he said.

"A woman is not a thing to be traded."

Farwell looked up then.

"You came early to tell me that."

"What happens at Fort Solomon—"

"Is not one thing," Farwell said.

"It is one thing," Elias said. "The trade in women."

Farwell regarded him steadily.

"You sat in that room and let me speak. You knew what it was and you let me mistake it."

"You spoke," Farwell said, "because the words were needed."

"She is a decent woman."

"That's not the question."

"It is to me."

"It isn't to the ground," Farwell said.

"The child needs her."

"The child needs feeding."

"It's not right."

Farwell's face altered slightly at that. Not anger. Weariness, perhaps, or the patience a man uses toward someone naming a weather pattern as though it were an argument.

"Right," he said, "is a word men use when they don't control the outcome."

Elias took a step closer.

"I have done what you asked. I stood where you put me. I said what needed saying."

"You did."

"This goes too far."

Farwell nodded once, as though that at least were honestly felt.

"It always does," he said.

Silence.

Rain.

Elias stood in it. The words he had used in that room. The words he had used at the grave. The words he had set in front of Bella Hawthorne like something offered rather than taken.

You have said enough.

She had been right.

He had not known it then.

"A priest cannot stand in a place and let this pass," he said.

He set the words down where they needed to land.

"If he does, then what he says elsewhere carries nothing."

Farwell removed his hat and placed it beside the ledger.

"You believe that."

"Yes."

The word came clean.

Too clean.

Farwell watched him a moment.

Then he said, "You still think this place is arranged around what ought to happen."

Elias said nothing.

Farwell went on.

"It isn't."

He rested one hand on the closed ledger.

"A man dies. A wife's left. A child's left. Another man across the water wants satisfaction for the one he lost. Men want whiskey. They want order enough to keep trading. They want not to wake up one morning with the wrong throat cut because nobody settled what needed settling." He looked at Elias. "That is the arithmetic."

"It is damnable arithmetic."

Farwell inclined his head a fraction.

"Yes."

The word landed harder than denial would have.

Farwell's eyes did not move.

"I am not saying it is good," he said. "I am saying it is what there is."

He turned the hat once against the wood.

"Little Soldier's camp. You walked in. You walked out." His thumb moved along the brim. "The service at the crossing. Solomon had men there. Not to pray."

Elias said nothing.

"He saw what you did with a book and a passage and a crowd that didn't know what it was feeling." Farwell's voice had gone quieter. "He saw it do work his guns couldn't."

He set the hat down.

"A man with that particular usefulness," he said, "does not need to limp north behind a Benton wagon."

Elias stood still.

He thought about Little Soldier's camp. The dogs circling. The child watching. Walking in and walking out. What the collar had done in that place and what he had told himself it meant.

He thought about Jacob at the crossing.

"I can't let the matter of the woman go," he said.

Farwell nodded. Not agreeing. Merely receiving the line exactly where he had expected it to fall.

"I thought not."

Silence.

Then Farwell said, "The Benton men ride to Whoop-Up."

Elias looked at him.

"I could put in a word," Farwell said. "A seat on the wagon. Provisions. A start."

The words sat between them.

Outside, faint through the rain, came a burst of laughter from the saloon.

Elias did not answer.

Farwell marked what wasn't said.

"You told me north," he said. "You told me Whoop-Up."

"That was before."

"Before what."

Elias thought of Bella. The grave. The room. The scarred man at the door.

"Before the road narrowed," he said.

Farwell's eyes held him.

The rain went harder for a moment and then steadied again.

Farwell touched the ledger with two fingers.

"If you ride with them, you leave these troubles behind. They're not yours."

Elias looked at him.

Farwell's face had not changed. No pity in it. No threat either. Only the plain stating of a thing.

"And if I stay."

Farwell gave the smallest movement of one shoulder.

"Then you stay."

"That all."

"No," Farwell said. "Nothing's all."

He stood then and came around from behind the desk. Not close enough to crowd him. Close enough that the room changed shape.

"You came here with a debt," Elias said. "You made me larger in it."

Farwell looked at him.

"You made yourself larger."

"I tried to keep peace."

"You traded for it."

Elias said nothing.

Farwell's voice stayed level.

"You spoke. I let you. Words were needed and you had them. I have no quarrel with that."

"This is not about a quarrel."

"No," Farwell said. "It's about what a place requires. And requires of a man."

He looked toward the door. Toward the rain beyond it. Toward the saloon, where the Benton men sat drinking within a hundred feet of them.

Then back at Elias.

"You've said your piece," he said.

You can leave," he said.

A small pause.

"If that's still a thing you can do."

Elias looked at him.

He saw the wagon again. The man in the doorway. The road out.

"No," he said.

Farwell's eyes narrowed a fraction.

"You said you were going," Farwell said.

"That was before."

Silence.

Elias drew breath.

"I spoke in your room," he said.

"Yes."

"I spoke to her."

"Yes."

"I have not spoken to him."

Farwell did not move.

"Moses."

A long quiet.

"That's not your ground," Farwell said.

"It is now."

Farwell regarded him.

Not permission.

Not refusal.

Recognition.

"Remember Jacob," he said. "Moses finishes things."

* * *

Elias put on his hat and walked through the open door.

The rain struck him full in the face.

The wagon still stood at the rail. One of the Benton men was in the saloon doorway with a glass held in both hands, not drinking, watching the yard. He turned his eyes to Elias when Elias came out and kept them there.

The glass did not move.

Elias walked.

Past the wagon. Past the horses. Past the place where the yard broke into street and the street sloped down toward the ford.

The mud gave under his boots. The creek had risen in the night. It moved fast and brown at the crossing, carrying the country south with it.

On the far bank, Fort Solomon.

He stopped at the edge of the water.

Behind him, Farwell's settlement.

The wagon from Benton.

The road he had thought he was taking.

Ahead, Solomon.

Bella.

The thing he had helped set in motion.

He stepped into the creek.

The cold came up through his boots.

His bad foot found the stones and held.

He crossed.

Fifteen

He crossed where the water ran brown and fast. The stones shifted under his bad foot. He did not hurry. The current pressed at his legs and moved on. On the far bank the ground rose out of the cut and flattened toward the buildings.

Fort Solomon did not present itself the way Farwell's did. No line of street. No suggestion of order. The structures sat where they had been put and stayed there because no one had yet required them to be otherwise.

A low house stood nearest the crossing. Wider than the rest. Light in the windows though the day had not yet failed. Voices came out of it. Laughter. A woman's voice. Then another.

The door stood open.

Inside, the air held heat and perfume laid over smoke and sweat. Lamps burned though there was still light enough to see by. A piano sat against one wall. A man struck at it without skill and without pause. Women moved between the tables. Dresses bright where colour had been found. One leaned against a man's shoulder. Another stood with a tray and watched the room without expression. Near the far wall a younger woman sat alone with nothing in her hands. Dark-complexioned. Assiniboine, or close enough. Her eyes moved across the room with the particular attention of someone who had learned that watching was safer than being watched.

The sound shifted when he stepped in.

Not stopped.

Adjusted.

The man at the piano missed a note and found another.

One of the women looked at him. Took in the collar. The coat. The mud on his boots from the crossing. A small smile touched her mouth. Not kindness.

He did not answer it.

A man at a table turned and laughed once through his nose.

Another voice from the back of the room said something low and the men near him laughed.

The woman with the tray set it down. Crossed the room toward him.

"You lost," she said.

"No."

She looked at him more carefully then. At the face. The set of it.

"Stay there," she said.

She went to the back without turning her back on him until she had to.

The piano went on.

No one asked him to sit.

No one offered him anything.

After a moment the woman returned.

"He'll see you."

She led him through a narrow passage where the air grew closer and the sound of the room fell away behind them. A door stood half open at the end of it. She knocked once against the frame and stepped aside.

He went in.

The room was smaller than Farwell's office.

Cleaner.

A table. Two chairs. A bed against the far wall with the cover drawn straight. A basin on a stand. A coat hung carefully on a peg.

Solomon stood by the window.

He turned.

His coat was buttoned. His cuffs straight. The same man as at the saloon table. Nothing out of place.

He looked at Elias.

Then at the collar.

"You found your way," he said.

"Yes."

His eyes moved once over the coat. The mud at the hem. The wet at the shoulders. He indicated the chair.

Elias remained standing.

"As you like," Solomon said.

He sat.

Did not offer drink.

"What is it," he said.

Elias said, "The woman."

Solomon's eyes did not move.

"A message," he said.

"Yes."

"From Farwell."

"No."

Solomon regarded him.

"Then from who."

"From me."

A longer look.

"You came a long way," Solomon said, "to tell me what a woman will do."

"She is not coming."

Silence.

Solomon leaned back a fraction in the chair.

"She may not do that work," he said. "Not at first."

Elias looked at him.

"There are other uses," Solomon said. "A house. Kitchen. A woman earns her place in stages."

He held Elias's eyes.

"You understand that."

"No," Elias said.

Solomon's fingers rested on the table.

"No," he said.

"Once she is here," Elias said, "she will not leave."

"That is generally so."

"And what she does here will not be her choice."

Solomon considered that.

"Choice," he said. "A word."

Elias did not answer.

Solomon went on.

"She will be fed. The child also. That is more than the ground offers her now."

"She is not coming," Elias said again.

Silence.

Solomon's eyes narrowed a fraction. Not anger. Attention.

"On what ground," he said.

Elias said, "On the ground that I say so."

The room held.

"You," Solomon said.

"A priest."

Solomon looked at the collar.

"Machray sent you," he said.

"I came on my own initiative."

Solomon's gaze moved over him. Measuring.

"A man on his own initiative," he said, "has no court behind him."

"No."

"No bishop within five hundred miles."

"No."

"No law."

"There is law," Elias said.

Solomon waited.

"Older than yours," Elias said. "Older than Farwell's."

Silence.

Solomon regarded him steadily.

"God's law," he said.

"Yes."

"And you carry it."

"The church carries it," Elias said. "I speak for the church."

Solomon looked at him a long moment.

Then he stood.

He crossed to the window and stood with his hands behind him, looking out toward the creek. The light beyond had gone the grey of late afternoon.

"A collar," Solomon said, "is a piece of cloth."

"Yes."

"What is behind it depends on the man."

"Yes."

Solomon turned.

"I have known men who wore that," he said, "who were worth less than what they stood in."

Elias said nothing.

"And I have known one or two," Solomon said, "who were not."

He crossed back to the table.

He looked at Elias.

"There is a matter," he said.

Elias waited.

"South of here," Solomon said. "Along the water. The ground between the forts."

Elias held still.

"Men cannot move freely through it," Solomon said. "Trade cannot move."

"Why."

Solomon's eyes did not change.

"The people camped in the bend," he said. "They hunt there. They cross at will. They have fired into my post. A man of mine was turned back last month."

"Turned back," Elias said.

"Yes."

"From the coulee."

Solomon inclined his head a fraction.

"From the ground between."

The room was very quiet.

"That ground," Elias said, "is where they have always moved."

"Yes," Solomon said. "And it is also where I need to move."

Silence.

"What you are saying," Elias said slowly, "is that you want an understanding."

"An agreement," Solomon said.

"Between you and Little Soldier."

Solomon's eyes held his.

"If a man carries authority," he said, "then it stands where he puts it."

The words sat between them.

Elias looked at the table.

He thought about Little Soldier at the fire. The food set before him on a piece of bark. The child who had come two feet closer and stayed. He thought about what an agreement might look like to him. Something carried by the church's name. Something that said the ground was seen. That it was certain. Known.

Something that could hold.

He saw, for a moment, a man standing in that same ground with paper in his hand and a gun behind him.

He let it go.

"And the woman," he said.

Solomon looked at him steadily.

"If a man carries authority," he said, "then it stands where he puts it."

He let that sit.

Elias held his gaze.

"I will need to meet with him," Elias said.

Solomon said, "Yes."

"On his ground."

"Yes."

Solomon regarded him.

"You have been there before," he said.

"Yes."

"He received you."

"He did."

Solomon nodded once.

"Then you know the way," he said.

Elias picked up his hat.

He did not put it on immediately.

"The woman stays where she is," he said. "Until this is done."

Solomon looked at him.

"Until it is done," he said.

Elias put on his hat.

He went to the door.

Behind him Solomon said, "Reverend."

He stopped.

"Little Soldier is not a simple man," Solomon said.

Elias said nothing.

"Do not mistake patience for agreement."

Elias went out.

The room opened around him again. The piano. The voices. The women moving through it.

One of them looked at him as he passed. The same one as before.

Not smiling now.

He stepped outside.

The ground had begun to dry at the edges where the afternoon had reached it. The mud holding in the low places and giving elsewhere.

He walked down toward the crossing.

The creek moved fast and brown.

He thought about the ground between the forts. The coulee. The willows along the creek bottom. The way Little Soldier had come up through it, south along the water, and the willows had taken him back.

He stepped into the water.

The cold came up through his boots.

He crossed.

Sixteen

The room was not empty.

It was only between uses.

Two teamsters near the stove with cups going cold. A man at the far table, hat beside him, plate gone mostly clean. The piano shut. The lamps unlit. Daylight through the front windows picking out every scar in the floor, every place the boards had been asked to hold more than they were built for.

Elias sat at the bar with the stew and half a heel of bread.

The coat was upstairs.

He had stopped going up for it somewhere in the past week. Not a decision.

The door opened.

His eyes went to the mirror behind the bar before he had decided to look. Two men, the sound of outside coming in with them and then gone. He located their hands, their coats, the way they moved into the room. Neither of them was the scarred man. He would be on the road by now. North-west. The wagon and the whiskey moving up through the hills.

Elias looked back at the stew.

He broke the bread without eating it.

Nora came from the back and took in the room the way she took in everything — efficiently, without appearing to. She refilled the teamsters without being asked and came toward him.

Set the coffee pot down.

"You've taken to the place," she said.

"Have I."

"Most men meaning to leave don't start eating regular."

He took a bite of the stew. The grounds had settled dark at the bottom of his cup.

"It's a room," he said. "And a plate."

She refilled his cup and set the pot between them. Did not move away.

He ate.

The door opened. He felt it before he heard it — the air shifting, the movement of the yard for a moment, then the door closing again. He let his eyes go to the mirror. One of Farwell's men. He had seen him before.

He looked back at the bowl.

"The camp," he said.

She waited.

"Little Soldier. His people trade."

"When it suits them."

He broke the bread into two pieces. "Word could be sent down there."

Nora set a glass on the counter and held it to the window light and set it down again. She was not answering him and she was not walking away.

"You've been there," he said.

"I've family there."

He looked at her.

"Métis," she said.

He nodded once.

"I brought you back," he said.

"You did."

The teamsters near the stove exchanged something low. A chair scraped back.

"He listens," Elias said.

She looked at him then. "You'll say one thing. He'll hear the other."

He let that sit.

"What does he want."

She was quiet long enough that he thought she had decided against it.

"What keeps his people through winter," she said. "And not to be the one who chose wrong."

He turned the cup once in his hand.

"I can go down there."

"You can stand there. That's not the same thing."

A pause.

"Stop before the lodges," she said. "Wait for someone to come to you. Men go down there thinking they're settling something." She picked up the pot. "They come back having started it instead."

The door opened.

His eyes went before he sent them. Two men, road-dirty, already talking to each other about something that had nothing to do with this room. He watched until he had what he needed. Then he looked at his cup.

One of the new men called out and Nora went to the end of the bar.

He thought about the wagon in the hills. The scarred man beside it. The look that had found him in the trading post and marked him without yet deciding when the matter would be taken up.

He was still thinking about it when she came back.

She refilled his cup and stood.

"The widow," she said.

He kept his eyes on the table.

"Men are speaking on it," he said.

"Men speak on everything."

He said nothing.

"The women have been going by," she said. "Food. Wood. Talking."

He moved the cup. Set it back.

"That holds," he said.

"Not long."

A chair scraped again near the stove.

"Fence is down on the south side," she said. "Won't keep anything out."

He said nothing.

"Women can bring food," she said. "They don't mend a place."

At the table behind him one of the new men said something about a horse taken. Said the next word plain enough.

Indians.

The other man answered lower. Not disagreement. Not quite agreement either.

One of them laughed.

"Where is she to be put," Nora said.

He moved the cup. Set it back. "Nothing's been settled."

She waited.

"Farwell's not pressing it."

"And Solomon."

He drew a breath.

"Solomon hasn't made a move."

She watched him. A long moment, the room going on behind them both.

"That won't hold," she said.

"It might."

"Men don't leave things unsettled."

"Farwell understands the situation."

"Farwell understands what's useful." She set the pot down an inch from where it had been. "That's a different thing."

Elias had nothing to say to that.

"If she's put right, she'll live," Nora said. "If she isn't, she won't. Men like to think there's time between those two."

He moved the bowl to the side. There was nothing left in it. There was nothing left to do with his hands.

"Solomon made a calculation," he said.

She waited.

He said no more.

He had stood in Solomon's room. He had spoken and Solomon had listened and weighed what was on the table against what was being asked. Elias had laid down what he had. Solomon had decided it was worth more than Bella Hawthorne. What that said about Elias he had not decided to consider.

“You’ll be going to the camp,” she said.

“Might be.”

She took the bowl. Set the pot back where it belonged.

Then she moved away down the bar.

He sat with the cup.

The two new men at the table were still at it. A horse. A rope cut in the night. One of them said men were getting bold. The other said they always had been.

The door stayed shut.

He thought about the coat upstairs. He thought about a fence down on the south side of Bella Hawthorne’s place. Wind getting in where it pleased. Stock gone through already or would be soon enough. Women arriving with food and leaving again. He thought about how long such things held before they stopped holding.

He picked up his hat.

Seventeen

The post would not sit.

He drove it once. The maul glanced and jarred his arms. The wood leaned a finger's width off true and held there as if it had chosen it.

He set his boot to the base and tried again.

The hole he had opened yesterday had closed on him in the night, the edges slumped back in. He dug it out with the shovel, shallow, not deep enough. He knew it as he did it.

The sun was already up and working.

The fence ran in a line that had once been straight. It dipped now where the posts had loosened, the wire sagging between them in a tired curve. There was a place where a man might step through without lifting his leg. He had seen it from the road. It had bothered him.

He set the post again. Held it with his left hand. Brought the maul down.

The blow landed. The wood sank an inch. Still not true.

He lifted the maul again.

A fly found the wet at his neck. He shook his shoulder and missed the post. He stood there a moment with the weight of it in his hands.

The camp was south. He thought of it briefly, the way a man thinks of a thing he has decided not to do yet. Then he set the maul to the post and struck again.

This time it went in. Not straight. Not deep enough. It stood.

He went to the wire. Took it in both hands and drew it toward the new post. It resisted, then came, the slack gathering from either side. He wrapped it once. Twice. The ends bit his palm. He twisted them together with the pliers until they would not take another turn.

He let go.

The line held. The curve lessened. It was not right, but it was better than it had been.

He stood with his hands on his hips and breathed.

Behind him, the house sat with its door closed against the light. The yard was bare where the grass had been worn down to dust. Heather's fence, he thought. Bella's garden wall he had noticed along the south side, the soil worked and thin. This was a place a woman had been keeping upright by herself.

A length of board lay along the bottom rail where it had come loose. He bent and lifted it. It was heavier than it looked. He set one end against the post and tried to bring the other up into place. It slipped. He caught it against his thigh and felt the bruise of it.

"You don't have to do that."

He did not turn at once.

He set the board down carefully, leaned it against the post, and then looked.

Bella stood a few paces off, the shade from the house cutting her in two. Her hands were empty. Her hair was tied back in a way that kept it from her face. There was dust on the hem of her dress where it met the ground.

"It's coming down," he said.

"It's been coming down."

She did not step closer. She looked past him at the line he had worked.

He followed her gaze. From where she stood the new post showed its lean.

"I'll set it deeper," he said.

She said nothing to that.

He picked up the board again, set it, tried to hold it in place with his shoulder while he reached for the nails. They lay in the dirt where he had spilled them. He crouched and gathered them, one by one, into his palm. The collar clung. He felt it when he bent. He put the nails between his teeth, straightened, and set the board again. The first strike of the hammer glanced. The nail bent. He pulled it out with the claw and tried another. The second took. He drove it in. Not flush. He struck again. The head sank crooked. He worked down the length. Two more. Three. Each one holding a little of the board.

When he was done, he stepped back. The rail sat where it should have been. It bowed between the posts.

He let the hammer hang at his side.

There was a tin cup in Bella's hand. He had not seen her go for it.

She held it out.

He went to her and took it. The water was warm from the sun. He drank it anyway. It ran down his throat and settled somewhere low. He drank again and felt it in his stomach, a weight.

"Thank you," he said.

She did not answer. She watched him drink.

He gave the cup back. Their hands did not touch.

She looked at the fence again.

"You set it too shallow," she said.

He glanced at the post.

"It will hold," he said.

"For a while."

He nodded as if that had been his intention.

He turned back to the wire.

"I can bring another post," he said. "Set it beside. Take some of the strain."

She said, "You don't have tools for that."

"I can manage it."

She watched him a moment longer.

"Why?" she said.

He took hold of the wire again, as if that answered it.

"It needs doing."

"It needed doing before."

He tightened his grip and pulled. The line drew taut. The twist at the post creaked.

He let it go.

He felt her looking at him.

"When?" she said.

He kept his eyes on the fence.

"When what."

She did not change her voice.

"When do I go."

He reached up and touched the collar, thumb finding the edge, lifting it from his skin. It stuck, then came away. The air against his throat was a relief that lasted a moment.

"It hasn't been set," he said. "There are arrangements—"

"Someone has set it."

He shook his head, small, contained.

"There are a number of interests—Farwell, Solomon—there are things to be worked through."

She waited.

"You were in the room," she said.

He took a step along the fence and bent to the wire. It gave him something to look at, something to do with his hands.

"It isn't decided in that way," he said. "It's a matter of—"

"A matter of what."

He twisted the wire again, though it would not take another turn.

"Of time," he said. "Of—circumstance."

She let that sit.

The yard held the heat. The flies had found the damp at his collar again. He shook his head once, irritated, and did not move his hands.

From the road, a man came down toward the fence.

Elias saw him only when he was close.

Dunn. Farwell's man.

He came without hurry. Hat low. Broken nose. Coat open. The same man who had stepped into the saloon and not stayed.

He stopped at the line of the fence and looked at the work. He took in the new post, the sag of the wire, the rail. Said nothing.

Elias straightened. He reached for the collar again, set it straight.

"Morning," he said.

The man rested a hand on the top wire and pressed down. It gave a little under the weight and then held.

"Farwell's asking," he said.

The words sat in the air between them.

"It's not time," Elias said.

The man looked at him over his broken nose. His look was flat.

"He sent me," he said.

Elias inclined his head.

"It's not time."

The man let the wire go. It rose back to where it had been.

He looked past Elias once, to the house, to Bella standing there with the cup in her hand. His gaze did not linger. Then he turned and went back the way he had come.

Elias watched him until he reached the road and took it. When he turned back, Bella was still there.

"You were in the room," she said again.

He opened his mouth.

No word came.

The fly settled at his throat. He did not brush it away.

"When," she said.

He took a breath.

"Soon," he said.

The word lay thin.

She looked at him a long moment, as if measuring the distance between what he had said and what was. Then she turned. She went back to the house and closed the door. The sound of it was not loud. It carried.

He stood in the yard with the hammer in his hand. The fence ran before him, a line that did not quite hold.

He went to the new post and set his shoulder to it. It moved under him, a fraction, the earth giving where he had not set it deep enough.

He stepped back.

He went to the wire and took it in both hands and drew it tight. The twist at the post creaked. The line straightened.

He held it there a moment, feeling the strain in his arms.

He still did not have the words.

Eighteen

The post had to come out again.

He put the shovel to the base and worked the earth loose around it. The ground was dry at the top and harder below. The blade bit and jarred. He leaned his weight into it and felt the complaint rise out of the bad foot and travel up the leg. The fence ran on either side of him in a line that had given up pretending. Wire sagged. One rail leaned. The repaired board already showed the shape of the strain he had asked it to carry.

He dug.

The sun was not yet high but had already begun its work.

The house behind him held stillness the way a place does when it has been emptied by force. Door shut. Window dark. No pan set out. No sound from within.

He had come because there was a fence and a yard and a house that had not yet fully admitted what had been done to it. Because labour was narrower than thought.

He got the post loose at last and lifted it free. Dirt fell from the base in small dry clots. He set it down, wiped his hand once against his trousers, and drove the shovel back into the hole to deepen it.

The door opened behind him.

He did not turn at once. He took one more cut at the earth. Then he looked.

Mary stood in the doorway with Heather beside her.

The child held to the woman's skirt with one hand. Her face had gone past crying and into something flatter. The look of a child who had been awake too early and had seen too much and understood enough.

Mary came down off the porch. She had no hat. The light caught the iron in her braid and the hard lines of her face. Heather came because Mary came.

Elias straightened.

"Morning," he said.

Mary looked at the hole. The post in the dust. The maul. The hammer. The length of rail he had tried to mend.

Then she looked at him.

"You found work."

He said nothing.

Heather's eyes were on him. He looked away first.

Mary stopped a few paces off. Not close enough for confidences. Close enough that nothing would be mistaken.

"They came before the light," she said.

The yard changed around him without moving.

"Who."

"You know who."

He did not answer.

"Two from Solomon's place. One on a bay horse with a split ear. One broad man with a yellow beard. They knocked. Then they opened the door."

Heather's fingers tightened in the cloth of Mary's skirt.

Elias said, "Bella."

Mary's eyes did not leave him.

"She was here when they came."

The heat in the yard altered. Went meaner.

"Heather was sleeping in the back room. Bella got her out first. Brought her to my place through the yard before they came in proper." Mary paused. "Then she went back because if she ran, they would come looking."

No one moved.

Elias felt the shovel handle in his hand as though it belonged to another man.

"She went with them," he said.

"She was taken with fewer blows than some women get."

The words landed flat and hard.

Heather looked up at Mary, then back at Elias.

He set the shovel aside carefully. Too carefully.

Mary watched that too.

"You still here fixing her fence," she said. "That a comfort to you."

"No."

"Good."

The child had not taken her eyes off him.

Mary drew one breath through her nose.

"There's more."

He looked at her.

"A man was brought into camp an hour ago. Little Soldier's people. Shot through." Her face did not change. "Found in the coulee."

The shovel, the post, the wire, the whole yard seemed suddenly part of one thing he had not yet named and was now too late to refuse.

"Who shot him."

Mary gave the smallest movement of one shoulder.

"A man with a gun."

"That could be any man."

She looked at him as though patience were a resource she had nearly exhausted.

“Dead men make things simpler,” she said.

He said nothing.

"Some in the camp want blood. Some want to know who did it. Some know they will never know." She took one step nearer. "And you are still here with a shovel."

Heather shifted closer into the woman's dress.

Mary's eyes stayed on Elias.

"You have said enough. You have stood enough. You have watched enough men arrange enough things." A beat. "Now go do something that costs you."

Silence.

Then she turned to Heather.

"Come."

The child looked once more at Elias. Not pleading. Not accusing. Merely seeing him.

Then she went with Mary back toward the house.

Elias stood in the yard with the hole open at his feet.

The post lay beside it.

The fence ran before him in a wavering line that still did not hold.

He bent once, picked up the coat from where he had laid it across the rail, and put it on. The cloth had gone hot in the sun. He took the revolver from the pocket where he had left it and checked it without needing to. Closed it. Slipped it back.

He did not take the shovel.

He left the fence as it was and went out through the gate.

* * *

The coulee lay to the north, between the two forts, a low break in the land where the creek bent and the grass gave way to willow and shade. The place where men disappeared from sight before they were gone.

He walked down the hill and took the trail south along the creek. The heat opened over him. He walked faster than the foot wanted.

He saw no one.

That was the first wrong thing.

The second was the birds. None.

He slowed.

Not by choice. Because the body knew.

Something moved in the willows to his left. Then to the right.

He turned and a man came out of the shade with a rifle levelled at his chest. Young. Assiniboine. The look on his face something past anger and not yet finished.

Two more behind him.

Elias held still.

He answered in the little Assiniboine he had. *Came to speak. Little Soldier.*

The young man said something sharp. The others moved to his flanks. His hand said: walk.

They took the gun. Not roughly. Efficiently. The revolver gone. His wrists seized and held.

One of them jerked his chin south.

Elias went.

The willow branches brushed his shoulders as they took him down through the shade and into the lower ground by the camp.

The smell reached him before the lodges did.

Not woodsmoke.

Blood.

* * *

They brought him in through the edge of the camp and people turned to look.

The dead man lay on a robe at the camp's centre, in a cleared space with men standing around it in a broken ring. Women farther back. Children drawn away. Little Soldier stood at the head of the robe. He saw Elias come in and said nothing. His hands were at his sides.

The young man with the rifle spoke loudly. Others answered. The sound moved through the ring and did not settle.

Then one of them turned and stepped into Elias's path and hit him across the face with a closed fist.

He went down.

The ground came up hard and he caught himself on both palms and felt the dirt on his tongue. He got one knee under him. Someone's boot found his ribs from the left side. The air went out of him all at once. He tried to rise and the boot came again, harder, and he went flat.

He got his arms up.

It didn't help much.

They were not trying to hurt him. They were trying to make him dead and hadn't quite decided how far to take it. That was the difference he felt in the ground — not cruelty. Grief with a direction.

A third kick found the bad foot.

Something gave.

The pain arrived at a pitch beyond description, beyond sound, a white and total thing, and his leg pulled itself toward his body by instinct and left him on his side in the dirt with his hands against his face and his mouth already filling.

He tasted iron.

Someone got a fistful of his coat and hauled him half-upright and struck him twice in the same place on his jaw. He felt the second one less than the first. The world tilted and offered him the ground again.

He did not go all the way down.

He did not know why.

His hands found the dirt and held.

He was on his knees in front of the dead man. That much was clear. The robe was two feet from his face and the shape beneath it was young. He could see that even now. Younger than expected. He had thought that before but had not yet understood it properly. At the edge of the camp, beyond the ring of men, he could see the picket line. Four horses. For a camp this size there should have been twenty.

A fourth man stepped up with something in his hand.

A word came through the camp like a stone thrown.

Once.

The man stopped.

Elias looked up.

Little Soldier spoke. The voice low, controlled, the sentences long enough that the interpreter had to wait until the end.

"He says Red Tail hunted in the coulee at dawn. He heard riders. He came up to see. He was shot and left there."

The crowd shifted. A woman made a small sound and swallowed it.

"No one saw who did it?" Elias asked.

The interpreter translated. Little Soldier answered without haste.

"He says tracks were there. Then other tracks. Horses from the north. Horses from the west. Men crossing over men. He says dead ground does not tell the truth."

Elias looked at the wound. Clean shot. No message left on the body but the body itself.

Little Soldier spoke once more.

“He says some men here want a white man dead before sunset.”

The young man who had first hit him said something in Assiniboine and slapped his palm against his own chest. Others answered him. Not all in agreement.

Little Soldier did not turn his head.

“He says some men want you.”

Silence moved through Elias like a blade finding its place.

“Why me.”

“He says because you are white. Because you come from the forts and walk between them. Because a man might be enough if truth cannot be found.”

Elias drew breath and felt it catch halfway. His jaw throbbed when he swallowed. Something loose at the back of his teeth. He tasted it again. Iron.

He looked at Little Soldier.

“If you kill me, the forts will say you did it.”

The interpreter translated.

Some of the men laughed once, without humour.

Little Soldier answered.

“He says the forts already say what helps them.”

True enough that there was no room to stand outside it.

Elias looked at the dead man. At the wound. At the mud drying on one side of the face. At the young men who had already been putting him beside it.

He said, “You want the man who did this.”

The interpreter spoke. Little Soldier answered at once.

“He wants a thing that will hold.”

Elias understood then why Little Soldier had held his men back.

Not mercy.

Cost.

His tongue found the split inside his cheek. He did not stop it.

He looked once at the crowd. At the young men, already leaning toward war because war gave grief a direction. At the women, measuring cost faster than the men.

He tried to draw breath and found he couldn't take it full.

Bella in the doorway.

He pushed it down.

Then he said, "The coulee."

The interpreter hesitated before translating, as if he had expected something else and not liked it.

Little Soldier listened.

Elias went on.

"The place between. The ground both forts move through. The place men cross armed and call it no one's."

The interpreter gave it to him.

Little Soldier's eyes stayed on Elias now.

"That place will keep taking men. Yours. Theirs."

He shifted his weight without meaning to and the bad foot gave under him. He caught himself before he went down.

"Any man who stands in it without rule."

The young man with the rifle spoke sharply before the interpreter could translate further. The interpreter answered him in Assiniboine without taking his eyes from Elias.

Little Soldier said one word. The camp went quieter.

Elias felt every step of what he was doing and stepped anyway.

"Give it."

The interpreter stared at him.

"Translate it."

He did.

There was noise then. Immediate. Angry. Several voices at once. A woman said something from behind the ring that cut across the others and lasted longer. The young men answered her.

Little Soldier did not move.

Elias heard the interpreter render Little Soldier's reply and knew from the man's face before he spoke English what the answer would be.

"He says it is already his."

"Yes," Elias said. "Which is why it is always at risk."

The eyes of the camp were on him now in a different way.

He did not let himself look at what he was doing.

"The forts are north and west of it. Men from Solomon move there. Men from Farwell move there. Traders. Hunters. Drunks. There is no way for you to keep that ground from becoming a killing place except by killing for it every time."

The interpreter gave it over.

Little Soldier's face remained unreadable.

Elias pointed south. To the open country below the bend. Beyond the willows. The broader land where the camps could range without sitting between two white men's hungers.

"Take land they can name and sign. Larger. South of the bend. To the low ridge and beyond if you want it. Hunting rights. Crossing rights. White men kept out. Horses besides. Payment for the dead."

The interpreter translated. Horses needed no help.

The camp's noise came slower now, because numbers and boundaries did work that rage did not. Men began speaking not in heat alone but in measure.

Elias watched Little Soldier instead.

The older man listened to his people. A long time. Then he spoke.

"He says you offer him his own coat and call it a gift."

Elias took that.

"Yes."

The interpreter blinked once, then gave it across.

Little Soldier's mouth moved. Not a smile. Recognition.

He said something more.

"He says your words are white man words. They make theft sound orderly."

Elias tasted blood again before answering.

"Yes."

The interpreter looked at him then as if something in him had given up expecting better.

Little Soldier asked a question.

"He asks what makes these words hold."

"Writing."

The interpreter translated.

Little Soldier did not react.

"Paper signed by both fort men," Elias said. "Marked. Witnessed. Bound."

"He says paper is not a fence."

Elias swallowed. It hurt.

"No," he said. "It is white man law."

The answer travelled through the camp and changed the sound of it. Not softer. Stranger.

Little Soldier said several sentences, none hurried.

"He says if white men honour paper, then paper is your rope, not his."

Elias felt the truth of that as a pressure at his throat.

"Yes."

Little Soldier spoke longer now.

"He says if he takes peace instead of blood, then peace must be costly enough that his young men do not think him afraid."

The young man behind Elias said something hard. Others answered him.

Little Soldier went on speaking over none of it and all of it.

Winter came whether a man chose war or not.

Some things a man could not eat.

The interpreter faced Elias fully.

"He says thirty horses."

The number entered the camp like a stone into water. Some men turned their heads. Others did not.

The interpreter looked at the fire before he continued. He said it the way he had said things before without being asked to translate them. "The bison are gone. What horses they had, they traded for provisions. For whiskey." He did not look at Elias when he said the last word. "Thirty horses is what a camp this size needs to move when winter comes."

"He says land from the bend south to the red ridge, and west to the broken poplar. No white hunting there. No white riders cutting through camp ground. No shots fired in the coulee by fort men. If one is fired, the paper is dead."

Elias heard the gap in it.

It would not hold clean.

He did not need it to.

The interpreter continued.

"He says the body is to be named in the writing. Payment for Red Tail. Not for general peace. For Red Tail."

The dead man lay between them in the hot morning, younger than all this.

"And," the interpreter said, with a pause that belonged to Little Soldier more than to him, "he says the priest brings the paper back himself."

The camp had gone quiet enough that even the dogs knew something had shifted.

Elias said, "Farwell may sign. Solomon may not."

The interpreter translated.

Little Soldier answered immediately.

"He says then you are the man who lied."

That sat where it ought.

Elias looked once more at the dead man. At the wound. At the young men who had been putting him beside it ten minutes ago and might yet.

Bella in a room that was not hers.

He did not know if she was alive.

He lifted his eyes to Little Soldier.

"I will bring it."

Nineteen

He crossed before the heat had finished gathering.

The water was lower than it had been. Stones showed that had been under a week ago. His bad foot found each one and he let it speak and kept moving. The bruising along his jaw had gone the colour of old leather. He could feel the socket of his eye when he turned his head quickly—a deep specific ache that had settled in without any intention of leaving. Mary had taped two ribs before he left. They held when he breathed shallow.

He kept his breathing shallow.

He climbed the far bank.

Fort Solomon sat where it always sat. Without apology. Without arrangement. Two men in the yard watched him come through the gate. They did not speak.

He went in.

The room had been altered for them.

Not cleared. Arranged. Tables pushed back. Piano shut. Lamps unlit in the day. The women gone from sight though not from the place; the air still held them. Coffee, stale smoke, perfume, and underneath all of it the older smell of men who had mistaken appetite for authority long enough that the room had taken it in.

Solomon sat at a table near the middle. Coat buttoned. Hat on the wood. Farwell was there already. A lamp burned on the table though the day was sufficient. Papers in front of Solomon.

His papers.

Bella stood near the stair.

That was where Elias's eyes went first. Not by choice. A new mark at her cheekbone, blue gone to yellow. A lip split and closed again. One sleeve torn and pinned. Her hair pulled back by someone who had needed it out of her face and had no further use for appearance.

She did not look at him.

Farwell gestured once. "Sit."

Elias remained standing.

Solomon looked at his face.

The room absorbed what that meant without naming it.

"You were struck," Solomon said. "In the camp."

"Yes."

"And still you came back."

"Yes."

Solomon's fingers turned his cufflink. "What did they want."

"Terms."

A pause.

"Let us hear the church."

"It is not the church," Elias said. "It is an agreement."

"With who."

"Little Soldier."

Solomon sat very still.

"And he gave you this."

"He gave terms. By word."

"And you wrote them."

"Yes."

"Read," Solomon said.

Elias unrolled the paper. It wanted to curl back into itself. He held it flat and read.

The land first. From the creek bend south to the red ridge. West to the broken poplar. No white hunting there. No riders cutting through camp ground.

Then the dead man. Red Tail. Payment for him. Not for general peace—for him.

Then the coulee. No shots fired. If one is fired, the paper is dead.

Then the horses. Thirty.

When he finished, he said the last thing. "The marks of both forts. Witnessed."

* * *

Solomon took the first page between two fingers and read it with the care of a man who distrusts translation—not the language but the distance between what words say and what they intend.

Farwell turned his hat once.

Solomon set the page down.

"Little Soldier wants the coulee," he said.

"He wants it recognised," Elias said. "That's what the paper says."

"Which is not the same thing."

"No."

Solomon's fingers rested on the edge of the page.

"He is not giving it up. He is keeping it. And I am agreeing to that."

"You are agreeing to the terms under which men move through it," Elias said. "That is different from ceding it."

"Is it."

"In law. Yes."

Solomon looked at him.

"In law," he said.

He turned the word over once. Not contempt. Something more patient than that.

He read the second page. Then the third.

"Thirty horses," he said.

"Split equally between the forts."

"Fifteen horses from my stock. As payment for a dead man."

"For the man and for a binding agreement."

Solomon set the page beside the first.

"He has not put his mark."

The sentence sat in the room like something placed on a scale.

Elias kept his hands flat on his knees.

"No."

"You bring me a paper from a man who has not agreed to it."

"He agreed. The mark follows."

"When."

"When I bring it back."

A small silence.

"When you bring it back," Solomon said.

"Yes."

"With my signature already on it."

"Yes."

Solomon's eyes stayed level.

"That is an unusual arrangement."

"It is."

"A man signs a paper the other side has not yet committed to."

"That is how agreements begin," Elias said. "One man first."

Solomon considered that without expression.

"And we trust the second man will follow."

"They are his terms. They are what he's asked."

"And if he looks at my name on this paper and decides he has won."

Farwell set his glass down.

"Moses," he said.

Solomon's eyes moved to him.

"A country without courts still wants law," Farwell said. He said it the way he said most things—practically, as though reading aloud a conclusion already established by the evidence. "It looks for something to work through. A channel." He nodded once toward Elias. "I've watched Elias walk into places I wouldn't send dogs and walk out carrying what was needed. Little Soldier fed him. That is not nothing."

"No," Solomon said.

"The three communities out here need a man they'll each take seriously." Farwell's voice had gone quieter, as though the observation required less weight than the others. "That is a useful arrangement to have."

Solomon looked at Elias.

"Farwell's lawman," he said.

"No," Elias said.

Both men looked at him.

He kept his eyes on Solomon.

"That is not how I work."

Farwell's jaw shifted once and settled.

"Then how," Solomon said.

Elias thought about the crossing. About Red Tail on the robe. About what he had told Little Soldier and what delivering it would require.

"A man in this territory with a collar and a gun and no authority but what he can hold in a room," he said. "Not Farwell's man. Not a bishop's man." He paused. "Just a man who has said words to Little Soldier's people and to you and has to stand behind all of them at once."

He stopped.

"That is the only kind of law that holds out here. Because it doesn't belong to any one of you."

The lamp burned.

Solomon's hands rested still on the table.

"You speak plainly," he said.

"When I can."

"And when you cannot."

Elias said nothing.

Solomon turned the pages once, aligning their edges.

"You promised him something else," he said.

Elias waited.

"A man does not walk out of that camp with a body on the ground and come back with a treaty that costs thirty horses without leaving something more behind." His eyes did not move. "What did you promise him."

The lamp held its flame.

Elias thought of the lie that was on the paper. About how Little Soldier had demanded no shots fired by white men. And how the words on the page read only no shots fired. He had not written the demand because Solomon would not have signed. Likely, Farwell would not have signed.

Solomon and Farwell would read the words. Little Soldier would not. Elias would tell Little Soldier that the words bound the white men. Elias would get all their marks. Because the truth and the possible were not the same, and the distance between them was the ground where Elias needed to stand.

Then Elias looked at Solomon, and said the words that were needed to make the three settlements hold.

"I told him that the paper would be witnessed," Elias said. "By someone neither of you holds."

"And that is you."

"I told him it was."

A pause.

"Are you."

Elias held his gaze.

"I am whoever the paper requires me to be."

Solomon studied him.

Outside the room a woman's voice rose and then fell away into something else.

"The coulee," Solomon said. "Men of mine move through it."

"The paper allows for safe passage."

"Armed passage."

Elias thought about the young man with the rifle. About grief finding direction. About what armed passage through that ground would look like when a man's blood was already running wrong.

"So long as no shots are fired, the paper will hold," he said.

Solomon's eyes narrowed a fraction.

"You keep offering me what you don't have."

"Yes."

A silence that contained several things.

"The dead man is named in the writing," Solomon said.

"He is."

Solomon read the line.

"Red Tail."

"Yes."

Solomon set the page down. He was quiet long enough that Elias felt it in his taped ribs.

"The widow stays until Little Soldier marks it."

The words went through Elias the way cold water goes through.

He did not look at Farwell.

"No," he said.

Solomon regarded him.

"She is my guarantee."

"She is a woman."

"In this country—"

"No." Elias kept his voice where it was. "She is not a guarantee. She comes with me now."

Solomon's fingers rested on the papers.

"I said no."

"I heard you."

He lifted his eyes.

"She comes with me now, or I walk back to Little Soldier's camp and tell him there will be no paper and I let what follows follow."

The room did not move.

Farwell's hand lay flat on the table.

"Moses," he said.

Solomon's eyes stayed on Elias.

"You would let it fall," he said.

"If I have to."

"Thirty horses. The land. The dead man's name."

"Yes."

"For the sake of a woman."

Elias thought about Heather.

"I know her," he said.

Solomon placed his hands together and rested his chin upon them. He considered Elias a long moment. Not hostility. Assessment. A final taking of the measure.

Then he sat back in the chair.

"She goes," he said.

Farwell nodded once.

Solomon reached for the pen beside the lamp. He read the last page over, the pen held above it. Slowly. Reading.

When he reached the coulee line, he stopped.

"One shot," he said.

"Yes."

"The paper's dead."

"That is what he said."

"No man owns the ground."

Solomon looked at him.

"And the coulee."

Elias felt the lie arrive. "The intention is that no man owns it by gun alone."

Solomon saw it.

The seam.

He signed.

The scratch of it was the only sound in the room for a moment.

He set the pen down. He aligned the pages.

"Reverend."

Elias looked up.

"I do not know what Little Soldier will do," Solomon said.

"No."

"I do not know what Farwell will do." He did not look at Farwell when he said it.

Farwell's mouth moved.

"I know what I will do," Solomon said. "Hold what is mine and wait." He looked at Elias. "And I know what you will do."

Elias waited.

"Whatever is necessary," Solomon said. "Whether necessary is honest or not."

He pushed the papers across the table.

"Get the mark," he said. "Before one of my men forgets himself. Or one of his."

He looked at Bella.

"Go."

She did not move at once.

Then she crossed.

When she passed behind Elias he caught the smell of soap over fear and old sweat and something sharper beneath it.

He did not turn.

* * *

Outside, the air was hotter than he expected.

Farwell stood a little apart.

No one spoke.

Bella looked at him.

She looked at his face the way she looked at everything—without softening, without flinching, taking in what was there. He looked at hers. Neither of them said what they were looking at.

They walked south to the ford, following the edge of the coulee. The land within was dark and quiet.

They crossed at the ford where the stones were flat and the current moved without urgency. The cold came up through his boots and his bad foot found the riverbed and held.

The ache in his foot was steady.

The taste of blood was not gone.

Farwell's side. Heather waiting.

Bella stopped and looked back once across the water.

Behind them, Fort Solomon.

The camp to the south. Little Soldier's mark not yet won. Thirty horses not yet gathered. The coulee still the coulee.

He had told Solomon it would be done. Had said it looking at the pen and thinking about Bella's sleeve and Red Tail on the robe and Heather with her hand in Mary's skirt and the young man whose grief still had a direction. He had said it the way he had learned to say things in this country—not as a lie exactly, not as the truth exactly, but as the shape a necessary thing had to take before it could become real.

Bella started walking.

He walked with her.

The creek moved behind them.

It carried what it was given, as it always had, indifferently, south.

Nothing held.

Something begun.

Twenty

The last post went in straight.

He had reset it twice. The third time he packed the earth tight around the base with his boot heel and the flat of the shovel and drove the maul down until the post stopped moving. He stepped back. It stood.

The wire ran from it in a line that held. Not quite level. The second post still showed its lean. But the whole of it stood now, and the gate closed on its latch without lifting, and the repair he had made to the board along the bottom rail had not pulled loose in the night.

He drove one more nail into the board anyway.

Then he stood with the hammer hanging from his hand and looked at the length of it.

It was not the fence Anderson Hawthorne had put up. That fence was in the ground with him, or had been, eight weeks now. In the far corner the earth had subsided — a slight depression where the ground had settled in around itself. A post stood near it. Elias had put it there without deciding to.

He set the hammer down on the rail.

Bella was working the garden along the south wall. What the season had left her. Carrots and potatoes coming out in the ground. A small harvest of pumpkin. Dried stalks where the tomatoes had given up. She worked with a short-handled implement, pulling and loosening the dry ground, moving along the row without hurry. She had been at it when he arrived, and she was at it still. She did not look at the fence.

He collected the tools and set them against the post near the gate.

Heather came around the corner of the house with a rag in one hand and held it toward him. He took it. He did not know what she intended. He wiped his hands on it anyway.

She watched him do this and then took the rag back and went around the corner again.

He heard Bella pull something from the earth behind him. The sound of soil releasing.

He picked up the shovel and carried it to the lean-to.

* * *

Midday came in long flat light. The grass on the hills had gone its autumn colour — a dry gold that gave nothing back but more sky, more distance. The shadows ran at a lower angle than they had a month ago. He felt the change before he named it.

He was coming along the back of the settlement when the movement caught him at the birch copse.

He went still before he decided to.

His hand found his coat.

The birch copse sat on the rise east of the settlement where the ground climbed toward the sky. He had come through it himself once, in the other direction, in different light. He watched the tree line now the way a man watches something that has already done him damage once.

Horses. Four of them. Riders.

He held.

They came through the copse in the unhurried way of men returning from somewhere they had been before and intending to be again. Métis, from the look — mixed dress, practical, the long rifles of autumn hunters across the saddles. Pack horses behind. Loaded. The season's work already done.

He let his hand fall.

The first man came through the last of the birch and saw him standing in the open ground.

He nodded once. The slight adjustment of a man who has placed something and moved on.

Elias did not move.

The riders came down off the rise and took the trail toward the settlement. Their horses' breath made small clouds in the air. The pack animals walked easy under their loads.

The last rider passed.

He stood there.

The light lay on the hills to the north and west in a way it had not laid in August. The grass held it differently. The distances had changed, not in measurement but in quality — the particular quality of a country that has begun its preparation and is not yet concerned with what that preparation costs the people inside it.

He thought about the road south. The way you think about weather you have already decided to be in.

He knew how the wagons ran in September. How they stopped in November. A man on a Benton wagon could reach the hills in October if he set out with purpose. In November he would not set out.

He breathed the air in.

The light was north and west.

He was already facing it.

After a time, he continued back toward the settlement.

* * *

Farwell's ledger was open on the desk when Elias came in. He did not close it.

He had the look of a man who has concluded a transaction he cannot quite fault and cannot quite approve. He looked at the collar, then at the coat, then at the mud still on the boots from the morning's work.

"Last of the horses went across yesterday," he said.

Elias said nothing.

"Fifteen head from my stock. Fifteen from Moses."

"And the mark."

Farwell looked at the ledger.

"Done." A pause. "Last week."

That was all he gave it.

"Price was high," he said.

"Yes."

"Could've been negotiated tighter." He turned one page without reading it. "The land especially."

"The land was his to begin with," Elias said.

Farwell made a small sound in his throat. Not agreement.

"Not a shot was fired," Elias said.

The room held that.

Farwell picked up his pen. He wrote something in the ledger. Brief. He set the pen down.

He closed the book.

"Well," he said. Then nothing further.

The creek moved behind the building in its ordinary way. Somewhere a door closed against the wind.

Elias put on his hat.

"Reverend."

He stopped.

Farwell had not looked up from the closed ledger.

"Winter's early this year," he said. "Feel it in the mornings."

It was not a question.

Elias went out.

* * *

The saloon was the same saloon.

Same boards. Same smell of old whiskey worked into the floor. The fire had been laid. It had not been needed yet and had been laid anyway — the kind of thing a place does when it has decided winter is coming and has stopped arguing about it.

He stepped in.

The nearest man looked up and tipped his hat before Elias had taken three steps. Then looked back at his glass. A pair at the table near the window lowered their voices when he came into the room — not in fear, in the adjustment a space makes around something it has incorporated. A man at the bar moved one step without looking at what had prompted him to.

Elias walked to the bar.

Nora set a glass in front of him and poured. Water. Not whiskey. The trade could go on without him.

He became aware of them the way he became aware of most things — by what the room was doing around them rather than by looking directly.

Two men. Sitting apart. Known to each other, or known enough — the angle of their bodies said the rest. A line between them that was not a line on the floor but might as well have been. Both with drinks they were not drinking. Both facing the room the way men face a room when they are waiting for something it will provide.

Their eyes came to him within a breath of each other.

He laid down the glass.

The collar was still on.

He had not removed it.

Ice had taken the edges of the creek.

Twenty-One

They did not call it a court.

He took a table near the middle of the room and turned it once so the light from the front window fell across it instead of behind. It rocked on one leg and settled. He left it as it was.

He set the book down.

A chair on one side. Two on the other. Not matched. Not arranged.

He sat.

The room went on as it had been. Nora behind the bar. A man at the far table with his hat still on his head and his drink in his hand. Two others near the stove, speaking low. The door opening and closing on the afternoon.

Elias opened the book to a clean page.

He wrote the date.

He left space below it.

He did not look up.

* * *

Word moved.

It did not arrive all at once. It came in the way of it—men drifting nearer without choosing to, a chair drawn back an inch, a conversation shortened and not taken up again. A woman from the settlement stood near the wall with something still in her hands she had not set down.

Nora watched it happen and said nothing.

Farwell took a place where he could see the table and the door both. Not close. Not far. He stood with one shoulder against a post, the way a man stands in a room he does not need to control.

Solomon was at the back. Hat on. Coat buttoned. He had come in and not announced it. No one asked him why.

Elias let the room settle around him.

* * *

The Scotsman came first.

He did not sit at once. He stood looking at the table, at the book, at Elias, scarred knuckles white where rope had burned them years ago, as if measuring whether the room would hold what he had come to say.

Then he took the chair to the left.

The Métis came behind him.

He did not hurry. He did not look at the Scotsman. The tobacco pouch at his belt was worn through at the seam, the leather thinned by the same thumb that had worn it smooth. He took the other side and remained standing a moment longer than needed before sitting.

Elias took their names. Wrote then in the book.

Thomas McLeod.

Jean-Baptiste Desjarlais.

McLeod reached into his pocket and set two coins on the table. Not pushed. Placed.

Desjarlais watched him do it. Then he set one coin beside them.

Not equal.

Elias looked at the coins.

He did not touch them.

"Mr. McLeod," he said. "Tell me the matter."

McLeod told it clean.

The watering bend off the coulee trail. His family's freight teams working it three years running. The bank they had cut to ease the approach. Brush cleared. A place made where a wagon could come down without breaking an axle.

Then Desjarlais's teams coming through and leaving it wrecked. Churned ground. Collapsed bank. Men using what they had not made and not caring what they left behind.

He did not look at Desjarlais.

Then his voice changed.

"His people," he said. "Drunk at the bend. More than once. Men from Little Soldier's camp coming down and disrupting my teams."

Desjarlais said something quiet in Michif. Not at McLeod. At the table.

McLeod went on.

"Second time, one of them came at my teamster with a hatchet."

He left that where it was.

"His people."

Behind the bar, Nora went still. Not obviously. The cloth in her hand simply stopped.

Elias wrote a line.

He let the silence stand.

"Mr. Desjarlais."

Desjarlais spoke as though each word had been placed before he picked it up.

"We have used that bend longer than he has," he said. "Since before the post. We will use it after." A small movement of his hand. "Water does not keep names."

He glanced once at McLeod.

"We do not quarrel with a schedule. We want access. The men he names are Assiniboine. From Little Soldier's camp." He did not soften it. "They are not my people. I do not answer for them."

"They come at the same—" McLeod began.

"Mr. McLeod."

Elias did not raise his voice.

McLeod stopped.

At the bar, a man gave a short laugh into his glass.

It hung there.

Nora did not look up when she said, "You can take that outside."

The man set the glass down. He did not laugh again.

The room held.

* * *

Elias looked at his notes.

"You have used the bend longer," he said to Desjarlais.

"Yes."

"You do not object to the work done there."

"It serves us."

"You want consistent access."

"Yes."

He turned to McLeod.

"You say the labour gives you claim."

"It gives a man something," McLeod said. "In any country."

"And the men at the bend."

"His responsibility."

"Not mine," Desjarlais said. His hands moved once on the table and stilled.

Elias looked at the page. The date. The names. The space below.

He began to write.

* * *

The pen moved.

The room waited.

When he looked up, both men were watching him.

"Here's what I've written," he began.

"McLeod's teams shall have the bend first light to midday, for working freight."

He let that land.

"Afternoons. Midday to four. Open use."

A shift at the wall. Small. Contained.

"Evenings. Four to dark. Desjarlais. His teams."

McLeod leaned forward.

"Evenings means his teams come through after mine have softened the bank," he said. "Every day."

"In September," Elias said, "yes. In October it is ice."

"Next September."

"Come back next September."

McLeod's jaw set.

Desjarlais had not moved.

"In autumn," he said, "light is gone by five."

"Yes."

"That is not enough."

"It is what holds."

Desjarlais looked at him a long moment.

Then he sat back.

"The drunks," Elias said, "are not the dispute."

Both men looked at him.

He let that sit.

McLeod spoke into that space.

"Next man comes at my team down there," he said, not looking at anyone now, "I'll put him down and be done with it."

No one moved.

Elias did not answer at once.

He looked at McLeod.

Then at Desjarlais.

Then at the room—the men at the wall, Nora at the bar, Farwell not moving, Solomon not moving.

He picked up the pen again.

"No arms at the bend," he said.

The room shifted.

"No rifles. No pistols drawn. Either side."

McLeod looked at him.

"And when a man does."

Elias met his eyes.

"He loses the bend."

Silence.

"For how long."

Elias considered it.

"Three days."

A breath moved through the room. Not relief. Measure.

"Is that clear, Mr. McLeod."

A pause.

"It's clear."

"Mr. Desjarlais."

"Yes."

Elias wrote the line. Set off from the rest.

He pressed harder than he had before.

When he finished, he turned the book so they could see.

Desjarlais read it.

McLeod glanced and did not.

"Morning's mine," McLeod said, as if to himself, already standing.

He took his hat.

Elias said nothing.

McLeod went out.

Desjarlais remained a moment longer.

He looked at the page again. Then at Elias.

A small nod. Not agreement. Not quite.

He stood.

He went out.

* * *

The room loosened.

Men turned back to their tables. Not immediately. In pieces.

A woman at the wall left without looking back.

Nora moved behind the bar as if she had never stopped.

Solomon straightened from where he had been leaning.

He came forward.

He looked down at the book. Not reading it so much as weighing the man who had written it.

He said nothing.

Then he went out.

* * *

Farwell stayed.

He watched the table. The chairs. The ledger.

He came forward and gathered the coins. He set them nearer Elias.

"You'll want those," he said.

Elias did not reach for them.

Farwell looked at him a moment.

"You've started something," he said. Then he turned away.

* * *

Elias held the book. The leather was rough in his hands.

He became aware of Gabriel Lavallee the way he became aware of most things in a room — not by looking directly but by what the room was doing around him. Nora had placed herself at the far end of the bar. The two men near the stove had gone quieter than their conversation required.

Gabriel stood near the door with his hat in his hands and the look of a man who had come to the fort but had not yet decided whether the coming had been worth it.

He came forward when Elias met his eyes.

"You need to come," he said. In English. Straight to it, the way a man speaks to someone he has already done hard work beside.

Elias waited.

"Wolf hunters put poison on the land. Down past the bend. On his ground." Gabriel set his hat on the nearest table as though he needed his hands free to say the rest of it. "Bison carcasses. Six, maybe eight. Laid out across the flat."

The room did not move.

"Little Soldier is asking what the paper is worth," Gabriel said. "He is asking it loud. In front of the young men."

A pause.

"You understand what I'm telling you."

Elias understood.

Gabriel had interpreted for Little Soldier across two winters and longer. His position in that camp was not sentiment. It was use. A man who speaks between peoples is valuable precisely as long as the people on both sides believe speaking is possible. If the young men carried the camp past that point, Gabriel Lavallee became a man standing in open ground between two closed doors.

"The young men," Elias said.

"Some of them have been waiting for this." Gabriel picked up his hat. Turned it once. "The ones who never believed the paper would hold."

"The paper has held."

"The bison say otherwise."

The words settled.

"They have not gone to the carcasses yet," Gabriel said. "They are waiting."

"For what."

Gabriel held his eyes.

"For you to answer."

Elias looked at the book on the table. The date. The names. The coins Farwell had set within reach and he hadn't touched.

He picked up his coat.

His hand found his rib as he put it on. The tape held. The ache beneath it was its own kind of memory — the ground coming up, the boot finding the same place twice, the taste of iron that had taken two weeks to leave him.

The light outside had shifted. The kind of light that did not last.

He went.

Twenty-Two

He asked Gabriel once, on the trail south.

"How will they receive me."

Gabriel walked ahead of him and did not turn around.

That was the answer.

His foot found the ground the way it found it now—careful, particular. One wrong step cost more than it should. The ribs moved under the banding with each breath. He had not thought about them in days. He thought about them now.

The grass moved alongside them in the low wind, indifferent. The creek sound came and went as the trail bent. The sun sat lower than it had a month ago and the light it made was harder, thinner, the kind that gives you the landscape without softening it.

Gabriel's pace did not adjust to the foot.

Elias did not ask it to.

* * *

The camp did not begin.

One moment the grass. Then a lodge where there had been nothing. Then another. Smoke running low to the ground. A child's voice and then no voice. Dogs that watched without sound. No gate. No line. No place where a man could say he had crossed.

"Here," Gabriel said. He looked at Elias once. "Wait."

Gabriel slowed and then stopped.

The ground here was different. Not in its appearance. In what the body knew of it. The grass had come back in most of it. Not all.

Red Tail had been laid out here.

Elias stood.

The camp moved around him without acknowledging him. A woman carrying water who looked at the ground near his feet and then past him. A man at a hide frame whose hands went on with their work without interruption. A boy who came to the edge of one lodge and looked at him and then went back inside. Near the nearest lodge a meat rack stood mostly bare. What hung on it would not see a family through to November.

At the edge of things, two young men stood together. Not speaking. Watching.

He kept his hands at his sides.

The gun was inside his coat. It did not make him safe. It reminded him of the ground, which was where a man ended up when things went badly. He had been on the ground here before. He knew the taste of it.

* * *

The young man came from between two lodges. No hurry. Direct. The walk of someone who had somewhere to be and had decided this was it.

He stopped a few paces off.

He looked at Elias the way a man looks at something he has already decided about.

Then he spat.

The spit hit the dirt between them and darkened it.

Elias felt it come up before he named it. Not thought. Something lower. The body shifting its weight without asking him. The foot settling. His hands moving slightly out from his sides.

The young man saw it.

He stepped in and swung.

Elias didn't get his hands up in time. The blow caught him high on the cheek and turned his head. The world went briefly sideways. He stepped back, caught himself, and moved in.

He closed the distance. His arms went around the man's shoulders. He drove him back. They went down together in the dirt and the impact said something about the ribs.

No clean lines. No space. Close work.

The young man was fast. He got a hand free and struck at the left side. Elias felt it go through the banding and settle somewhere deep. He tightened his grip and rolled. Found himself on top. He got one knee across the man's arm and his weight into it.

The free hand came up. Fingers at his throat.

He drove his forearm down across the wrist.

The young man bucked.

His coat was open.

The revolver was right there.

He did not reach for it.

He put his fist into the man's face. His weight behind it.

Again.

Then the hands came. Not one. Several. They took him by the coat and the shoulders and hauled him off—the way you take a man you've decided something about—and he was in the air briefly and then the ground came up again. He lay a moment where he was. The sky above the camp was the sky above any other place. White and enormous and without opinion.

He pushed himself up.

The young man stood a few feet away. Blood at the corner of his mouth. Chest moving fast. He looked at Elias with a thing in his face that was not finished yet.

Then a voice came from somewhere in the camp.

Not loud.

Enough.

The young man stepped back once. And again.

Elias got to one knee. Then to his feet.

Two men came and took his arms. Not rough. Not gentle. The way you take something you intend to move without damaging further.

They walked him through the camp.

As they passed between the lodges, the same two young men had shifted closer. One of them followed a few steps behind. Not intervening. Not leaving.

* * *

Little Soldier sat where Elias had seen him before. But not as he had seen him before.

Two others were with him.

To his right an older man. Broader through the chest. White at his temples and at the top of his braids. He held a pipe he was not smoking. His eyes were already on Elias when they brought him in and did not move from him.

To Little Soldier's left a woman. Perhaps sixty. Her face had done more weather than the men's. A blanket across her shoulders despite the afternoon. Her hands were in her lap and they were not still.

Elias was released and stood.

Gabriel took his place a little behind and to the side of the three—the particular position of a man between two languages who has learned not to stand too close to either.

Little Soldier looked at Elias. At his cheek. At the sleeve. At the mud on the knee.

Then he spoke. Gabriel waited until he was done.

"He says: I hear you are still a man after all."

No one smiled. Neither did Elias.

He said nothing. His shame was enough.

The older man spoke. His voice came from low in the chest. Gabriel let it run to its end.

"He says: the paper was meant to keep white men from this ground. The ground is wide. Still you must come to ours."

Elias looked at the man.

"I came because the paper is being tested," he said. "Not by me. By men I didn't send."

Gabriel gave it over.

The older man received it. He set the pipe on his knee.

"He says: then where were you when they came."

There was no answer that was not true.

Elias said nothing.

The woman spoke then. Her voice was not raised. It did not need to be. She looked past Elias when she said it, as if addressing something he had brought with him that she did not wish to look at directly.

She spoke for longer than the others had.

Gabriel waited until she was done.

"She says the sky is changing. Frost bends the grass. Soon the snow will come. This is the time when her people work. When the meat is laid in and the roots are pulled and the skins are made ready."

He paused.

"She says in her mother's time the animals came in numbers that darkened the plain. You did not wonder if there would be enough. You wondered only how much you could carry home. She says she has watched the herds go smaller since before her children were born. Not drought. Not sickness. White men who take what they came for and leave the rest where it falls."

Gabriel looked at the fire.

"She says seven animals on the flat is not something her people have not seen before. It is only that this time she can see them."

A pause.

"She says this is not a time for problems that belong to white men."

Another.

"She says who will answer when her daughter's children go hungry."

Elias held still.

"Tell her I understand," he said.

Gabriel translated.

The woman looked at him for the first time. She said one short thing.

"She says: then go fix it."

* * *

Little Soldier spoke.

Gabriel gave it over in pieces.

"He says the men who hunt with poison came from the south. He says his young men did not see them come in. They saw only what was left behind." He stopped, then continued. "He says: this is not a man's way to hunt. It is not good for the animal. It is not good for the man who comes after and does not know what was done to the meat."

The older man spoke without waiting.

"He says the hunters take the skin and leave the rest. In the old way, nothing is wasted. In the white man's way, everything is wasted." Gabriel paused. "He says: this is a way of hunting that does not know what hunting is."

"These men are not from the forts," Elias said. "Not Farwell. Not Solomon. They come up from Montana. They cross where there is no border post, no line a man can see. We don't want them either."

Gabriel translated.

The older man said something once. Short.

"He says: whose country do they cross to get here."

Elias looked at him steadily.

"Yours."

No one spoke for a moment.

"And if your young men shoot them," Elias said, "the men from Fort Benton will come north. They will not ask whose ground they are riding through. They will not ask whose ground the hunters were on. They will come and they will be many and they will not come alone."

Gabriel translated.

The older man's hands tightened once on the pipe. He did not speak.

Little Soldier was watching Elias. Not with the stillness of a man waiting. With the stillness of a man who had already considered this possibility and set it beside the others and was now watching to see what it looked like in another man's mouth.

The woman spoke. Her hands came briefly out of her lap.

Gabriel: "She says: white men come when white men are killed. This is not a reason for her people to suffer wolf hunters. It is a reason for the white men to stop wolf hunters."

Elias said, "Yes."

She looked at him. A small movement of something in her face. Not agreement. Acknowledgement that he had heard her.

"If you can find them," he said, speaking across all three of them now, "I can bring them to answer for it. Not in Farwell's saloon. Not before Solomon. Here."

Gabriel translated.

The older man spoke. One sentence.

"He says: finding them is not justice."

"No," Elias said. "But it is where justice starts."

Little Soldier looked at him a long moment. Then he stood.

He said something to Gabriel without looking at him.

Gabriel looked at Elias.

"He wants you to see."

* * *

They walked.

Little Soldier. The older man. Gabriel. Elias.

Behind them, at a distance that was not accidental, the young man with the blood at his mouth came as well.

Over a rise where the grass gave way to shorter growth and the ground flattened into a wide shelf above the creek bottom. The sky had nowhere to go but down.

He smelled it before the rise.

Then he saw it.

Bison. Six of them. A seventh beyond, at the far edge of the flat.

Down.

Not hunted. Not taken.

Down.

They lay where they had fallen or been driven to fall, hides removed in pieces, bodies swollen. Flies moved over them in black shifting masses, lifting briefly when the wind moved and settling again. The smell was enormous—sweet and wrong and occupying the air so completely that it was a moment before Elias understood he was still breathing.

He stopped. Covered his mouth with his coat. His eyes watered.

The older man stood beside him. He did not look at the flat. He looked at Elias looking at the flat.

The tracks in the ground around the carcasses—shod horses, men's boots. A fire ring a little north of the nearest animal. Two nights, maybe three. Strychnine worked into the meat and the hunters riding out before it did its work, come back for the wolf pelts, come back for what they had come for and nothing else. The wolves would be somewhere nearby in their own version of this.

He made himself look at the nearest animal.

A cow. Good size. She had rolled near the end, or been driven to it by what was happening inside her. The ground around her bore that out. One eye was to the sky now and the flies had made it their own.

Seven animals. Seven families fed, made lean, carried through to spring. Now a problem on the land.

He thought of the woman's hands in her lap. The frost on the grass. Snow coming in.

Little Soldier spoke.

Gabriel: "He says: this is your paper."

Elias did not answer at once. He looked at the flat. He let it be what it was.

He lowered the coat. Breathed through his mouth.

"I'll find them," he said.

Little Soldier did not look at him. He looked at the flat, the way Elias had looked at it. He spoke quietly. The older man beside him answered equally quietly. A brief exchange that Gabriel did not render.

Then Little Soldier looked at Elias.

"He says: tell me what the paper is worth," Gabriel said. "He is asking you. Not the paper."

Elias held his gaze.

"As much as the man who carries it," he said. "No more."

Gabriel gave it over.

Little Soldier received it. He turned and walked back toward the camp.

* * *

They came back to the place of the elders.

The woman was where they had left her. The fire between them had been fed. The smoke ran low and south, the way smoke runs when the air has decided it is autumn.

The young man from before stood off to the side. He had a cloth at his lip. He watched Elias come in and did not cover what was in his face.

Little Soldier sat. He spoke to the older man. Then to the woman. The conversation moved between the three of them and Gabriel did not translate, because it was not for Elias and Gabriel knew the difference.

Elias sat. No man objected.

The woman spoke the longest. Her hands came out of her lap once. Gestured south, toward the flat. Went back.

The older man answered. His voice was lower now than it had been. Not softer. Considered.

Then Little Soldier looked at Elias.

He spoke. Gabriel translated without pausing between sentences.

"He says: you have one day. Before the sun is here again." Gabriel glanced up briefly. "You bring the men who did this to this camp. Not to Farwell. Not to Solomon. Here."

Elias held still.

"Or," Gabriel said.

His eyes moved once toward the young man.

"Or the young men go themselves."

Silence.

Little Soldier held his eyes.

Elias nodded.

He did not trust his voice and did not use it.

No one dismissed him.

He stood.

Then he turned.

He passed the place where Red Tail had been. The young man followed, then stopped and watched him go. The camp gave him its back the same way it had given him its side—not hostility, merely the ongoing business of people whose lives would continue whether or not the man walking north solved what he had said he would solve.

The grass opened ahead.

The smell of the flat stayed with him.

His foot found the ground the way it had learned.

He had one day.

Twenty-Three

He did not go to the saloon.

Not because he had decided against it. Because he already knew.

He had stood on the slope above the bend as the evening light began to come on and looked up the hill to Fort Solomon and to the coulee that lay beside it.

The coulee ran between the two forts like a seam in the land, low and willowed, dark even in afternoon. Water. Cover. A clear line of retreat in two directions. Men who knew how to live rough and wanted no one's notice.

He walked up the hill.

* * *

Fort Solomon received him without ceremony, as it always had. The gate open. Two men in the yard who did not ask him his business. The same piano, the same low light, the same smell of the place carried in the air before the door.

He went in.

The room was full. Food. Music. Girls laughing sharp and false. In the corner, four men drinking without talking, looking at their cards. A woman at the far table with her head against a man's shoulder, eyes open, looking at nothing. Another behind the bar who looked up with a red smile that stilled at the sight of him. She did not need to work for the Reverend.

He stood at the threshold and let his eyes move through the room.

Three men near the window.

He took in the coats first. The cut of them. The stain along one hem that was not mud but old fat, the kind that gets into wool from skinning work and does not leave it. Boots caked in the particular grey dust of the southern coulees. A rifle leaned against the wall behind the nearest chair with the ease of a man who sleeps beside his tools.

Enough.

The nearest man turned to say something to the one beside him.

Elias went still.

The face was broader now than it had been. A scar along the jaw he had not had before. More beard. The same small eyes that moved to new things the way a dog's move — not in curiosity but assessment.

Elias turned before the man's eyes completed their circuit of the room.

He went out.

He stood in the yard with his back to the wall of the building and let the air do what it did.

He had seen enough inside.

He left the rest where it lay.

* * *

He was still standing when Solomon came out.

Solomon took in the yard, the gate, and then Elias, in that order. He adjusted his coat at the button and came forward without hurry.

"Reverend."

"The men inside," Elias said. "When did they arrive."

"This afternoon."

"Did they pay for rooms."

Solomon regarded him.

"They have not."

"Then they're camping in the coulee tonight."

"Likely."

"I need one of them."

Solomon waited.

"Wolf hunters from the south have poisoned seven bison on Little Soldier's ground. Left them to rot. It was them or men they ran with. I need one to bring before the camp."

Solomon's eyes did not move from his face.

"That," he said, "is your arrangement."

"One man given up," Elias said. "That's all. The others walk."

"And if they don't want to walk," Solomon said, "in the direction of an Indian camp."

"I'll manage it."

A small pause.

"You'll manage it," Solomon said.

He said it the way he said most things — not with contempt, but with the weight of a man recording what he has heard.

"These are Montana men," he said. "They came here for whiskey and they'll go back south when the season closes. Little Soldier's problem is not my problem."

"It will be if his young men come to the coulee to settle it."

"The agreement," Solomon said, "says the coulee is ours."

"It says no man holds it by gun."

"It says no shots get fired."

"They won't need rifles."

Solomon's gaze held.

"Seven animals," Elias said. "On his ground."

A silence.

"They'll come quiet," he said. "And they won't take the one they mean."

Solomon turned the cufflink once.

"Reverend, you know what they do to a man they mean to punish."

Elias held his eyes.

"Yes."

"Then you understand what you're asking."

Elias said nothing.

"Might not even be the right men," Solomon said.

"Your girls hear things."

The yard held.

Solomon was still for a moment. Then something moved across his face that was not a smile and was not its opposite. The expression of a man who has received new information and is deciding where in the ledger it belongs.

"That," he said, "is not law."

"Might not be."

Another silence, of a different quality.

Solomon looked toward the coulee. The low break in the land south of the fort. The willows already darkening in the late light.

He looked back at Elias.

"You'd give him up."

Elias did not answer.

The silence held.

"And if I don't," Solomon said.

Elias met his eyes.

"Then you'll have them in the coulee before morning," he said. "And whatever happens there won't stay there."

Solomon studied him a moment longer.

Then he nodded once. Not agreement. Measure.

"Come back," he said, "in two hours."

He turned and went inside.

* * *

Elias stood in the yard alone. The smell of the flat was still with him, if he breathed wrong.

He thought about the man inside.

He did not think about him long.

Twenty-Four

The coulee first. Then back.

He told himself he went to confirm what he already knew. He walked south along the creek in the dark, the water beside him carrying the last of the light south with it, and did not think about what he was going to do.

The camp sat in the bottom where the willows opened into a rough flat. Two fires. Men around them. He smelled the whiskey and the grease of the season's work before he saw the light. He stopped at the edge of the willows and looked.

Three men. Four. One asleep against a saddle. Another feeding the near fire with a branch he dragged without rising.

A rifle leaned against the nearest tree.

He looked at the rifle.

He looked at the men.

One of them said something. Another laughed. The sound ran up through the dark and past him and was gone.

He stood there long enough to know he was not looking for guilt.

He turned and walked back.

* * *

The yard was lit by the lamp above Solomon's door.

He waited at the edge of the light. Not close enough to be seen from the window. The creek ran behind the fort. The smell of the evening came down off the hills.

He did not pray.

He had tried, on the walk back, and the words had not come. Not because he was not a praying man. Because a praying man asks for something he does not yet have.

He had already decided.

The door opened.

Solomon came out first. He stood on the step and looked at the yard the way he looked at every room—taking in the gate, the dark, Elias standing in it. He adjusted his coat at the second button. Straightened his cuff. Something in the movement suggested he had already finished whatever required finishing inside, and this was the next item in an ordered sequence.

He nodded once.

The blond man came through the door. Then one of the girls—a young woman, dark-haired, a shawl pulled over her dress against the cold. She stood in the doorway with her arms crossed and looked at Elias without expression.

Then Doyle.

Two of Solomon's men had him by the arms. He was not unconscious. He was past it. His feet worked but not reliably. His head hung forward and lifted and hung forward again. The whiskey came off him in a warm invisible wave.

They brought him forward.

At the edge of the lamplight Doyle's head came up. His eyes found Elias and held there. Something moved through them. Not recognition yet. The effort before it.

Then:

"John."

The word came out flat and certain.

"My name is Elias Wilson," he said. "Reverend Wilson."

Doyle blinked. He looked at the collar the way a man looks at something that has been put in the wrong place.

"John Heath," he said.

"You're drunk," Elias said. "Can you walk."

The men released him.

He swayed. Found his feet. Looked at Elias with the eyes of a man whose body had been taken from him but whose mind was still working to hold something.

"I know you," he said.

"I'm going to help you back to your camp," Elias said.

He took Doyle's arm.

Doyle let him.

He looked back once at Solomon's door. The girl had gone inside. The blond man remained, watching. Solomon stood at the edge of the lamplight with his hands at his sides, his face doing nothing at all.

Elias walked Doyle through the gate.

* * *

The hill was steep and the dark was complete past the fort's light.

Doyle's weight came against him. Not resisting. Trusting. The way a drunk man trusts the nearest solid thing.

He smelled of whiskey and old work. His coat was rough under Elias's hand.

They went down toward the creek.

Doyle said something into his chest that Elias did not catch. Then he said it again.

"Where we going."

"Your camp," Elias said.

"Camp's in the coulee."

"Yes."

Doyle's feet found the easier ground at the bottom of the hill and he straightened somewhat. He looked at Elias. His eyes were working harder now.

"You're the priest from Farwell's."

"Yes."

"John Heath was a bookkeeper out of Fort Benton."

"You're thinking of someone else."

Doyle's mouth worked. He was looking at the collar. At Elias's face. Back at the collar.

"Maybe," he said.

They walked.

The creek bent south. Elias followed it. The willows came up on either side and the dark thickened. Doyle's weight was steady against his arm, not fighting. The sound of their boots in the grass and the sound of the water and nothing else.

"Where's your camp," Doyle said again.

"We're almost there."

* * *

The fires had burned lower.

He stopped at the edge of the willows and looked at the camp. One fire still going. Dogs at the perimeter. The lodges dark against the dark.

Doyle had gone quieter. Elias could feel the man's attention sharpening, the way whiskey sometimes releases the mind just before the body gives out.

"This isn't my camp," Doyle said.

Elias walked him forward.

The dogs came. Not barking. The low circling angle of dogs that know the difference between alarm and ceremony.

"Little Soldier," Elias said.

His voice settled into the still air and stayed there.

A child called from somewhere and was hushed. A light moved inside the nearest lodge. Doyle had stopped walking. He was looking at the fires, at the lodges, at the dogs moving around them.

A man came out. Then another. Then the young man—the one whose lip Elias had split, the one who had put him in the dirt. He looked at Elias. He looked at Doyle. Something moved through his face that was not yet what it would become.

Little Soldier came last.

He was dressed for sleep. He stood at the edge of the firelight and looked at the two men without expression.

Elias let go of Doyle's arm.

Doyle took one step and stopped. He was looking at the young men gathering. At Little Soldier. He turned to look at Elias and the sharpness was fully in his eyes now.

Elias looked at Little Soldier.

"This is the man," he said. "One of the men who put poison on your ground."

Doyle said, "What—"

"This is what the agreement allows," Elias said.

Little Soldier looked at Doyle. Then at Elias. He said something in his own tongue. Low. Too quick for Elias to catch.

Then, in English:

"Not paper."

Elias held his gaze.

"White man law," he said. "Justice."

Little Soldier's face did not change.

"No."

"It is."

Little Soldier looked at him a moment longer.

Then he said, "Land. Not law."

The words sat in the dark between them.

Elias said, "Take your justice."

Little Soldier said something to the young men that Elias did not catch.

Doyle moved.

He was fast, even drunk. He went for the gap between two of them and almost found it.

Almost.

They had him before the willows.

"He can't—" Elias said.

He did not finish it.

Little Soldier looked at him.

"You stay," he said.

* * *

Elias did not watch.

He fixed his eyes on a point of darkness above the fire where the smoke rose and thinned into the same darkness as everything else.

He had not considered that they would not be quiet about it.

He had not considered that at all.

His breathing went wrong against the taped ribs. He made it shallow. The cold came in through his coat and stayed.

The creek ran behind him.

He thought about the fence at Bella's yard. The post that still showed its lean. The board he had nailed with the crooked nail and driven anyway. These thoughts arrived without invitation and he held them because they were the only ground available.

Doyle's voice changed.

He could not help but hear it.

He turned to Little Soldier. "Stop it," he said. "Kill him clean. Stop."

Little Soldier did not move.

He said it again.

His own voice reached him as from a short distance away. He had heard it in the lodge with Jacob. At the crossing. At the grave. It sounded the same as it always sounded.

No one was listening to it.

His hand went inside his coat.

The grip found his palm.

He did not take it out.

Not here. Not with them. Not with the fort up the hill and men who would ask where the shot came from. Not with Solomon's yard close enough to hear it and remember.

He held the gun where it was.

Then let it go.

The young man nearest the fire turned and looked at him. There was nothing in his face that Elias had a name for. It was not cruelty. It was something older than cruelty and more patient and it had been waiting longer than Elias had been in this country.

He looked back at the dark above the fire.

Doyle's voice changed again.

Then, from somewhere low:

"John."

Not accusation. Not a cry for help. Something between those things. Something that knew exactly what it was saying and said it from a place past caring whether it was heard.

The sound of it moved through him the way cold water moves—all at once and everywhere and then gone and you are left standing in the fact of it.

The fire burned.

The creek moved south.

The young men continued their work and the night held all of it without difficulty, the way the night holds everything that men do in it.

* * *

He did not know when it ended.

He became aware of the silence after it had already settled—the way you become aware of a sound only once it has stopped, when the shape of it is already past.

He was still standing.

His hands were at his sides.

Little Soldier stood near the fire. He looked at Elias with the expression of a man who had seen what he came to see and would carry it a long time.

Elias said, "He can't be found."

Little Soldier did not answer.

"If he is found," Elias said, "men will come. Not asking who did it. More will die."

Little Soldier looked at him a long moment.

Then he said something to the young men.

Elias did not understand the words.

He understood the work.

Little Soldier looked back at him.

"Go," he said.

* * *

Elias went.

Through the willows. Up along the creek. The dark was the same dark it had been an hour before when he had come down through it with a man leaning on his arm and the man trusting the collar and the collar meaning what it had always meant to men who needed something to trust.

He did not think about Doyle.

He thought about the colour of the creek in the dark. The sound of frost-stiffened grass underfoot. The lamp still burning in Solomon's window across the water, the same lamp, burning as it had been burning when he left.

He crossed at the ford.

The cold came up through his boots.

His bad foot found the stones and held.

He climbed the far bank and stood at the top of it with the creek behind him and the cold coming off the hills and Solomon's lamp in the window and he stood there until he could not have said how long he had been standing.

The creek moved south.

It carried what it was given.

He walked.

Twenty-Five

He woke before the light.

Not from rest.

The room. The smell of the place below, old whiskey worked into the boards. He lay still until the sounds of the settlement separated themselves into their parts. The creek. A horse against a rail somewhere. Wind at the sacking.

He sat up.

His ribs said what they said. He let them.

He dressed without hurry. The boot over the bad foot, laced to the second eyelet and no further. The collar. The coat.

* * *

The men came midday.

Two. The season's work was on them. Hides and grease and the grey dust of the southern coulees worked into the wool. Rough men. Dangerous in the way of men who were tired and had been drinking and had come a long way for something they had not found.

They came through the saloon door with the particular quality of men who have been redirected more than once.

Elias was at the table near the window. A glass of water. The book closed beside him.

The nearer man looked at the collar and then at the book and then at Elias.

"You the one keeps records," he said.

"Sit down," Elias said.

They sat. Neither removed his hat.

Nora moved behind the bar without looking toward them.

"One of our party hasn't come back," the nearer man said. "Walked out of Solomon's two nights ago. Drunk. Hasn't been seen."

Elias opened the book.

He turned to a clean page. Wrote the date.

"His name," he said.

"Hardwick. Doyle Hardwick."

Elias wrote it.

Doyle Hardwick.

He looked at it a moment. Then at the men.

"Give me the details."

The nearer man told it. Solomon's place. Evening. Hardwick had been drinking since before supper. They said he walked out sometime after dark. Last seen heading for the coulee. He hadn't come back.

"Anyone else see him go."

"Men in the yard. Saw him head south."

"You searched."

"This morning. Creek bottom. Coulee as far as it runs. Nothing."

The other man shifted in his chair. "Man that drunk falls in a creek, he doesn't always come up where you look."

"No," Elias said.

He wrote.

"I spoke with him briefly that evening," Elias said. "He was drunk. Said he was heading back to camp."

"He say anything else."

"Not much worth recording."

The nearer man leaned forward with both forearms on the table.

"We've got pelts to collect. Then need to head south before the snow falls. We already overstayed on account of Doyle."

Elias set the pen down.

"Where are the pelts."

"We ain't skinned them yet. We laid out the bait south of the creek bend three days ago. The flat below the low ridge. We been wasting time searching while the wolves likely lying dead and rotting. We don't have time to search for a man."

"That's Little Soldier's ground," Elias said.

"It's open country."

"It was open country." Elias looked at him. "There is an agreement. Land from the bend south to the red ridge. West to the broken poplar. It belongs to his people. No white men hunting there. No riders cutting through."

The nearer man's jaw set. "We don't know of no agreement."

"The agreement stands regardless."

"We've got property out there."

"You've got dead wolves you haven't found or skinned on ground that isn't yours," Elias said. "And I'd advise you strongly against going to collect them."

The other man straightened. "Why."

Elias looked at them both.

"Because it isn't safe."

A silence.

"Because of them," the nearer man said. It was not a question.

"Relations with Little Soldier's camp have been peaceful," Elias said. "I intend to keep them that way."

The other man looked at the nearer man. Something passed between them.

"You think they did it," the nearer man said.

"Did what."

"Doyle." He said it flat. "You think they killed him."

Elias picked up the pen.

"A wolf hunting man," he said, "drunk in the dark, gets turned around. Ends up in a native camp uninvited." He looked at the page. "That is not a good prospect for anybody."

The nearer man's hands came together on the table.

"Then there's your answer," he said. "They killed him."

"I didn't say that."

"You as good as."

"I said it's a dangerous situation for a man who doesn't know where he is." Elias looked up. "I don't have proof of anything beyond a man who was drunk and is now missing."

"So go ask them."

"I intend to make further inquiry."

"Ride down there," the other man said. "Ask them straight out. You're the law here."

"What I'm not going to do," Elias said, "is go down to that camp making accusations without proof and undo months of peaceful relations."

The nearer man pushed back slightly from the table. Not leaving. Deciding something.

"A white man's dead," he said.

"Possibly."

"Possibly." The word came out with something bitter behind it. "That's all you've got."

"That's what the evidence gives me."

"The evidence." He looked at the collar. Then at the book. "You know what I think. I think those Indians killed him and I think somebody ought to go clear them out before they do it again."

The room held.

Nora had gone still behind the bar.

Elias looked at the man steadily.

"Relations with that camp have been peaceful," he said again. "Men from both forts have moved through these hills without incident. I am not going to send armed men onto treaty land over a missing drunk." He set the pen down. "And neither are you."

The nearer man's eyes stayed on him.

"You can't stop us."

"I can make it considerably more difficult for you to operate out of either fort," Elias said. "And I can make certain that whatever happens down there next is laid at your feet and not anyone else's."

Silence.

The fire in the stove breathed.

The other man touched the nearer man's arm. Once. Low.

The nearer man looked at the table.

Then he looked up.

"The pelts," he said.

"Gone," Elias said. "Count them as the cost."

A long quiet.

The nearer man stood. The other with him.

"You'll continue the inquiry," the nearer man said.

"I will."

"And if you find something."

"Word will be sent south." Elias picked up the pen. "Give me a name. Where to send it."

The nearer man gave a trading post on the Teton River. A town. A name.

Elias wrote it.

Then: *Survived by a brother. Thomas Hardwick. Montana.*

"That all," the nearer man said.

"For now."

The man held his eyes a moment longer.

Then he went out. The other behind him.

* * *

The door closed.

Farwell had come in at some point without Elias hearing it. He stood near the back with one shoulder against the post, his hat in his hands. He looked at the door. Then at Elias.

"Well," he said.

Nothing after it.

He put the hat on and went out through the back.

Nora set a glass on the bar and looked at it and did not move it.

Elias looked at the window.

The two men crossed the yard. At the rail their horses waited with their heads down. The men mounted. They sat a moment. The nearer one looked back at the saloon, at the window, at nothing.

Then they rode south.

He watched them until the country took them.

He looked at the book.

Thomas Hardwick. Montana.

He looked at it a moment longer than he needed to.

Then he closed the book and went out.

* * *

The morning had gone cold in the way of October mornings—not winter yet, but the cold of a country that has begun its preparation and is no longer asking anyone's opinion of it.

He walked to the creek.

The ice was thicker than a week ago. Spreading out from the banks like gums on a mouth.

He stood at the bank.

He was still standing there when Bella came around the corner of the building with a pail in her hand. She saw him and did not change her pace.

She came to the bank. Set the pail down. Broke the thin skin of ice with the edge of it and let the water take.

Elias watched her do it.

The creek moved south.

She straightened. The pail full.

She looked at him.

Not a question.

"You'll be speaking," she said.

It wasn't a question.

He held her eyes.

"Yes."

She nodded once. As if something had been confirmed.

She bent to take the pail again.

"Come," he said.

The word did not move.

She did not look at him.

"Sunday."

She lifted the pail. Water sloshed once against the rim.

"I don't hold with it," she said.

"No."

"Anderson did."

He said nothing to that.

She looked past him toward the settlement. The buildings. The low smoke. The men moving in it.

"They'll come," she said.

"Some," he said.

"Enough."

She shifted the pail in her hand.

"And what will you tell them."

Elias did not answer at once.

The creek moved. The ice at the edges held.

"What holds," he said.

She looked at him then. Direct.

"Does it."

The question stayed where she put it.

He did not take it up.

After a moment, she nodded once. Not agreement.

"I'll see," she said.

She looked at him once more.

Then she went back the way she had come.

Twenty-Six

The cold had come in the night and stayed.

Not winter. October's announcement of it. The grass on the hills had gone the colour of old rope and the breath of the horses at the rail made small clouds that the air took and dispersed. The creek ran lower than it had in September, the stones along its edge gone white with the first thin rime that the morning sun had not yet reached.

They came bundled. Men with their coat collars turned up and hats pulled to the ears. Women with shawls doubled over and children pressed against their sides. They came down the slope toward the ford the way they had been coming since the summer — without being summoned, without ceremony, the settlement finding its way to the water's edge the way a settlement will when it has decided something is worth finding.

Bella came with Heather.

They took their place not near the front and not near the back.

Farwell stood where he always stood. Off to the side. Hat in his hands. Two of his men a little behind him.

Mary came after. She did not stand beside Bella. She stood where she could see the ford and the far bank and the trail south, the way a woman stands who has learned to keep the approaches in view.

A few from Fort Solomon came and stood as well, Solomon among them, standing still and measuring. They did not stand close but close enough to hear.

Whites and Métis. Men and women. Believers and non-believers. It being Sunday, they came and stood.

Elias stood at the water's edge.

He had been there when the first of them arrived and he was still there when the last came down the slope and the gathering quieted by degrees, the way it always quieted — not all at once, but in pieces, one conversation ending and then another, until only the creek remained.

He held the book.

He opened it.

* * *

"Dearly beloved," he said. "The Scripture moveth us, in sundry places, to acknowledge and confess our manifold sins and wickedness."

He led them in the words. His breath made a cloud. The air took it.

He left space and they filled it. When he had first come they had come with curiosity. Many not knowing or having forgotten the words. Now they answered.

The wind moved once across the gathering and released it.

He led them through the general confession and the voices came in behind him— uncertain at first, then settling into the words as into something the body remembered before the mind did.

He read the litany.

"From all the deceits of the world, the flesh, and the devil."

And the voices that knew it answered: *Good Lord, deliver us.*

"From battle and murder, and from sudden death."

Good Lord, deliver us.

"In the hour of death, and in the day of judgement."

Good Lord, deliver us.

The creek ran.

The cold sat on the gathering without apology.

He led them through the Lord's Prayer.

More voices now. The words known in the body even by those who had not used them in years.

Amen.

* * *

He put the prayer book aside and opened the bible. Turned to the passage he'd marked. He no longer read the words in the margins. He knew them.

"The Gospel according to Saint Matthew," he said. "Chapter the twenty-sixth."

He had chosen it. He did not examine the choosing. The passage was what it was.

He read it plainly.

"Now Peter sat without in the palace: and a damsel came unto him, saying, Thou also wast with Jesus of Galilee."

The creek ran. The cold held.

"But he denied before them all, saying, I know not what thou sayest."

A man near the front moved his hat from one hand to the other.

"And when he was gone out into the porch, another maid saw him, and said unto them that were there, This fellow was also with Jesus of Nazareth.

"And again he denied with an oath, I do not know the man."

He looked up once. Then back at the page.

"And after a while came unto them they that stood by, and said to Peter, Surely thou also art one of them; for thy speech betrayeth thee.

"Then began he to curse and to swear, saying, I know not the man. And immediately the cock crew."

He closed the book.

The sound of it was small.

He lifted his eyes.

"Peter was not a coward," he said.

The gathering held.

"He had said he would die first. He had said it plainly, and he had meant it."

The cold pressed at the coats.

"And still he stood in that yard and said: I do not know the man."

No one moved.

"We know this about ourselves." He looked across the gathering. "We have all stood in that yard."

A woman near the back inclined her head.

"He said it once. He said it again. He said it a third time."

Silence.

"And then he went out and wept."

A man removed his hat.

"This is not a man who was weak." He held there. "This is a man who declared himself. Who stood up and said: I will follow. I will be true. I will not fail you."

The cold came off the creek.

"And yet."

He turned. His foot said what it always did. He let it.

"He did not make excuses. He did not explain. He did not reason out. He did not justify. He went out. And he wept."

A breath.

"That is where grace begins."

His voice had gone quieter. Not softer.

"Not in the perfection of the man. Not in his having done what he swore to do."

He looked at his hands.

"In the declaration itself."

Silence.

"Say what you mean to be. Say it even knowing you will fail it." He looked up. "Say it again after you have failed it."

Amen. A different voice.

"Grace is not earned." His voice carried across the water and the cold and the bundled people standing in it.

"It is not apportioned to the deserving.

It is not withheld from the man who has said the words and then broken them."

He held there.

"It was not earned.

It was never earned.

It will never be given as we deserve."

The last word went out over the ford and the creek took it south.

Amen. Several voices now.

He lowered his head.

He opened the book again.

"The grace of our Lord Jesus Christ, and the love of God, and the fellowship of the Holy Ghost, be with us all evermore."

Amen.

The gathering held a moment.

Then it broke.

* * *

The rotation of hospitality had brought it to Bella's this time.

The men had not decided. The women had a logic to these things that operated without announcement.

Bella had laid the fire before the service. The coffee was on when they arrived.

The house was warm and close with people. Men stood where chairs were not. Women moved between them with borrowed cups and plates. The Hawthorn house held the particular sound of a settlement indoors — lower than the yard, more careful, the voices finding the register a room required.

Elias came in last.

Heather stood near the stove with a cup held carefully in both hands, the way a child holds something she has been trusted with. She looked at him across the room with the gravity of a child performing an important errand.

She carried the cup to him.

He took it.

"Thank you, Heather."

She looked at the cup, then at him, then went back to her mother's side.

Bella was pouring at the table. She did not look up.

Farwell found him near the window.

He stood beside Elias and looked out at the yard, the creek, the hills beyond. He held his cup and did not drink from it immediately.

"You keep finding the words," he said.

Not quietly. The room could hear it.

"When they're needed."

He drank.

He did not look at Elias when he said it. He said it the way he entered a figure in a ledger — not as opinion but as fact recorded for future reference. Several people nearby had heard it. He had known they would.

Elias said nothing.

Farwell looked at the hills.

"About time this place had something to gather around," he said. "Other than trouble."

He set the cup down on the sill.

"Been talking with McLeod," he said, after a moment. "And a couple of others."

Elias waited.

"The cold won't hold services at the ford much longer." He turned the cup once. "Come spring, a man might think about something more permanent."

A woman nearby had been listening without appearing to. She turned at that.

"A church," she said.

Farwell gave the smallest movement of one shoulder. "Somewhere the settlement could use."

"A proper one," the woman said. "With walls."

"Walls would be a start." He looked at Elias. "If a man intended to stay."

The room had shifted slightly toward the conversation. Not all of it. Enough.

A man near the door said he knew where there was timber. Another said the ground east of the post was level. A third said it would need to wait on the thaw.

The talk moved around Elias the way the room moved around Bella — taking him as a fixed point, building around him, not asking his permission.

He looked at his cup.

Mary was across the room. She had not moved toward the conversation or away from it. She was looking at Bella. Then her eyes came to Elias. She held them there a moment, flat and certain, the look of a woman who has already concluded something and sees no reason to revisit it.

Then she looked away.

* * *

People left by degrees.

The cold outside received them one by one. Coats pulled tight. Children gathered in. The particular reluctance of a gathering breaking up when the warmth inside is known and the weather outside is not.

Elias set his cup on the table.

Bella was stacking plates at the far end. She worked with the efficiency of a woman who had been managing other people's comfort all afternoon and was now quietly reclaiming her house.

A cup had been left near the edge of the table. He moved to it. Took it up. Set it with the others.

Bella reached for the same space at the same time.

Their hands met on the rim of the cup.

She stilled.

He did not take his hand away.

"I can manage my own table," she said.

She kept her eyes down.

A moment.

"Yes."

He set the cup down with the others.

She went on stacking.

He put on his coat.

He moved toward the door. Stopped.

Heather was at the stove with her doll. She had positioned the doll upright against the leg of the stove and was explaining something to it in a low voice.

He looked at her a moment.

Then he went out.

Twenty-Seven

The cold had settled in for good.

Not October's announcement of it but December's occupation — the kind that moved in and set down its things without asking. The creek had gone ice, thick and hard enough to step on without the sound of cracking. The hills were white above the treeline and the wind came off them at an angle that found the gaps.

The first Wednesday, Mary had brought two of the fort children herself, one under each arm, and delivered them to Bella's door with a look that said the matter was settled and anyone who felt otherwise could take it up with the weather.

After that they came on their own.

Twelve of them, in the end. Five was little Heather, who already knew her letters and treated this fact as a credential. Thirteen was the McLeod boy, who arrived the first morning with the manner of someone who had been given a choice between this and something worse, and had chosen this without enthusiasm. Between them were the others — Farwell's people, a few from Fort Solomon, children who could not yet be put to full work and had been delivered to the Hawthorne house two mornings a week in various states of willingness.

Bella ran the room the way she ran everything. No praise that wasn't earned. No correction that left a mark beyond the correction itself. She had painted a section of board black and hung it where the window light fell across it, and she moved between the children with a piece of chalk and the patience of a woman for whom patience had long since become a tool.

Elias worked the numbers.

He had not known he would find it satisfying. But there was something in the specific quiet of a child understanding a thing for the first time — the small shift in the body that came just before they said it aloud — that held him in the room more reliably than sermons sometimes did. He worked down the rows. Threes and fours. Simple additions carried over. The McLeod boy, who had arrived to be difficult and found no purchase for it, had been working his column sums for twenty minutes without looking up.

He watched Bella at the board.

She wrote the letters large and even. When a child gave a wrong answer she did not say it was wrong. She said try again in a voice that made trying again seem like the obvious next thing, which of course it was.

He watched her hands when she wrote.

Working hands. He watched them without meaning to.

Heather appeared at his elbow.

She had been given her own slate at the start of every class. She used it with the focused urgency of a child performing an important errand, tongue at the corner of her mouth, chalk gripped like it might make a break for it.

She held the slate toward him.

He looked at it.

Five additions. Simple sums. She had done them all correctly. The numbers were large and somewhat uneven in their proportion but they were right, every one, and she had checked them — he could see the small marks at the side where she had gone back.

He looked at her.

She looked at the slate. Then at him. Waiting.

"Every one," he said.

She took the slate back with both hands. She carried it directly to her mother and held it up without a word.

Bella looked at it.

"I see," she said.

Heather returned to her corner and began another row.

Bella looked up and found Elias watching her. Something crossed her face before it settled back into the ordinary expression of a woman managing a room. She looked away first.

He looked back at the McLeod boy's column.

By three o'clock the light had gone flat and grey. Parents came to the door, some stepping inside, some standing in the cold, and the children went out in their coats and boots, one by one. The woman from Fort Solomon took her boys by their collars and gave Bella a nod that carried more than a nod usually carried. The McLeod boy went out last and Elias thought he heard him spelling something under his breath on the porch.

The room emptied.

Then it was only Bella, Heather in her corner with the slate, and Elias at the table with the addition sheets for next Wednesday.

The house held the warmth of twelve children and then held the absence of them.

Bella stacked the small slates against the wall. Elias folded the papers and set them in the book. Neither of them spoke.

Heather was doing another row of sums.

Bella set the kettle on. She came to the table and sat across from him. Not close. The width of the table between them. She folded her hands.

He waited.

"I want to ask you something," she said.

"All right."

"I'd like a plain answer."

He set the book aside.

"You came here shot," she said. "Mary dressed that wound for eight days."

"She did."

"A man shot you. You killed him."

"Yes."

"That isn't an ordinary thing."

"It is not."

"Some might say not a godly thing."

He said nothing.

She looked at her hands, then at him.

"I want to know what kind of man draws that kind of trouble."

The kettle breathed on the stove. Heather's chalk made its small scraping sound in the corner.

He looked at the table.

"My father was a merchant in Fort Garry," he said. "Dry goods, mostly. A plain man and a careful one. He wanted something different for his sons than counting bolts of cloth." He paused. "He sent me east to seminary. Ontario."

Bella watched him.

"I came back and presented myself to Bishop Machray. He is a serious man and the territory was large and I was young and untested. He thanked me and said there was nothing available yet."

He looked at his hands.

"I'd heard about Fort Benton. That it was growing quickly. That there was work for men willing to go where no comfortable post was waiting. It seemed like the kind of place that needed what I had."

"Fort Benton," Bella said.

The way she said it was the way she might confirm a child's wrong letter. Not unkind.

"The whiskey trade was everywhere in Benton. I knew it before I arrived. I hadn't understood the shape of it. Men buying horses for a crate of bottles. Women. Children in some cases."

He glanced at Heather.

"I preached against it," he said, lowering his voice. "More than once. More than was wise."

"Men warned you."

"Some did." He held there a moment. "A man came to see me one evening. A bookkeeper with the trade. A decent man, I thought, in an indecent arrangement. He told me I had made enemies. He told me there were men who had decided I was a problem and that he was telling me because he lacked the courage to stop them and wanted someone to know he had tried."

The kettle had begun its first low sound.

"I left that night."

Bella said nothing.

"I had a little money. I thought if I reached the North West Territory there was nothing they could do — crown jurisdiction, however untended."

He drew a slow breath.

"A man named Crews followed me out of Benton."

He stopped.

Bella waited.

He looked at Heather.

"I won't say the rest of it with the child in the room," he said. He said it quietly. Not as an excuse.

Bella held his eyes a moment. Then she rose.

"Heather," she said. "Go and see to the chickens."

"It's cold," Heather said.

"Yes," Bella said. "It is."

Heather set her chalk down with the careful resignation of someone who has learned there are categories of argument that do not benefit from entering. She put on her coat, pulled her hat down over her ears, and went out.

The door closed.

The house was very quiet.

He told it plainly. He kept it short. Crews had come at him at the creek crossing and he had killed the man. He was not proud of it. It was in him still, the way these things are in a man, the way a healed bone remembers the break. He said only that it was done and that it was the man or himself and that he had chosen himself.

He stopped.

Bella poured the coffee. She set a cup in front of him and sat back down.

She looked at him.

The silence held.

"You arrived here with a dead man behind you," she said.

"To Fort Farwell. Yes."

She held her cup without drinking.

"And the bishop's parish."

"Machray sent word eventually. A post in the territory, when one became available." He paused. The lie had reached the place where one more word would thin it. "That was the last I heard."

She looked at the window. The light outside had gone grey-blue, the colour of December at four o'clock when the sky has given up trying.

"I believe you were in Benton," she said.

He waited.

"I believe a man followed you."

She set her cup down.

"What I don't know," she said, "is whether I have all of it."

Not accusation. An observation entered into the record. She had the ability to state a thing in a way that left no room for argument because she was not arguing.

He looked at her.

"You have what I can give you," he said.

It was the most honest thing he had said all evening.

She received it the way she received everything — weighing it, finding its measure, not in any hurry about the outcome. The way she looked at the slates the children brought her. Measuring the work against what she understood the student to be capable of.

She did not tell him it was enough.

She did not tell him it wasn't.

"The coffee is getting cold," she said.

He drank.

* * *

Heather came back from the chickens with cold on her face and a complaint about the frozen ground that she delivered to the room in general before shedding her coat onto the chair and resuming her sums as though they had been waiting for her.

He stayed another twenty minutes. When he rose Bella walked him to the door in the ordinary way, which was not quite the ordinary way.

He put on his hat. Stepped out into the dark.

The cold was immediate and full. The hills were white under a sky gone black and specific with stars. The creek lay quiet in its ice. Bella's lamp burned in the window behind him as he walked and he did not look back.

He was already thinking about the next time she would ask him something.

He had not answered her plainly. He had answered her carefully, which in a man of his particular history was not the same thing. He had given her the shape of the truth and withheld its bones and she had known it, and knowing it she had let him stay and poured his coffee and said the cup was getting cold.

He did not know what to call that.

He walked on.

The cold took his breath and gave it back to him.

The light in her window held behind him longer than it should have.

Twenty-Eight

The summons came in the middle of the afternoon.

Not shouted.

Nora at the saloon door, coat already on, saying his name once in the tone of a person who had no use for repeating herself.

He set the book down.

The room had gone to its winter dimness though the hour was not yet late. Frost had filmed the inside edge of the front window where men's breath and stove heat had not reached. Two teamsters near the fire looked up as he rose and then looked back down as if the looking had cost them something and they preferred not to spend more.

Nora did not wait for him to ask.

He took his coat from the peg and followed her out.

The cold met him clean.

Not the early season edge of it. The full thing now. The kind that set itself in the lungs at once and stayed there. Snow lay hard along the packed street where boots and hooves had ground it grey. The creek beyond the buildings was white and flat under the sky.

Nora crossed toward Farwell's place without speaking.

He kept pace with her.

"What is it."

"A woman came in."

"From where."

"North of Solomon's."

That was all she gave him until they reached the house.

Farwell's door stood open to the warm and closed again behind them as soon as they entered. Mary was there, moving from stove to table with the economy of a woman who had already assessed the room and found no advantage in haste. On the hearth, half in the firelight and half out of it, sat a Métis boy of six or seven with his boots still on and a blanket around his shoulders. He was turning something in his hands. A strip of leather, worked soft with use, with a few trade beads knotted into it in a pattern too regular to be accidental and too worn to be decorative anymore. He turned it and turned it, not looking at anyone while he did.

Nora went at once to him and crouched.

"You warm enough."

The boy nodded without lifting his eyes.

On the far side of the room sat a woman Elias had not seen before. Dark hair badly pinned. One sleeve torn at the seam and stiff where it had dried. Snow still melting at the hem of her skirt. One cheek gone red from wind and something older than wind beneath it. She held herself upright with the flat exhausted composure of a person who had been past fear for some time and had come out the other side into necessity.

Farwell stood by the table. Hat in his hand. Dunn near the wall with his coat still buttoned and his shotgun leaning against his leg as if it had been brought in only because setting it outside would have meant more trouble later.

The woman looked at Elias.

"This is him," Farwell said. "Reverend."

The title entered the room and did less than it usually did.

Elias took that in.

"What happened."

The woman answered him herself.

"My name is Marguerite Bouchard." Her voice was flat with cold and used hard. "My husband tried to kill me this morning."

No one spoke.

"I took Luc here and went to Solomon's place. Moses wouldn't have me." She did not put anger into it. She did not need to. "Said he'd not send men a mile north in this weather for a husband and wife quarrel."

Farwell made a small sound through his nose that did not amount to surprise.

Marguerite went on.

"There are two more at the house. My girls."

"How old," Elias asked.

"Eight. And four."

She looked at the floorboards between them.

"He cut them."

The room altered around the sentence.

"How bad."

"The little one I don't know. The older one can still stand." She swallowed once and went on. "He's been drinking what he made himself. Since yesterday. Maybe before." A pause. "He said they weren't his anymore."

The boy by the fire kept turning the bit of leather in his hands.

Elias looked at Marguerite.

"What's your husband's name."

"Armand."

"Does he have a gun."

"He has one. I didn't see it." She drew breath. "He had the knife."

"The children are still with him."

"Yes."

Farwell put his hat on.

"No point going to Solomon. He already had his chance."

That was all he said on that subject.

He looked at Dunn, then at Elias.

"We'll go."

Mary had stopped moving. She stood with one hand against the table and looked at Elias the way she looked at weather that had already decided itself.

"The house," Elias said. "How far."

"Up the coulee and out," Marguerite said. "Maybe a kilometre. On the high side. You can see the roof once you clear the cut."

Farwell nodded once.

"To the post," he said to Dunn. "Fetch my rifle."

Dunn took up his shotgun with the other hand and went.

Farwell looked at Elias. "You armed."

"Yes."

"Bring the right hope."

He went out after Dunn.

Nora remained crouched by the boy. Mary crossed to Marguerite and set a cup into her hands. Marguerite took it because it had been given, not because she wanted it.

Elias stood a moment in the house heat.

The boy on the hearth turned the beaded leather once more in his fingers. Something taken down from a shelf without permission. Something held because the hands required occupation and there were no other tasks yet suitable for them.

Nora looked up at Elias.

"Bring them back."

He touched his hat and went.

* * *

They took the coulee north.

Farwell ahead with the rifle across his saddle. Dunn on foot beside him with the shotgun broken open in one hand until the wind became enough that he stopped pretending caution and snapped it shut. Elias walked with the revolver under his coat and his collar against his throat like a thing someone else had put there.

The creek ran under ice in the bottom of the coulee, hidden except where dark water showed through at bends and under the roots of willows. The banks rose white and wind-cut on either side. Their boots found the frozen track where others had passed in better weather and not recently.

No one spoke for a time.

The cold did the speaking.

It found the eyes. The knuckles. The places where cloth failed. Breath came and went white and was taken at once. The willows stood black against the snow and did not move unless the wind got a clean angle at them.

Halfway up the coulee Dunn said, "If he's gone over hard, there's not much to say to him."

Farwell did not turn.

"Then say it once."

Dunn made no answer.

They climbed.

The light had the hard flat quality winter gives the country when the day is already thinking about ending. The sky above the cut was fast with low cloud moving east. No birds. No dogs. No smoke until they were nearly on the place.

Then the house stood above them.

Small. One room and a lean-to. Sod roof gone white and thick at the edges. Smoke coming weak from the pipe and lying low in the wind instead of rising. No tracks visible fresh enough to trust. The yard drifted over and silent.

They came out of the coulee and crossed the last open ground without hurry.

The silence was wrong.

Not empty.

Occupied.

Farwell halted them ten paces short of the door and looked once at the house, once at the yard, once toward the lean-to and the low pen beyond it.

Then he nodded at Elias.

Elias stepped forward.

He stopped at the door and listened.

Nothing.

Then something from inside. Not words. The dull shift of a chair leg on plank. Or a body against wood.

He called through the door.

"Armand Bouchard."

The wind took some of it.

He said it again.

"I'm Reverend Wilson from Fort Farwell. Your wife reached the fort. We've come for the children."

No answer.

The smell came through the cracks before anything else did.

Sour mash. Human waste. Blood gone old in heat.

Elias looked back once. Farwell had the rifle ready but not raised. Dunn stood to the left of the door with the shotgun down and his eyes on Elias, waiting for the room to tell them what sort of room it was.

Elias put his hand on the latch.

Lifted it.

The door gave inward.

Heat met them. A bad wet heat held too long in a room sealed against winter.

The smell had been worse inside than outside had allowed.

Moonshine. Piss. Blood. Unwashed wool. The close sweet wrongness of a place where fear had been breathing for hours.

The room was dim though it was still daylight. One shutter half closed. Stove going low. Table overturned near the wall. A chair on its side.

The man sat in the only upright chair near the stove.

Bareheaded. Shirt open at the throat. Beard gone wet and clotted where something had dried into it and then been drunk through. A long hunting knife in his right hand, the blade dark to the hilt. His eyes had the bright depthless look of a man no longer under the authority of ordinary cause and effect.

One child sat on the floor beside his knee.

The older girl.

She was upright because upright had been decided for her somehow and not because her body had any business doing it. Blood dried down one side of her dress from a cut across the upper arm and another at the scalp that had run into her hair and stopped there. Her hands were in her lap. Her eyes were open and aimed somewhere near the stove but not at it.

The younger one lay by the wall on a folded blanket, eyes open, face pale with a cut along the cheek and another at the neck too near the thing that mattered.

Alive.

Still.

Too still.

Elias took that all in before he knew he had.

Armand looked at the collar.

Then at Elias's face.

Then at the men behind him.

He did not rise.

He said, "There."

The word held no meaning on its own and yet was spoken as though it concluded something.

Elias stepped inside.

The floorboards felt soft with spilt things.

"Your wife is safe," he said.

Armand's mouth moved once.

"Whore."

The knife stayed low against his thigh. Not relaxed. Waiting.

"The children need seeing to."

Armand looked at the girls as if Elias had named furniture he had forgotten owning.

"No."

It came out mild. Nearly conversational.

Farwell and Dunn had entered behind Elias and spread slightly without discussion. Farwell to the right where he could see the child by the wall. Dunn nearer the door, the shotgun now held in both hands and kept low.

Armand's eyes moved to Dunn.

Stayed there a moment.

Then returned to Elias and the collar.

"Look at him," Armand said. "Brings the black thing in with him and stands there like Sunday."

Elias felt something move once through the room and settle nowhere he could use.

He kept his voice where he kept it with the dying and the frightened and men with knives who still inhabited the language of other people.

"Armand. Set the knife down."

"No."

"The girls are hurt."

"They bled." He looked at the older one. "They had the wrong blood." He looked back at Elias. "She made them wrong."

The words were not shouted. They came with the patient explanatory tone of a man clarifying a matter simple enough that only malice could have missed it.

"Your wife's at Farwell's," Elias said. "Your boy too. They're warm."

Armand stared at him.

Then he smiled with only one side of his mouth.

"Boy."

He turned the knife once in his hand.

"Mine."

The older girl flinched at the movement and did not otherwise move.

Elias said, "Yes."

It bought him Armand's eyes again.

"You know that," Armand said.

"Yes."

"Do you."

"I do."

The stove settled with a soft metal sound.

Armand looked at the younger girl by the wall and then at the older one beside him and then at Elias with a look almost tender in its certainty.

"They weren't his anymore," he said.

Elias said, "Let the children come outside."

Armand's eyes narrowed a fraction.

"Outside."

"Yes."

"Snow's deep."

"They'll be wrapped."

He gave no sign he had heard.

Elias said, "The little one needs a doctor."

"There is no doctor."

"Then Mary."

At that name something crossed Armand's face and was gone before Elias had it.

The man's eyes went past Elias's shoulder toward Dunn and back again.

"You hear them," Armand said. "The ones behind you."

"No."

"I do."

He lifted his chin toward the corner above the stove.

"They don't stop."

The room held.

Farwell had not spoken. Dunn had not shifted. The older girl's breathing was visible now that Elias had found it—small, quick, held shallow against pain.

Elias said, "Armand."

The man looked at him.

"Give me the older one."

Armand's eyes dropped to the child at his knee.

His face altered slowly into concentration, as if the request were technical and required review.

"She'll tell."

Elias said nothing.

"She saw."

Still Elias said nothing.

The man looked up again and found the collar waiting for him.

"Blood," Armand said. "There's one for blood. You know it. The blood and the—"

He stopped. Looked at the child by his knee.

"Tell it right."

Elias felt the failure before the words came.

"There is mercy," he said.

Armand's face did not change.

"There is forgiveness."

No change.

"The Lord—"

At that Armand leaned forward in the chair with a sudden intimate focus, as if Elias had at last reached the true subject.

"The Lord."

"Yes."

Armand's eyes shone.

"You brought the dark one in with you and say Lord."

The knife lifted an inch.

"Don't."

The word came not as plea but warning.

Elias tried once more.

"Your children are leaving this house."

He did not raise his voice.

"They are going out now."

The older girl turned her eyes toward him for the first time. Not trust. Not hope. Simple animal attention to the changed current in the room.

Elias kept his eyes on Armand and said to her, "Stand and come to me."

Nothing happened.

He said it again.

The child by the chair moved.

Not much. Enough.

Armand saw it.

The whole room changed.

He came out of the chair fast enough that for an instant the mind refused the fact and registered only height and steel and the violent upsetting of distance.

He lunged toward the older girl, then toward Elias, then perhaps toward no single thing at all but through them.

Dunn fired.

The shotgun broke the room in two.

For a second there was no hearing in it. Only force. The chair going over behind the man. Smoke and stove heat and splintered sound striking the walls and coming back wrong.

Armand hit the floor beside the stove and did not rise.

The older girl screamed.

The younger one by the wall began crying then, not loudly, but with the thin stunned sound of a body returning to itself.

Elias was already at the children.

He did not look at Dunn. He did not look at Farwell. He went first to the girl by the chair, got his hands under her arms, felt how little she weighed, and moved her away from the spreading dark near the stove. She made a sound when he lifted her but did not resist. He set her near the door.

Farwell had crossed to the younger one and was kneeling badly in the cramped space, getting his big hands under shoulders and blanket with more care than the hands suggested they would possess.

"Alive," Farwell said.

The word came as if from another room through the ringing in Elias's head.

Dunn opened the shotgun and fed it another shell by habit.

Elias took off his coat and wrapped it around the older girl. Her eyes were fixed on something over his shoulder. He put his body between her and the room.

"You're going outside," he said.

He could not hear his own voice properly. The words seemed to arrive in the air already spoken.

Farwell stood with the younger one in his arms and nodded toward the door.

Elias took the older girl's hand. It was cold despite the room. He led her into the white light.

The cold hit like a correction.

He got her clear of the threshold and sat her in the lee of the wall where the wind struck less hard. Farwell came a moment later with the younger child and set her down against Elias's folded coat over the snow. The girl's crying had gone thin and steady.

The older one looked at him.

Blood had dried into the hair above her left temple. The cut on the arm had gone tacky and dark.

"What's your name."

She worked at the answer.

"Claire."

"And your sister."

"Anne."

"All right."

He looked at the younger one.

"Anne."

The child's eyes found him and stayed.

Behind them the house stood with the door open to the bad heat and the dim interior beyond.

Dunn came out last and pulled the door nearly shut behind him but not fully.

He looked at neither Elias nor Farwell.

"The road back won't improve."

Farwell looked at the children. Then at the sky moving fast over the ridge.

"No."

Dunn shifted the shotgun once in his hands and set it against his shoulder.

Still no one mentioned the shot.

Farwell said, "Take the older one."

Elias bent and lifted Claire into his arms. She winced once and then held still the way frightened children hold still when they have concluded movement worsens the terms of things.

Farwell took Anne.

Dunn went ahead down the rise.

They started back toward the coulee.

After ten paces Elias looked once over his shoulder at the house.

The door stood almost closed. Smoke still came thin from the pipe. Nothing in the yard moved.

He turned back.

The girl in his arms had one hand caught in the front of his collar. Not tightly. Just there.

The coulee took them down.

The wind found the cut and ran along it. Snow at the edges had drifted blue in the gathering light. Dunn's boots made the first track. Farwell followed with the younger child under his coat and the rifle banging lightly against his back. Elias came last with Claire held high enough to spare her the jolting where he could.

No one spoke for some time.

Then Farwell said, without looking back, "We'll go for him before full dark if there's enough of it left."

"Yes," Elias said.

That was all.

The child in his arms had gone heavier with trust or exhaustion. He could not tell which.

Below them the frozen creek held its white line through the bottom of the world. Ahead, somewhere past the bend and the black willows and the coming blue of evening, was Farwell's fire, Mary's hands, the woman waiting, the boy with the beaded leather still turning in his fingers unless something better had finally been given him to do.

The light lowered.

The coulee took them south.

The collar sat against his throat.

It had said nothing in that house.

The gun had said nothing either.

There had only been the room, and the knife, and the children, and the fact of what men did when words no longer reached the place a man had gone.

Twenty-Nine

The house held more people than it was built for.

Not by number. By what they carried.

Marguerite sat at the table with her hands flat on the wood as though she had set them there and had not yet been told she could take them back. One sleeve still torn. The cloth stiff where it had dried and been warmed again by the room. Her eyes moved when spoken to. They did not settle.

The boy slept in the chair by the stove with his boots still on.

Bella had not taken them off.

There are ways to sleep that mean a person is not to be woken for anything that is not fire.

The older girl sat on the floor with her back against the wall. A blanket around her shoulders. She held it closed with both hands. Not from cold. From keeping herself inside it.

The small one lay on Bella's bed.

Mary had cleaned the cut as best she could. Her hands moved with the quiet certainty of someone accustomed to injury — the wound assessed, wrapped, checked once. She set the cloth aside.

The child's breathing came light and quick, then slowed, then found something that might hold.

Bella moved between them.

Water. Fire. The small adjustments that make a room possible.

She did not speak unless she had to.

When she did, it was to ask for a hand. To turn a shoulder. To take a cup.

Marguerite took what was given. Drank when told. Said nothing about the house she had left.

Mary stood once by the bed and looked at the child a moment longer than the work required.

Nora behind her.

Mary said, "We'll go."

Not a question.

Bella did not look up from the stove.

"All right," she said.

Nora crossed to the table and set a cup near Marguerite's hand. She crouched once by the boy, touched the blanket, adjusted it without waking him.

She looked at Bella.

"If he comes," she said.

Bella set another piece of wood against the iron.

She did not answer.

Nora stood.

They went out into the cold.

The door closed.

The house held.

* * *

The saloon had been cleared without being emptied.

Tables pushed back. Chairs turned. Men standing where they stood when there was something to see and no one had told them where to put themselves.

Farwell sat near the middle. Not the head of anything. A place that saw the door.

Elias stood off to one side. Hands clear of his coat.

Nora moved behind the bar. The bottle came down. Glasses set. No one asked for them.

Mary stood near the wall. Arms folded. Watching the room as though it were weather that had not yet decided itself.

Farwell turned his hat once in his hands.

"Cold one," he said.

No one answered.

The door opened.

Solomon came in with his coat buttoned and his hat low. The blond man behind him. Another at the door. Close enough.

Solomon crossed to the table and took the chair that faced the room.

He did not remove his coat.

He did not reach for the glass.

Farwell did not offer it.

A moment passed.

Then the door opened again.

Little Soldier entered with two of his men. Gabriel with him.

They did not look at the room. They came to the space and stopped.

The room settled.

Farwell said, "There's a matter."

No one spoke.

"There's a man dead in a house north of Solomon's," he said. "Woman. Three children. No ground to put him in."

The words sat where they were placed.

Solomon's eyes moved once across the room and came back.

"Wrap him," he said. "Set him outside. Bury him when the ground takes a spade."

"And the rest of it," Farwell said.

"It's her house."

The blond man shifted once near the door and went still again.

Farwell's fingers rested on the table.

"That house won't hold," he said. "Not through this."

Solomon's mouth moved once.

"Then she should have chosen better."

Mary did not move.

Nora set another glass on the bar and did not look at it.

Farwell said, "It's your side of the creek."

Solomon looked at him.

"Then keep to yours."

The room narrowed.

Elias had seen the room already.

The child on the bed. The girl holding the blanket. The way the boy slept as though the body had taken what it needed and would not be argued with.

He said, "You cannot leave them there."

No one turned.

The words went into the room and stayed.

Solomon's eyes found him.

"You've taken a great deal on yourself lately, Reverend."

Elias did not answer.

Farwell's jaw set once and settled.

"The ground is what it is," he said. "We're not talking about the ground."

Silence.

Little Soldier looked at the table between the men. Not at Farwell. Not at Solomon. At the space between them where the matter lay unresolved.

He was quiet long enough that the room began to fill with the sound of its own waiting.

Then he spoke in his own language.

Gabriel's voice carried it across.

"They will come south."

No one spoke.

Farwell looked at him.

"That wasn't in the agreement."

Little Soldier did not look at him.

He said something else. Shorter.

Gabriel said, "The ground does not hold a man in winter. The people do."

The room held that.

Across it, Mary's arms came loose at her sides. She did not step forward. She did not speak. But she uncrossed them, and the movement was not nothing.

Solomon leaned back slightly in his chair.

"That's your choice," he said. "Not mine."

Little Soldier did not answer.

Farwell looked once at Elias. Then at the table. Then back at Little Soldier.

He nodded once.

"All right," he said.

No one marked it as a decision.

It was one.

Solomon stood.

He adjusted his coat as though it required it. Looked once at the glass he had not touched.

"We'll see what comes of it," he said.

He turned and went to the door.

His men followed.

The cold came in with them and went out again.

The door closed.

The room stayed.

Then it began to move.

* * *

The house was warmer than the saloon and not warmer enough.

Elias stood in the doorway a moment before stepping in.

The room had shifted.

The boy by the stove now lay on his side with the blanket pulled up to his chin. The older girl had not moved far but her head rested now against the wall with her eyes closed. The small one slept on the bed with her mouth open slightly, the breath coming easier than it had.

Marguerite sat where she had been.

Bella moved at the table.

A cloth in her hand. The same cup. The same small work that does not end.

She looked up when he came in.

He closed the door behind him.

"They'll go south," he said. "To the camp."

Bella watched him. "All of them."

"Yes."

She nodded once. "There's nowhere else."

She said it as one might say the time.

Elias stood with that.

The boy stirred in his sleep and made a small sound.

Elias moved without thinking.

He set a hand on the back of the chair to steady it.

The boy's hand came out from the blanket and found his sleeve.

Held it.

Not asking.

Elias stood there.

The hand remained.

Bella watched it.

Then she turned back to the cloth in her hand. The movement was quiet and deliberate and it was not indifference.

He eased his sleeve free without waking the child.

He stepped back.

Bella set the cup down.

"There's wood by the door," she said. "If you're staying."

He nodded.

He crossed to the pile and took up an armful.

The work went on.

No one spoke.

The house held what it could.

Outside, the cold settled deeper into the ground that would not yet take the dead.

Thirty

By February the cold no longer announced itself.

It had settled into the boards and the hinges and the pail handle by the door. It lived in the mornings and did not leave much when the fire came up. Snow lay banked along the fence in a hard grey line where wind had worked it over and left it. The creek was white and flat beyond the houses, the sort of white that did not suggest purity to anyone who had lived through enough of it. Only distance. Only cold made visible.

School had ended an hour ago.

The room still held the shape of it.

Chalk dust on the board. A slate left on the bench and returned to the stack only because Bella had seen it there and not because the child who left it had remembered. The heat of bodies gone but not gone long enough for the house to forget them. Heather sat at the table with her tongue at the corner of her mouth and a scrap of paper laid flat under both hands as though paper might blow away indoors if not properly supervised.

Bella was at the stove.

Not cooking. Managing what came after. Pot moved back from the hottest part. Cups rinsed. The ordinary work of returning a room to itself.

Elias stood by the door with his gloves in one hand and his hat in the other.

He had not put on either.

He had stayed to stack the slates and wipe the sums from the board and carry in the split wood from the lean-to though there had been enough wood already beside the stove for the evening. Bella had not asked him to do any of it. She had not told him not to.

He stood a moment looking at Heather's bent head.

"What's that," he said.

Heather looked up as though she had nearly forgotten he was still there and was pleased to discover the mistake.

"A thing."

"Yes."

"For you."

She said it with the straightforward gravity of a child delivering official business. She lifted the paper from the table with both hands and brought it to him.

He took it as he took most things from her now. Carefully. As though handed something that mattered because it mattered to the giver and that was enough.

The paper had been cut from the blank end of an old broadside or handbill. On the back some printed letters showed through faintly and upside down. On the front Heather had written a word in pencil with the painful concentration of someone who had learned that each letter had to be wrestled to the page separately.

ELIA

He looked at it a moment.

Then at Heather.

"You wrote my name."

She nodded once.

"Nearly all of it."

She considered this. Looked at the paper. Found the defect. Looked back at him.

"I ran out of room."

"Yes."

He folded the paper once. Not sharply. Put it in the inside pocket of his coat.

"I'm obliged to you," he said.

Heather watched where he had put it, satisfied by the seriousness of the placement.

Bella had turned from the stove at some point during this exchange. He felt her eyes on them and looked up. Something moved at one corner of her mouth and nearly became a smile before it set itself right again.

He felt it in him with the force of things that arrive quietly and do more damage for it.

Heather went back to her chair. Climbed onto it rather than sitting in it. Took up the pencil again and bent over the table with the solemn industry of a clerk.

Bella turned back to the stove.

"You needn't keep every paper she hands you," she said.

He set his hat on the chair by the door.

"I know."

"She'll write twenty more by spring."

"I've room for them."

Bella moved the kettle to the crane and set another stick of wood against the iron with the toe of her boot. She made a small sound in her throat. Not approval. Not disapproval either. The sort of sound a person makes when another has answered in a way that prevents easy objection.

The room held for a time in the ordinary noises of itself. Pencil at paper. Iron settling on the stove. Wind finding the edge of the roof and moving on.

The hour had come where a man who was neither husband nor kin nor invited guest took his hat and stepped back out into the dark and the snow and whatever room he occupied elsewhere. He knew the hour. He had known it from the moment the last child's boots had gone down the porch steps.

He remained where he was.

Heather lifted the pencil and frowned at what she had made. Bella crossed to the table and stood over her.

"No," she said. "That one begins higher."

She took the pencil from the child, bent over, and formed the letter on the margin with the clean even certainty of a woman who did not waste motion.

He watched her hand do it.

She gave the pencil back to Heather.

"There."

Heather tried again. This time the line held.

Bella remained bent a moment longer than the correction required. Her hair had come loose behind one ear. She reached and tucked it back.

The curve of her neck sat in his eyes.

He became aware of the coat still on him. Of the heat along the back of his neck where the collar sat. Of the distance between the table and the stove and the chair by the door. Ordinary distances. Not ordinary.

Bella straightened.

"Sit down if you mean to stay," she said.

She had not raised her voice. She had not turned the sentence into a question. She stood with one hand on the back of Heather's chair and looked at him directly, and what she had said was not invitation but refusal of pretence.

He crossed to the table and sat.

Heather, without consulting anyone, pushed the second cup toward his place.

He took the cup when Bella poured.

Their hands met at the handle.

Only for the taking of it. Nothing a room could object to. Nothing anyone could name. Her fingers were cool from the basin. His had gone warm inside the gloves he had not put back on.

She did not move first.

Neither did he.

Then the handle turned fully into his hand and the moment had passed and was no less there for passing.

Bella went back to the stove and set the coffee pot down. Then she sat across from him, the width of the table between them, and Heather between in the way children sometimes are and are not. She picked up the mending from beside the lamp. A mitten of Heather's gone through at the thumb. She threaded the needle and bent her head.

The lamp had not yet been lit. The last of the afternoon held at the window, thin and colourless, enough to see by for now.

Heather reached for the cup nearest her and found it empty.

"May I have more."

"No," Bella said. "It's done."

Heather took the correction with the quiet resignation of a child who had tested the matter because testing is what children do and had learned nothing surprising from the result.

Elias drank his coffee.

The room had entered that evening hour in winter when light goes before the day is finished and everyone inside a house has to decide whether what remains is still afternoon or has already become night.

Bella rose and lit the lamp. Turned the wick. Set the chimney in place. The flame steadied and grew.

He looked at the table.

"How is the little one," he said.

He meant Marguerite's girl. Bella knew it at once.

"Better," she said. "Mary stops in. Nora too."

"And the others."

"They've a place." Bella put the mending in her lap and drew the thread through. "That's enough for a child."

He nodded.

Bella sewed in silence for a few moments.

Then: "Now that you've got a place."

He looked up.

She had not looked up herself. The mitten sat in her hands. Needle in, needle through, the small necessary labour of repair.

"Yes."

"Will you write to them."

He did not ask who.

Fort Garry stood at once in the room between them. Not the town itself. The word of it. His mother. A sister.

He answered before the answer had fully arrived.

"I intend to."

The words went into the room and were accepted by it at once. A man with a place intending to write home. Nothing in that required notice.

The lie did not cost him less for being smaller.

Heather, satisfied by the answer though no one had asked whether she required satisfying, said, "You can tell them I wrote your name."

Bella's eyes came up then. To him.

Not hard. Not soft either. Simply present.

"You may," she said.

He held Bella's look.

"Yes," he said.

Heather returned to the paper.

Bella took one more stitch. Then another.

"A man writes when he means to stay."

He nodded.

She watched him a moment longer. Then nodded once.

Nothing settled. Not fully. But something had been placed where it could be seen.

The light lowered another degree. The room shrank around the lamp and stove and the three people holding to both.

Heather set the pencil down.

"Done."

She lifted the paper and brought it around the table. This time the word had all its letters, though the A had gone strange and ambitious and the S again leaned like a fence post set in thawing ground.

ELIAS

She offered it to him with both hands.

He took it.

"This one came right," she said.

"It did."

She looked at the first pocket where he had placed the other.

"Same place."

"Yes."

He slipped it away into his coat with the other one.

"You'll fill your coat with scraps if you encourage her in this," Bella said.

"I have carried worse things."

Heather watched to ensure the procedure had been properly executed. Then, because she had accomplished all that a child could reasonably accomplish in an evening, she leaned against his shoulder without warning and looked at the lamp.

He went still.

He could feel the weight of Heather against the sleeve of his coat. Small and absolute. The sort of trust that is not granted after review but simply lives where it lives and reaches where it reaches.

He raised a hand and set it lightly at the child's back. Nothing more than enough to keep her from slipping on the smooth wood of the chair.

Bella's eyes sat upon him.

For a moment the mending in her lap stopped mattering.

The thing at the corner of her mouth. Not a smile. The almost of one.

She looked down first.

"Bed," she said to Heather.

Heather did not move.

"I'm not tired."

"No. You're merely hanging off a guest."

"I'm not hanging."

Bella set the mitten aside.

"Heather."

The child straightened with a sigh proportioned to the injustice.

Elias removed his hand at once.

Heather took the paper scraps and pencil and put them in order on the shelf because bedtime did not exempt a person from order in Bella's house.

Bella rose and helped her with the buttons at the neck of her dress. Not because the child could not do them. Because mothers do such things while they still may.

Heather looked over Bella's shoulder at him.

"You won't go before morning."

"No," Bella said.

He said at the same time, "I'll be gone before then."

Heather considered the discrepancy and chose the answer that pleased her less.

"Goodnight," she said.

"Goodnight."

Bella took the lamp from the table and led the child into the back room. Their shadows passed across the wall. Quiet words. The shape of blankets being turned down. Then only Bella's steps returning. She set the lamp back on the table and sat again. The room had altered in Heather's absence. More space in it. More risk.

The mitten remained unfinished in her lap.

He should have taken his hat then. He knew it with full clarity and remained seated with his coffee gone cold.

Bella threaded the needle again and did not look at him.

"You mean to make this difficult."

It was not accusation. It was observation.

He answered with the truth nearest the surface.

"I wasn't aware I had a choice."

That brought her eyes up.

"No," she said. "I suppose you weren't."

He let that stand.

The wind touched the wall once and moved on. Somewhere outside, a horse knocked a rail with its hoof.

Bella set the mitten down and folded her hands over it.

"If you stay after the child has been put to bed," she said, "you ought to know how it looks."

He looked at her.

"Yes."

"And if you know."

He waited.

"That leaves only whether you mean it."

He felt the room narrow around the lamp.

He could have stepped aside from it. Could have answered with courtesy. With indirection. Could have given her enough fog to live inside for another week or two while the winter held and the school carried them and the house kept putting them in one another's way.

He did not.

"Yes," he said.

The word was very quiet.

Bella looked at him as if the trouble with plain answers was not that they said too much but that they left too little to hide behind.

She gave a small nod. No more than that. Not acceptance. Not refusal. The acknowledgement a person gives when another has set his hand to a thing and she has heard the sound of it.

Then she took up the mitten again.

"Very well," she said.

The needle went through the wool. Came back. Drew the gap closed a little further.

He sat a while longer and did not try to improve what had been said.

At last he stood.

She did not look up immediately.

"I'll come Wednesday," he said. "For the sums."

"Yes."

He took his hat from the chair.

At the door he put on the gloves and then paused with his hand on the latch.

Behind him the lamp burned. The stove held. Bella sat at the table with the child's mitten in her hands, mending what would be needed again tomorrow.

He said, "Goodnight."

This time she did look up.

"Goodnight, Mr. Wilson."

That too was a decision.

He opened the door.

Cold came in clean and hard enough to hurt the teeth. Snowlight lay over the yard and the fence and the road beyond in a colourless sheen. He stepped out into it and pulled the door shut behind him.

The papers rustled once inside his coat when he moved.

He stood a moment in the frozen dark, then put his hand flat against his coat where the papers were. Through the cloth he could feel the two folds of paper, and beneath them the old wound in his ribs where the cold had found it.

He had said yes to her.

He had said it looking at her hands and meaning it.

Then he went back through the snow to the place that was said to be his.

Thirty-One

The light had changed.

Not the temperature. The cold was still there in all the places it had taken up residence — the hinge of the door and the rope handle of the pail and the air that found the lungs on the first breath of morning. But the light had done something. The sun sat higher than it had in December. It came across the eastern hills at an angle that fell differently on the snow, making shadows that ran shorter and bluer, as though the country had remembered something it had set aside and had begun, in no particular hurry, to pick it up again.

He was filling the pail from the clean snow at the edge of the yard.

Heather stood beside him with her own pail. Small. She had filled it to approximately the depth of her hand and seemed satisfied with this.

She had been beside him for some time.

"Why is winter so long."

He bent with the shovel.

"It isn't always."

"It feels always."

"Yes," he said. "It does feel that way."

She considered this and found it acceptable.

"Why is your hat round."

He straightened but did not touch the hat.

"It was the hat available."

She studied it.

"Mr. Farwell's hat is flat."

"Mr. Farwell's hat suits him."

"Does yours suit you."

He paused in the work.

"I expect not."

She accepted this and scooped a quantity of snow into her pail with her mittened hand.

"Why are children not allowed in the saloon."

"Because the business done there is for men."

"Nora said I could come in."

"Nora is kind."

"She gave me a piece of sugar."

"That was kind too."

Heather processed this, watching her breath cloud and disperse.

"My tooth came out," she said.

"I know."

"Why."

"The small teeth make room for larger ones."

She ran her tongue across the gap with brief scientific interest.

"Does it hurt," he said.

"No." She moved on from it with the ease of a child for whom the body is not yet a source of worry. "Why does Ma look at you like that."

He did not break his rhythm.

"How does she look at me."

"Different."

He said nothing.

"Different from how she looks at Farwell," Heather went on. "Or Gabriel. Or Mr. McLeod." She looked up at him. "Different than she looked at Pa."

He put the shovel in.

"She'll have to answer that herself."

Heather received this and found it insufficient but unarguable. She moved to her next approach.

"Is Pa watching from heaven."

He stopped.

She was looking at the hills to the east where the light came from. Her face had the plain attention of a child who asks hard questions expecting honest answers, because nothing in her experience had yet taught her otherwise.

"I don't know," he said.

She turned.

"You're a priest."

"Yes."

"Doesn't that mean you know."

"No," he said. "It means I believe. Which is not the same."

She considered this with the same gravity she brought to column sums.

"But you think he might be."

"I think he might be."

A pause.

"Where is heaven."

"I don't know that either."

"The Bible says."

"The Bible says there is one."

She looked back at the hills. The light on the snow had the particular quality of late February — hard and thin and briefly beautiful, not promising anything.

"All right," she said.

She picked up her pail.

* * *

The room was warm. The stove had been going since early and the house had taken the heat into its boards the way a house does in deep winter, holding it close, giving it back through the day in small particular ways. The window held daylight. The lamp sat unlit on the table.

Bella was at the table with a cloth. She looked up when they came in and took the measure of the pails without comment.

Heather set hers down and went to work on her mittens.

"Elias says he doesn't know where heaven is," she announced.

"Heather."

"He said so."

"Take your coat off."

"He said believing isn't the same as knowing." She pulled at the buttons with the focused competence of a child who has learned that speed and accuracy are not the same thing. "And that his hat doesn't suit him."

Bella glanced at the hat. Looked back.

"Your coat," she said.

Heather peeled it from her shoulders and hung it on the peg. She turned back to the room.

"And he said why Ma looks at him isn't his to answer."

"Honestly," Bella said. She looked at her daughter. "Go outside."

"I just came in."

"See whether the chickens want anything."

"They won't."

"Go and make certain."

Heather looked at Elias.

"You don't mind, do you."

"Listen to your ma."

She retrieved the coat from the peg with the resignation of someone whose objection had been fair and had been overruled anyway. She rebuttoned it with precision and went out.

The door closed.

The room settled around itself.

Bella looked at the door, then at the cloth on the table. She reached for it.

He crossed to her.

She had begun to turn — toward the stove, toward something, her hands already finding their purpose — and he took her wrist.

Gently.

Not letting go.

She went still.

Her hand stayed where it was in his. She did not pull away.

"Bella."

She did not turn yet.

"Bella."

She turned.

He was closer than the room usually allowed. She looked up at him. Whatever she had been about to arrange in her face, she had stopped arranging.

He did not speak.

Her eyes held his. Waiting.

She said, "You never asked my father's permission."

The words came level. Proper.

"I would have," he said. "If I could have."

She watched him.

"I asked Farwell instead."

A small shift at her mouth. Not quite approval.

"That would suit him," she said.

"Yes."

She let that sit. Her wrist still in his hand.

"I kept my house," she said.

It was not a complaint. It was a fact.

"I know you did."

She held him there with it.

The room was quiet.

"You didn't tell me everything," she said.

Not loud. Not accusing.

Just placed.

He did not look away.

"I told you what there is."

She watched him.

The answer did not satisfy. It did not break.

It held.

Her eyes dropped once. To his hand at her wrist. To the place where she had not taken it back.

She did not take it back.

He said, "I would be very much honoured if you would be my wife."

The words arrived more formally than he had intended.

Bella looked at him.

Her hands, still in his, tightened once.

The room held.

Something moved at the edge of her face that was not quite a smile and not quite grief.

"Mrs. Wilson," she said.

"If you would have it so."

She held his eyes.

"I think I might," she said.

He brought his other hand to her chin.

She lifted her face.

He kissed her.

Her mouth was warm and real and for the first moment she was simply still, and then her hands came out of his and found the front of his coat and she kissed him back the way she did everything — without half measures, having made up her mind.

He set his forehead against hers.

They stood.

Outside, the sound of boots on the porch steps.

He stepped back.

Bella turned to the stove. A small movement at one corner of her mouth that she was not managing.

Heather came through the door.

"They don't want anything."

"No," Bella said.

"I told you."

"You did."

Heather looked at Elias. At Bella. At the room between them.

Children have a gift for reading rooms. She read this one.

"Well," she said.

She hung up her coat with care.

"Are we having tea."

Bella set the kettle on.

"Yes," she said.

Heather climbed onto her chair and folded her hands on the table with the satisfied readiness of someone who had decided tea was an excellent outcome and had no further questions at this time.

Elias sat.

The light outside had moved the way it moves in late February.

A degree. An inch.

Not much.

But different from what it had been.

Thirty-Two

The room above the saloon was as it had always been. The rope bed. The basin. The window above the creek showing March sky, pale and cold and committed to nothing yet. He had slept in this room since August. He would not sleep in it again.

The fact did not ask anything of him.

He sat up.

His things were already reduced — most of them moved to Bella's house over the past two weeks in stages, without ceremony. What remained was the coat. The Bible. The collar on the washstand. His razor and the small steel mirror.

He shaved.

The mirror showed him the same face it had always shown him, the break running through it where someone's carelessness had cracked the glass.

He dressed.

The collar last.

He held it a moment. Then set it at his throat and went down.

* * *

Farwell was already in the saloon.

The room had been transformed in the manner of a place asked to become something it was not built for and had complied without enthusiasm. Tables pushed to the walls. Chairs arranged in two rough lines facing the front. Someone had hung a piece of cloth along the back wall — dark wool, Farwell's trading stock — and it did what it was meant to do, which was to make the front of the room look like the front of something.

Farwell stood near the window with his hat in both hands.

"Morning," he said.

"Morning."

He turned the hat once and set it on the nearest table.

"Mary's at the house." He looked at the room. "Women started early."

Elias said nothing.

Farwell looked at him. The measuring quality was gone from it.

"You eat."

"Not yet."

He lifted his chin toward the bar. Nora had left bread and cold meat and a cup of coffee gone lukewarm. Elias ate standing while Farwell continued to assess the room without appearing to.

"You know the service," Elias said.

"You pointed it out."

"You're comfortable with it."

"I have read aloud in front of men before, Reverend." Farwell looked at him without heat. "Managed a few court proceedings in my time."

He picked up the book from the bar and opened it. Anderson Hawthorne's book of common prayer that would now provide the words of holy matrimony. The ribbon lay at the Form of Solemnization of Matrimony.

"The secrets of all hearts," he said, as he might read a clause in a ledger.

Neither adding weight nor removing any.

He set the paper down.

"I'll manage it," he said.

* * *

They came at midmorning.

Without announcement, without arrangement, simply arriving. Farwell's people. Métis from along the creek. A few from Solomon's side of the water. The women who had been at Bella's since before light came now with everything set and themselves in their better dresses.

Gabriel Lavallee came and stood near the back with his hat in his hands.

Solomon sent one man. He took a place near the door, coat buttoned, hat on.

The room settled.

Then Bella came through the door.

The dress was her own — the best one, worked over in the days before. Her hair pinned with a care that had required time. Heather beside her in a clean dress that had been let down at the hem and taken in at the waist for a child who had grown since the last occasion requiring it.

Heather looked at Elias when she came in.

She took her place beside her mother and faced forward.

Farwell moved to the front. He waited until the room had settled entirely — the stillness of a collection of people who have decided that whatever comes next is worth attending to.

He looked at the book.

"Dearly beloved," he said, "we are gathered together here in the sight of God, and in the face of this company, to join together this Man and this Woman in holy Matrimony."

His voice had the quality Elias had heard in it before. Practical. Carrying. The voice of a man who had said necessary things in front of other men for a long time.

"Into this holy estate these two persons present come now to be joined. Therefore, if any man can show any just cause, why they may not lawfully be joined together, let him now speak, or else hereafter for ever hold his peace."

No one spoke.

The fire in the stove breathed.

The creek moved beyond the buildings. A horse shifted at a rail. The wind came once across the open ground and went.

"I require and charge you both," Farwell said, "as ye will answer at the dreadful day of judgement when the secrets of all hearts shall be disclosed—"

He read it plainly. As he read everything. The words had their own weight and required no addition.

"—that if either of you know any impediment why ye may not be lawfully joined together in matrimony, ye do now confess it."

Silence moved through the room.

Through the men near the back. Through Solomon's man at the door. Through the women who had arranged this and would live beside it after.

No one spoke.

Farwell lifted his eyes from the book. He looked at Elias.

Elias held his eyes.

Farwell looked back down.

He led them through the questions. Elias answered his. Bella answered hers. Their voices in the room, one after the other, in the plain declarative form the liturgy required.

Then the vows.

Their hands were joined.

Elias took hers.

"I, Elias Jonathan Wilson, take thee Isabella Heather Hawthorne to my wedded wife, to have and to hold from this day forward, for better for worse, for richer for poorer, in sickness and in health, to love and to cherish, till death us do part, according to God's holy ordinance; and thereto I plight thee my troth."

The words came as they were given to him.

He did not pause.

He meant them. He may have meant them more completely than he had meant anything.

Bella's voice.

"I, Isabella Heather Hawthorne, take thee Elias Jonathan Wilson to my wedded husband, to have and to hold from this day forward, for better for worse, for richer for poorer, in sickness and in health, to love and to cherish, till death us do part, according to God's holy ordinance; and thereto I plight thee my troth."

She did not ask. She stood.

The ring. Plain. Right for her. He had taken it from Farwell's trading stock two weeks before with no ceremony at all.

He placed it on her finger.

"With this ring I thee wed, with my body I thee worship, and with all my worldly goods I thee endow."

Farwell stepped forward. He took their joined hands in his and held them once.

"Those whom God hath joined together let no man put asunder."

Elias looked at Bella.

She looked at him. Not warmth, not softness. Decision. The face of a woman who has made a calculation and committed to its result.

The door shifted.

Solomon's man stepped out into the light and was gone.

The cold came briefly in and left.

Elias kissed her.

The room exhaled.

* * *

The fiddle started before the ceremony had fully broken apart.

Gabriel's cousin — a Métis man Elias had seen at the ford and along the creek, compact and unhurried — had the instrument out and was into it before the chairs had been pushed back. The tune was not a hymn. It was the sound of this country celebrating itself, and the room responded to it the way rooms respond to fiddle music when enough whiskey is available and the occasion is right.

The food appeared as if it had always been there waiting. Bread, cold meat, preserves, a pot of beans. A cake made with what the season offered, sufficient for the occasion if not ornate. Mary set down two covered dishes without comment — the gesture itself the whole of what she intended. Nora set a small wrapped thing beside Bella's place. The quilt came out, shaken and laid across a chair — deep blues and greens, the work of several pairs of hands through the winter months.

Farwell gave Bella an iron pot. Good and heavy. New.

"For the house," he said.

She looked at it, then at him.

"Thank you, Abel."

He nodded once and the matter was concluded.

Men drifted toward the bar with the naturalness of water finding its level. Glasses set down. Glasses lifted. The fiddle going. A hand drum joining it from somewhere, setting the rhythm beneath.

The women gathered around Bella the way women gather around a bride — without announcement, without arrangement, simply there. The quilt examined. The dishes praised. Heather, who had spent the morning in solemn performance of the occasion, had by the second hour loosened entirely and was eating something given to her and watching the fiddle player with the frank attention of a child who has located the most interesting thing in the room.

Elias stood at the bar with a glass.

The whiskey was Farwell's best, brought out for the day. He drank with the care of a man who knows the evening has not yet arrived.

He was a married man.

The fact arrived in pieces. He had spoken the words. Bella had spoken the words. Farwell had read the paper and the room had witnessed it and it was done. The ring was on her hand. The quilt was on the chair and the fiddle was going and the settlement had gathered because of it.

He drank.

* * *

Mid-afternoon. The fiddle still going. The food reduced to its last portions. Heather fighting sleep in a corner with the resignation of a child losing an argument she entered too late.

Elias found Farwell and Mary together near the far wall.

Not touching. As they always stood — proximate, self-contained, each sufficient.

He came to them with his glass.

"A good day," Farwell said.

"Yes."

Elias looked at them both. The whiskey had taken some of the careful distance out of the room.

"I could do it now," he said.

Farwell looked at him.

"If you wanted it."

A moment. The fiddle went on behind them.

Farwell turned the glass once in his hand. Something moved across his face — not refusal. The expression of a man receiving an offer he has long since considered and put in a particular drawer.

"A man has to be careful," he said slowly, "what he changes about an arrangement that's working."

He said it without looking at Mary.

Mary looked at Elias.

She held his eyes a moment. Then she looked at Farwell.

"What we have," she said, "does not require your book."

She said it without heat. The way she said most things.

Then she looked at Elias once more.

"But I am glad you thought to ask."

She crossed the room toward Heather.

Farwell watched her go.

"There it is," he said. He did not elaborate.

He lifted his glass.

"You did well today," he said.

Not praise. Something entered into the record.

He turned toward the room.

* * *

Mary took Heather without making a matter of it.

She crossed to the child where she had finally surrendered to sleep against someone's arm, crouched, gathered her, and wrapped her coat around her with the efficient tenderness of a woman who has attended to sleeping children too many times to make ceremony of it. She looked once at Bella. A look that required nothing and gave nothing. Then she went out with the child and the door closed behind them.

Nora watched it happen from behind the bar.

She met Elias's eyes briefly. Then turned and refilled the nearest glass.

Bella had seen it too. A stillness came into her face — the moment of reception before the surface settled back. She was still in conversation. She did not change the substance of her expression.

But something had shifted in her.

She knew what the night was.

* * *

They came at dark.

The fiddle first, distant, then suddenly not distant. Then the pots. Then voices — the settlement condensed into noise, the old Métis custom of the charivari moving toward the house in a wave of affectionate demand. Fiddle and drum and pots struck together and laughter underneath all of it.

Elias heard it from inside the house. He looked at Bella.

She was at the stove. She did not turn. But the corner of her mouth.

He opened the door.

The yard was full of them — most of the settlement still standing, Gabriel's cousin with the fiddle going and his eyes closed, men with pots, women with the particular laughter of people doing a thing that is silly and ancient and entirely serious. They shouted things he could not fully hear above the noise and did not need to.

He went back in and came out with the bottle.

A sound went up.

He brought it out to them and it went around and the noise kept going. Bella came to the door and the noise went up a different register for her, the warmth reserved for the one given and received, and she received it as she received everything — without pretending the room did not see her.

The bottle made its circuit. The fiddle went on. The cold sat on all of them and none of them moved.

Then, by ones and twos, they pulled back into the dark. The fiddle receding down the street. Voices thinning. A last shout from somewhere already distant.

Silence.

The yard empty.

He closed the door.

* * *

The lamp on the table.

He crossed to the chair and took off his coat.

Set it over the back.

The weight of the day came away with it.

He stood.

The gun sat on the table beside the lamp. Not hidden. Not put away. Placed.

He looked at it a moment.

Then turned.

Bella stood near the window. She had been watching him. She did not acknowledge that she had been watching him and he did not ask.

He crossed to her.

She was warm from the room and the day and the press of people. He set his hands at her face. She let him lift it. She looked at him with the eyes of a woman who has made her decision and requires nothing further from it.

He kissed her.

She came into it without ceremony, her hands finding his chest, the lapels of his shirt, moving upward. He felt her warmth through the cloth.

Her hands came to his chest. The shirt. The line of the buttons.

Then higher.

The collar.

Her fingers rested there.

He reached up.

Unfastened it.

Drew it free.

He took it and held it a moment — the worn pewter, the cloth, the thing that had spoken for him in every room since the road south of the line.

He set it on the table beside the coat.

He turned back.

There was nothing between them now that was not his own.

She reached for his shirt buttons.

One.

Then the next.

He stood in the lamplight and let her.

She was unhurried. Her fingers moved with the same certainty he had watched at a dying man's bedside, at a fence in summer, at a school board in the frost. Moving differently now. Directed toward him.

He found the hooks at the back of her dress.

The fabric came free.

Beneath it the warmth of her, the specific gravity of a woman who has decided to be known, and he understood what the liturgy meant — *with my body I thee worship* — not as form. As fact.

Outside, the wind whispered its cold harsh truth.

Inside, the lamp burned and the room held the shape of them.

* * *

Later.

The lamp turned to its last light.

Her breathing beside him, slow and settled. His hand at her side, the warmth of her real beneath his palm.

On the table the gun sat in what remained of the lamplight.

Beside it the collar.

Two things laid down.

He lay still.

The house had gone to the deep quiet of a winter night with the fire burned low. The wind moved through the land in its ordinary way, indifferent and continuous, as it had moved when he came down off the rise on one knee in the dirt, as it had moved through everything that had happened since.

He did not sleep.

He lay with his hand at her side and listened to the wind and to her breathing and to the house settling around them in the cold.

He had spoken the words.

He meant them.

Those two things remained where they were.

Thirty-Three

March came in without ceremony.

The cold did not leave. It settled into a different register — still present in the mornings, still finding the gaps in the walls — but the light rose earlier and stayed longer. The settlement felt it before anyone named it. Men moved differently in that light. Work that had been deferred through the worst of winter was taken up again and the sound of it — an axe, a hammer, a bucket chain at the creek — carried the quality of a place that had survived something and was prepared to say so.

He woke before Bella most mornings.

The house was quiet in a way the room above the saloon had never been. No boots below. No voices rising through the boards and settling again. He woke into the stillness and lay in it a moment before rising, attending to what it was.

He put the kettle on.

Heather came out before Bella.

She came with her Bible under one arm and climbed onto the bench as though the morning had been arranged around that purpose. The little book he had given her at Christmas was already softened at the corners from use. She set it on the table, opened it to Genesis, and looked at him with the seriousness of a person prepared to justify her presence.

"I'm practising," she said.

"I can see that."

She climbed onto his knee without asking and began.

She read the first verses carefully, her finger keeping place. Then by the third day the finger slowed and the words came from memory instead. Her eyes remained on the page. Her voice settled into the cadence of something that had ceased to belong only to the book.

He did not correct her.

He held the lamp angle steady and listened to her render the firmament from memory in the voice of a child who had made the words her own.

Bella came out when she came out.

She stood in the doorway a moment, shawl pulled close, her hair not yet put right. Not fully awake. There was something about her in that state — the face before the day had arranged itself upon it — that continued to catch him unprepared.

She saw them.

She did not smile. She did not speak. She went to the stove, took the coffee he had left there for her, and stood at the window with it, looking out toward the yard and the creek beyond.

Heather's high voice rose and fell.

And the evening and the morning were the third day.

The lamp cast its flickering light. Bella looked out at the yard and said nothing. The morning held the three of them in it without asking for anything more.

* * *

"Ice is breaking," Bella said one morning in the second week.

He looked up from the book.

"On the creek."

He listened.

She was right. Something in the sound had changed in the night. The flat silence of the frozen creek had given way to something with more articulation in it — water no longer frozen and held.

"Won't hold much longer," he said.

Bella looked at him over the cup.

He turned back to the page.

He had heard the weight in his voice only after it had arrived — the way a man becomes aware of what he has carried when the carrying eases by one small measure.

The creek moved.

He read the same line twice.

* * *

The school ran Saturdays and Wednesdays.

Twelve children through the winter. That had held, which meant something. A settlement keeps what it uses. Or most of it.

James McLeod had turned fourteen in February. His father let him finish out the month. Then he came to Bella's door on the first Wednesday of March with his hat in both hands and the look of a man delivering words he had not chosen himself.

"The boy won't be coming."

Bella stood in the doorway. Elias at the table behind her could see only one side of McLeod's face and the brim of the hat turning once between his fingers.

"There's work," McLeod said. "Thaw comes and there's work."

Bella said nothing.

"He's old enough."

She nodded once.

"Thank you for telling me."

McLeod inclined his head and went.

Bella closed the door.

James had not come himself. That said something too. Three days before he had been bent over a column of long division with the focused aggression of a boy who had discovered he was better at a thing than he had expected and did not yet know what to do with that discovery. He had finished the sums. Checked them. Then checked them again.

He was not here now.

The younger ones filled the room without knowing it was smaller.

Elias worked the numbers at the far end of the table and did not raise the matter. Bella moved among the children with the chalk. She felt it too. He could tell by the way she did not once look at the empty place on the bench.

After the children had gone she made coffee. They sat at the table with the slates stacked and the room returned to itself.

"The McLeod boy," he said.

"I know," she said.

That was all.

* * *

Sunday the settlement came to the saloon.

The arrangement had begun in October when the cold made the crossing less certain and Farwell had offered the room without troubling to call the offer generous. He had pushed the tables back himself the first Sunday and said no more about it.

It was not a church.

The smell of the place remained what it was — old whiskey in the boards, tobacco, damp wool, the stale closeness of a room shut too long against winter and opened too briefly. The piano had finally been covered with a cloth. The bottles still stood behind the bar. The children looked at them when they came in and then looked away when their mothers saw them doing it.

Some of the women had not come since October.

Two families from the far side of the settlement had attended the creek service through September and had not once appeared in the saloon. Whether from principle or distance or simple dislike of the place, Elias had not asked. A man did not keep that sort of tally unless he wanted resentment for a harvest.

From Solomon's side a few still came. The Renauds. A Métis family with young children who crossed regardless of weather. Solomon's girls did not come and had not been invited to, and Elias had formed no opinion on that beyond the observation that God was not waiting on their attendance to continue His work.

The room was what it was.

He read the service and the words went into it and were received according to what each person had brought to the receiving.

Farwell sat in back some Sundays with his hat on his knee and his face doing nothing at all. Whether he was worshipping or auditing remained, Elias had decided, none of his business.

Afterward the settlement spilled back out into the cold and separated along its accustomed lines.

The men remained in the street for a time in the way of men recently gathered who are not yet ready to disperse — speaking of spruce, of labour, of foundation depth, of whether the thaw would make a liar of any plan begun too early. The church had become the settlement's chief collective ambition, which meant that half the men spoke of it as though it already stood and the other half as though speaking of it too plainly might offend the weather.

The women went to Bella's.

That had begun without arrangement. Gravity had simply shifted in that direction, as it does when a settlement acquires something it lacked and does not yet know how to name it. Bella met it the way she met most things that came to her without her asking: she put the kettle on.

She was good at it.

That had not surprised him exactly. It had instructed him.

She set no great store by faith — she had never pretended otherwise with him, not even in the private hours — but she understood what the role required and met it without complaint and without performance. She did not testify. She did not lead prayer. She poured coffee. She remembered what each woman had said the week before and asked after it the next Sunday. She listened without needing to be seen listening, and the women trusted her in the particular way women trust a person who pays attention and keeps what is told.

Whether she had made peace with the contradiction or merely set it aside, he did not ask.

He hung up his collar and left them to it.

* * *

The matter came before him on a Thursday.

Two men. Henri Lacombe, Métis, a freight driver on Farwell's run. Beside him William Pratt, English, a hand at the trading post who had come up from Benton two seasons earlier.

They sat on opposite sides of the table. Neither comfortable. Not uncomfortable in the same way.

Elias opened the book and wrote the date.

"Mr. Pratt," he said. "Tell me the matter."

Pratt told it plainly. A grey gelding, fourteen hands, sound in wind and limb. Lent to Lacombe in November for a short haul to Fort Solomon and back, the animal being better on ice than Lacombe's own horse. Lacombe had taken it. Lacombe had returned it. The horse had come back with the near foreleg soft and a cut at the pastern. The cut had gone septic through December. Cost him the season's work from the animal.

"And still not right," Pratt said.

Elias wrote.

"Mr. Lacombe."

Lacombe spoke carefully. The horse had been sound when he took it. He had not driven it hard. The cut was not his doing in any deliberate way — ice crossings were rough on horses and that crossing had been rougher than most. He had returned the animal and told Pratt of the leg when he brought it back.

"You told him."

"I told him. He was there."

Pratt's jaw tightened. "He said it was nothing."

"It was not much," Lacombe said. "At the time."

Elias looked at the notes. Set the pen down.

"The horse was not returned as it left," he said. "The cut was there when it came back. You reported it, Mr. Lacombe. Mr. Pratt accepted the animal back in that condition. The sepsis came after."

He looked at both men in turn.

"Mr. Lacombe. The cut occurred while the horse was in your keeping. You did not cause it deliberately. But it was your keeping."

A pause.

"Half the winter feed for the horse. Paid to Mr. Pratt. Not for the sepsis. That came after your responsibility ended. For the cut on your watch."

Lacombe's face went still in the careful way of a man keeping his objection from becoming offence.

"Half the winter feed," he said. "For a cut from crossing ice."

"For the cut," Elias said.

"That is a great deal of money for ice."

"It is the cost of damage while the animal was in your care."

Lacombe looked down at the table. Drew one slow breath through his nose. Said something low in Michif that did not require translation.

Pratt had been watching with the expression of a man expecting complete vindication and receiving only a portion of it.

"And the sepsis," Pratt said.

"Is not Mr. Lacombe's liability."

"The sepsis came from the cut."

"The sepsis developed after you accepted the animal back."

"He told me the leg was stiff. He did not tell me—"

"You had the horse in front of you, Mr. Pratt."

Pratt's hands came together on the brim of the hat in his lap. He looked at the wall, then at the table, then somewhere over Elias's shoulder.

"So I am stolen from," he said, "and then told I should have looked more closely at what was stolen."

"The horse was lent."

"Lent and returned broken." He said it to the room rather than to either man. "And I am to take half a remedy and be grateful."

No one spoke.

Lacombe kept his eyes on the table. The set of his face suggested a man who had come prepared to be found wholly without fault and was now making the necessary room for disappointment.

"It isn't right," he said quietly.

Not to Pratt. Not to Elias. To the table between them.

Elias picked up the pen.

"Is it refused."

A silence.

Lacombe let the breath out.

"No," he said.

Pratt said nothing for a moment longer. Then, with the compressed dignity of a man receiving less than he had budgeted for:

"No."

Elias wrote the terms. Turned the book. Both men made their marks without looking at each other.

They went out.

He heard Pratt say something in the yard that the closed door mercifully reduced to tone.

Nora stood behind the bar with a glass in her hand. She set it down and did not move it.

Elias sat with the open book.

Two men came with a dispute and left with a ruling. Neither satisfied. Both bound.

He closed the book.

* * *

Farwell found him at the church site.

He came up the trail from the post with his coat buttoned high and his hat pulled low against the wind off the coulee. He did not appear surprised to find Elias already there. He stood at the edge of the staked ground a moment, looking at it, then walked the perimeter without speaking, the way a man walks land he has already been considering in his head.

The coulee ran close on the north side. The willows there were still bare but beginning, perhaps, to consider otherwise. South lay the trail back to the post. Beyond it the creek. The saloon roof showed above the trees. The hills rose westward under the pale March sky.

"Five minutes," Farwell said. "Ten in February."

Farwell looked the distance over.

"Ten," he agreed.

He nodded toward the north.

"McLeod knows where there's spruce. Two hours that way. Men who owe labour can fetch it. Ground will need to wait for thaw."

"May."

"May."

They stood on opposite sides of the stakes.

Farwell looked once at the coulee, once back toward the settlement, then at Elias.

"I won't put men and timber into ground a man is standing on temporarily," he said.

Elias looked at the staked corners. The open space they described.

"No," he said. "I wouldn't either."

Farwell waited.

Elias knew what the waiting was for. He did not resent it. A man like Farwell did not build for shadows.

"I'm staying," he said.

Farwell nodded once. The way a figure is confirmed in a ledger.

"Then let's build it properly."

He turned and went back down the trail.

* * *

Solomon came in the afternoon.

He came alone. Coat buttoned. Hat low. He crossed the saloon with the unhurried ease of a man making a courtesy call on another man he has no intention of rushing.

He looked at the table. At the book. At the two empty chairs still turned from the morning.

Then he sat.

Elias did not move the chair for him.

"A matter this morning," Solomon said.

"Two men. A horse."

"Settled."

"Yes."

Solomon nodded once. Looked at the book.

"That is a useful thing you've built," he said. "Men who would not have taken a ruling from Farwell — or from me —marked the page."

"They weren't pleased."

"No." A small pause. "That is how you know it held."

Elias said nothing.

Solomon rested both hands flat on the table. The cufflinks took the afternoon light.

"I have a matter," he said.

"Tell it."

"A man. Runs a trap line along the lower coulee. Uses the creek crossing on my side of the water. Has done so freely for some years."

"Before the fort."

"Before the fort." Solomon acknowledged. Then: "One of my men has lately decided the crossing is Fort Solomon's right of way. He has turned the man back twice this month."

"On your instruction."

A pause.

"No."

Elias held his eyes.

"Then correct him."

Solomon's fingers moved once on the tabletop and stilled.

"I could," he said. "Or the matter could come before the book. The crossing written down. Rights of access established." He held Elias's eyes. "A settlement with something written knows where it stands."

"What rights," Elias said.

"His access. Formalised."

"And yours."

Solomon looked at him.

"Whatever the record shows," he said. "That is all I ask."

"I'll need to speak with the man," Elias said. "And hear the history of the crossing."

"Of course."

"It may take time."

"There is no urgency."

Solomon stood. Looked once more at the book.

"A fair process," he said. "That's all."

He put on his hat and went out.

The room settled around the space he had left.

Nora moved a glass from one place to another without purpose and then stood with both hands flat on the bar.

Elias sat with the closed book.

The request was reasonable. That was plain enough. The process proper. That too.

He turned the pen once in his hand.

A man came with a grievance and the shape of the grievance told you something about what he wanted. Pratt had wanted the horse made whole and someone made responsible. Lacombe had wanted to be found without fault. Those were legible. He had known within minutes what each man had come for and what truth in the matter could be had.

Solomon was not legible.

That was not quite right.

He knew what Solomon had asked for. He did not know what Solomon wanted. In his experience, those two things were seldom the same in the same man. But they were seldom so far apart as this.

Whatever the record shows.

He set the pen down.

Outside the window the creek moved in its new register, the ice gone thin at the margins, the current pressing up through it from below.

He put on his coat.

If Solomon wanted the record to show something, then the record had to be laid down before Solomon could bend it. The man had crossed there since before either fort stood. What he knew — who had used it, when, and on whose understanding — was what the matter would rest on.

"The man who uses the crossing on Solomon's side," Elias said. "Where does he camp."

Nora looked at him a moment.

"South bend of the coulee," she said. "This time of year."

He picked up the book and went out into the March afternoon.

Thirty-Four

He crossed the creek where the stones showed.

The ice was gone from the edges and the current at the open centre moved with the authority of melt — fast, clear, carrying nothing. His bad foot found the familiar footing. He crossed without stopping.

Little Soldier's camp sat in the bend below the forts, where the creek curved east and the ground opened south toward the flat. He had been here often enough now that the dogs knew him before his shape resolved. The nearest lifted its head from the place it had been sleeping and set it down again. A woman carrying hides from the drying rack looked at him and looked back at her work. A boy stopped and watched with the open attention of someone whose elders had decided to go on with their business.

He was a known thing here.

Gabriel Lavallee was crouched at a fire outside the second lodge, cleaning a knife on a strip of hide. He looked up without appearing to have been waiting. He folded the hide and set it beside him. He did not put the knife away.

"Reverend."

"I'm looking for the man at the coulee's south crossing," Elias said. "Solomon's man has been blocking him."

"I know."

"Can you bring me to him."

Gabriel looked at the fire. Long enough that it was not casual.

"He won't want you there," he said.

"I know that."

Gabriel stood. He sheathed the knife. He picked up his hat from the ground beside the fire and put it on.

"His people are not Little Soldier's," he said. He said it the way he stated most things — not by way of warning but by way of precision, placing the fact where it needed to be before they moved. "He came through here last autumn. He trades when he has something. He uses the creek. He answers to no one in this camp."

"Whose is he."

Gabriel began walking north along the bend.

"His own," he said.

* * *

They followed the water. North of the ford, the coulee took them in. The willows grew close on both sides, their branches still bare but beginning to redden at the tips. The ground was soft with the last of the melt working down through it. Gabriel moved through it without effort, the way a man moves through land he has read in several seasons.

He was quiet for a while.

The coulee bent east and the light shifted. They were below the line of both forts now, the hills holding them on either side, the creek moving low and fast between the banks.

Gabriel stopped at a place where the high bank had been worn into a long smooth depression above the waterline, the earth rounded and old, the kind of shape that takes years to make.

He said a word in a language Elias did not have. Not to Elias. Not to the water. He said it the way a man says a name he is still owed.

Then he walked on.

Elias followed.

"Every people who came through here used this ground," Gabriel said, after a time. He did not slow. "Before the Assiniboine were strong in this country. Before my grandmother's people. The hills hold the wind and the creek brings the deer down." He stepped over a branch without breaking stride. "Some of them fought over it. The ground held." He said nothing further about it.

Elias walked.

He thought about the agreement. About what it meant to write a name over land that had been absorbing names for centuries without keeping any of them.

He let it go.

"Solomon says his man acted without instruction," Elias said.

Gabriel made a sound low in his throat.

"His man does what Solomon wants," he said. "Solomon is careful about the distance between those two things."

"Yes."

"Then you don't need me to tell you."

"No."

They walked.

"He was turned back the second time with a gun present," Gabriel said. "He came to the camp two nights after. He was not quiet about it. Little Soldier listened. That was all Little Soldier did."

"What does Little Soldier want from this."

"He wants to see what you do."

The camp came into view through the willows.

* * *

It was small. One lodge and a lean-to built against a spruce at the clearing's edge. Four traps hung from a branch — cleaned, set, waiting. Two horses on a picket line behind the lodge. Good animals. Fed through. A meat rack beside the lean-to holding what a late season could provide — not much, but taken and kept. A fire that had been tended recently.

The man came out before they reached it.

He was perhaps forty, with the particular economy of someone who had lived alone through many seasons — nothing wasted in movement, nothing open in the face. He looked at Gabriel first, then at Elias, and what moved across his expression at the sight of the collar was not surprise. It was the settled recognition of a man who had been expecting exactly this and had already decided how to receive it.

He spoke to Gabriel.

Gabriel answered. His voice was level.

The man looked at Elias and spoke again. Brief.

"He says he did not ask for you," Gabriel said.

Elias waited anyway.

The man's eyes stayed on Elias. He spoke at some length, and his voice was measured throughout.

"He says he has done nothing wrong," Gabriel said. "He does not steal. He does not damage. He crosses water that belongs to no one. The man who blocks him is the one who has done wrong. He asks what you are here for."

"I can make a ruling," Elias said. "Written, at Fort Farwell, with witnesses. It will say the crossing belongs to no fort. That he has the right to use it."

Gabriel translated.

The man said something short and flat.

"He says: then say it. And move the man."

"I can't move the man," Elias said. "But a ruling puts him in the wrong if he blocks again."

Gabriel began to translate. The man spoke over him. He had enough English for the word ruling. He said something in his own language, level and long.

Gabriel listened.

"He says a ruling is for men who disagree about what is right," Gabriel said. "He does not disagree. He knows what is right. The man blocking him knows what is right. They do not have a disagreement. He has a man with a gun."

Elias held that.

"He's correct," Elias said.

Gabriel did not translate it.

"Ask him what he will do if the ruling doesn't come."

Gabriel asked.

The man looked at Elias. He said one thing, without heat.

Gabriel looked at the fire for a moment before giving it over.

"He says he will wait until he doesn't need to."

The coulee was quiet around them. The creek moved below the bank.

Elias understood what that meant. He heard the floor of it, and he heard how close to it the man was standing.

"Fort Farwell," he said. "Three days. I hold the hearing in the saloon. He does not have to come. He does not have to accept any ruling. But I will make it." He paused. "I will write there what I have said here."

Gabriel translated.

The man listened. Then he turned to Gabriel and said something Elias didn't catch. Gabriel answered. His voice shifted — lower, something in it that was not translation. He made an argument of some kind. Brief.

The man shook his head once.

He looked at Elias.

In English he said: "Go away."

He went back inside the lodge. The door flap closed.

The horses moved on their picket. One looked toward the creek, toward something Elias couldn't see or hear.

Gabriel stood with his hat in his hands.

"What did you say to him," Elias said.

"I told him you will honour your word."

Elias waited.

"He said it doesn't matter."

They stood in the clearing a moment.

Elias turned north.

Gabriel fell in beside him.

* * *

He held it three days later.

Late afternoon light through the saloon windows. Nora had set the chairs. The book was open to a clean page.

Solomon came.

He came alone, crossed the room with the unhurried ease of a man who knows how to attend proceedings without appearing to need them. He sat in the chair across the table and looked at Elias with composed patience. He looked once at Gabriel standing near the wall.

Gabriel did not acknowledge the look.

The room held the usual afternoon. Men who had drifted in and not left.

The man did not come.

Elias waited. He was deliberate about it. He let the silence work.

Then he opened the book.

"The matter before this hearing concerns the creek crossing at the south bend of the coulee," he said. "A man who has used that crossing freely for some years was turned back twice this month by a man in Fort Solomon's employ."

He did not look at Solomon.

"The crossing predates both forts. That is not in dispute."

He let that sit.

"The coulee agreement, signed by both forts, holds that no man is to be impeded by force in his passage through the coulee. It holds further that no shots are to be fired." He looked at the page as though reading, though he had not needed the page since autumn. "The act of turning this man back, twice, with a firearm present, does not break the agreement as written.

But it breaks what the agreement was made to prevent."

Solomon's hands rested flat on the table.

"My man acted without my instruction," he said.

"I know that," Elias said. "This finding does not name your man."

He held Solomon's eyes.

"This finding holds the crossing as free passage," he said. "Not Fort Solomon's right of way. Not subject to the discretion of Fort Solomon's men." He wrote as he spoke. "Any person who moves through the coulee in the ordinary course of their travel may use it. Any man in Fort Solomon's employ who blocks the crossing does so in violation of the coulee agreement, which Fort Solomon signed."

He set the pen down.

"Furthermore." He let the word stand a moment. "The terms of the coulee agreement continue in full. No gunshots. No violence in the coulee. This finding operates within those terms." He looked at Solomon steadily.

The room was quiet.

Solomon sat very still.

There was a long moment in which Elias could not read what moved behind the man's eyes.

Then: "You've found a way to write it so it lands where you want."

"This is my finding," Elias said. "Will you sign it."

He turned the book across the table.

Then Solomon nodded once, in the way a man nods when he has confirmed something he had already supposed.

"No."

He stood. Straightened his coat. Looked at the book.

"Farwell's law," he said. "Or yours. Not mine."

He said it quietly. Not with contempt. With the precision of a man placing a thing in its correct location.

He put on his hat and went out.

The door settled behind him.

No one moved.

Then Nora set a glass down on the bar. The ordinary sound of an afternoon resuming.

Elias looked at the page. The date. The ruling. The space below it where no one had signed but himself.

When he looked up, Gabriel was still at the wall. His eyes were on the closed book. Then he put his hat on and went out.

Thirty-Five

The man spent the winter finding him.

Not the name on the collar. The other one. The one that had travelled ahead of him and waited.

There had been enough to start with. A face half-remembered through rain. A priest who wore a gun in the manner of a man who knew it. A ledger entry copied and carried south.

By February he had confirmation enough.

By March the ground was moving.

John Heath's debt was on record. Its recovery was the minimum acceptable outcome. Better was delivery — Heath breathing, under guard, moving south.

The money was gone. That left two outcomes.

He rode north with four men.

* * *

The creek was running again.

Elias lay still a moment and listened to the change.

Beside him, Bella slept.

He rose without waking her.

He set the kettle. Early light caught the hills to the west and held there before it reached the creek. He stood at the window and watched it come.

He had a ruling to write — a land dispute, two men who had sat across from him the day before with their embarrassment and their legitimate grievance, which the law required him to take equally seriously. He would write the finding this morning and deliver it.

It was an ordinary morning.

Then Dunn knocked.

* * *

The knock was not urgent. It did not need to be. Dunn's presence at a door communicated what urgency would have communicated and spent less effort doing it.

Elias opened.

"Farwell wants you," Dunn said.

Nothing else. The blunt waiting of a man who has said what he came to say.

"Now," Elias said.

"He said when you can."

He meant now.

* * *

He told Heather to tell her mother he'd be at Farwell's. She looked at him with the face of a child who had come to trust his word.

"All right," she said.

He took his coat. His hat.

The gun sat on the table beside the lamp where he had left it the night before. He went out.

The yard was soft underfoot. Below, the creek ran brown and fast with the melt. The ford's rocks showed above the surface as they always did, worn smooth.

He walked through Fort Farwell, Dunn beside him.

* * *

Farwell was alone in the trading post.

The room held its ordinary smell: dry goods, last night's fire, the ledger open on the counter to the current page. Farwell stood near the window with his hat in both hands. He looked at Elias when he came in and said nothing for a moment, in the way of a man deciding where to begin.

He dismissed Dunn.

Elias noted it.

"Delivery from Fort Benton," Farwell said.

Elias waited.

"Murphy. Four riders with him."

"Murphy," Elias said.

"Broad through the shoulders. Scar here." He indicated his own face, temple to jaw. "Asked after the Reverend Wilson."

Something moved through the room. Maybe only the fire.

"He say what it was he wanted," Elias said.

"He did not." Farwell made a notation. Closed the pen. "Said he had a private matter."

Farwell's eyes lifted then. Rested on him.

"He asked me to direct him to the Wilson residence."

Elias's right hand moved to his jacket pocket. Empty.

"I told him I'd pass the message along. That I don't direct men to private residences without an introduction. He didn't care for that."

"What else."

"He said he'd stay the night. He said he'd be back this morning. Same time. He said to have you here."

The fire ticked.

Elias kept his face where it needed to be.

"He at the saloon," he said.

Farwell studied him.

"I didn't like the look of it." Farwell said it with the flat affect of a man stating a property valuation. "I told him there was no room."

Elias nodded. Not thanking. Noting the rightness of a thing.

"What do you make of it," he said.

He asked it square and without weight.

"I think that Murphy selected four particular men for his whiskey run this year. And arrived at my fort seeking a particular conversation. A conversation I'd like to understand."

A long quiet.

"I don't know what he is," Elias said.

He said it plainly. The way he said most things — the complete, level sentence, nothing extra in it.

Farwell received this.

“He’s not a man from your congregation,” he said.

“No.”

“Not a man from the east.”

“I don’t know him.”

Farwell looked at him with the attention he had always looked at him with — the attention of a man who has decided to hold a door open and is watching who comes through it.

“He went across,” Farwell said.

Not a question.

Elias did not speak.

He heard himself breathe.

Fort Solomon’s door. Solomon with a glass set down at the right moment. The careful extraction of a story from a man who did not know he was being extracted. What Solomon would hold when the man rode away. What Solomon would do with it.

Elias looked at the ledger on the counter. The date at the top of the open page. The ordinary accounting of a settlement that had survived a winter and was moving into spring.

“He’ll be back in the morning,” Farwell said.

“Yes.”

Farwell waited.

“I’ll be here,” Elias said.

A silence in the room that neither of them filled.

“I’ll have Dunn nearby,” Farwell said.

“All right.”

He put on his hat and went out.

* * *

He did not go home directly.

He walked east. Down the hill to the ford. The ford where he had preached. The ford he’d passed through going to Little Soldier’s camp.

The water moved fast and cold past his boots. The crossing stones showed above the surface, worn smooth by the passage of men going south and north and back again, as though the divide were a thing that could be managed with sufficient repetition.

He looked northeast.

Fort Solomon sat quiet on the hill. The scattered buildings. The larger one where the girls worked and the men drank and lowered their guard for an hour or two.

The coulee dark beside it.

His hand lay on his empty jacket pocket.

Nothing moved.

He turned and went back up the hill.

* * *

Heather was still at the table when he came in.

Bella was up. She stood at the stove with her back to him and did not turn when he came through the door, but her shoulders changed in the way a person's body registers a familiar arrival. The morning smelled of coffee and the last of the night's warmth in the walls.

"You were a while," she said.

"Farwell needed a word."

She turned then.

She looked at him.

Bella had known loss in its specific form. She had stood beside the specific grave of it and come through the other side. That experience had made her face precise about certain things — about the difference between a man who has had a difficult morning and a man who has had a difficult morning he is not going to name.

"Heather," she said. "Go get the eggs."

The girl slipped from her chair without argument and went out the back. The door swung closed behind her.

Bella looked at him.

"What happened," she said.

She was exactly what she was. He looked at her and knew it.

"There's talk," he said. "About the church. Where it sits."

Her eyes hardened.

"The men got no right to make that decision."

She turned away. Took the broom. Set it to the floor with more force than it required.

"Nothing's decided," he said. "Farwell will handle it."

She rounded on him.

"No, he will not. Who was it speaking against it? McLeod?"

"I'll ask him."

"You didn't."

"No."

"Fix it, Elias."

"I will."

She held him there.

"When."

"Tomorrow," he said.

He went to her and took her arms in his hands. She stilled.

"It's not just you now, Elias."

He did not answer.

Thirty-Six

The stillness he'd learned to love felt different this morning.

It lay on the room like a held breath. Like the pause between the thing and its consequence.

He dressed in the dark without lighting the lamp. Trousers. Shirt. He reached for the collar and fastened it at his throat before he reached for anything else. Then the coat. Then the gun from the table beside the lamp. He turned the cylinder by habit. The click of it moved through the room with the particular clarity that small sounds have in the hour before light.

He held still.

Bella was watching him from the bed. The pale shape of her face in the grey coming through the window. Her eyes open and quiet and saying nothing.

He did not speak.

He set the gun in his coat and went to the door.

* * *

He did not put the kettle on.

He did not open the Bible on the shelf.

He stood at the window and looked out at to the east, where the light was trying to come and not managing it. Low cloud pressing down. A westerly working over the ridgeline with spitting rain in it. The sun somewhere behind all of it, not yet decided what kind of morning this would be.

April the first.

He had a ruling to write. Two men with a legitimate grievance required a finding entered into the book. He would write it today. He would sit down after and do it properly.

He put on his hat and went out.

* * *

He did not go to Farwell's front door.

He came around the long way, below the fence line, past the pole barn where the horses stood with their heads down in the wet. He came up along the east side of the yard and stopped at the corner of the trading post.

He heard them before he saw them.

Horses. Not one or two. The sound of a party arrived and settled. The knock and creak of a loaded wagon. The low exchange of men who have come a long way and are now deciding how they want to stand.

He came around the corner.

The wagon stood in the yard with its canvas lashed. Five men. Murphy at the front of them, broad through the chest, a scar running temple to jaw on the left side of his face. He stood with the stillness of a man who has been patient long enough and is content to be patient a while longer because he knows how it ends.

Farwell was there. Dunn to his left, the shotgun low in his hands.

Elias walked forward.

He kept his pace even. His hands at his sides. He came across the yard and stopped ten feet from Murphy and looked at him.

Murphy looked back.

He studied the collar first. Then the face above it. He took his time.

"You say you're Wilson."

"I am."

"Not as I hear it."

"You heard wrong."

Murphy moved his jaw slowly. He looked at the trading post window. The ledger visible on the counter inside. Then he looked back at Elias.

"There's a man been missing out of Fort Benton since last summer. Worked for T.C. Power." He paused. "Goes by the name John Heath. Has your exact likeness."

"I don't know him."

"No."

Murphy looked at the collar again. At the coat. At the gun on the hip of the man wearing both.

"Funny thing about Heath," he said. "Man had a talent with a ledger. Could make a figure go where he wanted it. Lost money comes to rest someplace, Reverend — and Heath was particular about where he rested it. Set the short columns down against other men's names. Let them carry the weight of what he took. Men who had nothing to do with it." He let that sit. "I had some dealings with him. Kept books for a time at a place I moved through. Told me the ledger was clean." His eyes did not move. "It wasn't."

The yard held its quiet. The rain had eased to nothing. A horse shifted at the wagon rail.

"I had some dealings with him too," Elias said. "Some years back. He moved on. I don't know where he went."

"That right."

"That's right."

Murphy looked at the scar on his own palm for a moment, as though checking something he already knew.

"Hundred dollars posted for Heath. Alive." He looked up. "Fifty for the other outcome."

"Then I hope you find him."

"I think I have."

Farwell spoke then, without moving from where he stood.

"You've got a claim the Reverend looks like a man you barely knew." His voice carried no particular heat. "Ain't enough to take a man from my town."

Murphy looked at him.

"Heath came out of Fort Garry. You from there, Reverend."

"A lot of men came from Fort Garry."

"Not so many who left Fort Benton in a hurry last summer."

"It ain't enough," Farwell said.

The same words, the same cadence, with the flat authority of a man who has decided on a line and is not in the business of explaining it.

Murphy looked at the five men behind him. A slow survey. Then back.

"I'm not talking about taking a man," he said. "I'm talking about a man coming south to stand before T.C. Power and answer for what he did. For what he set on other men." He let his eyes rest on Elias. "Men who worked clean and came up short because of what he wrote against their names."

A long quiet.

The spitting rain came again and then stopped.

Elias stood still. He could feel the weight of the gun at his chest with the clarity of a man who has stopped thinking about anything else. He could count the distance to each man. He could read the hands.

"My name is Reverend Elias Jonathan Wilson," he said. "You'll get no money for me."

Murphy pulled his coat aside. The gun on his hip was plain and he let them look at it.

"These men know how to deliver a man south. Alive or otherwise." He looked at Farwell. "T.C. Power has a good business arrangement with Fort Farwell. That trade runs both ways. Shame to let a misunderstanding put it at risk."

Farwell did not move.

"It ain't enough."

Dunn shifted his weight. The shotgun came up a degree. Not aimed. Present.

The silence in the yard held.

Then the sound of a horse.

Then two.

Solomon came through the gap in the fence with two men behind him. He rode at the unhurried pace of a man who has nowhere to be and so takes his time arriving everywhere. He pulled up at the edge of the yard and looked at the wagon. At Murphy. At the five men arranged around the yard. He looked at them the way a man looks at a bill he is deciding whether to pay.

"Mr. Murphy," he said.

Murphy looked at him.

"I wasn't informed of a delivery today."

"Whiskey run. Thought I'd stop in."

"You've stopped." Solomon looked at the arrangement of men in the yard. At Farwell. At Dunn. At the wagon sitting in the middle of it all. "You've had a conversation."

"Private matter."

Solomon looked at Elias then. The same composed attention he brought to everything. He looked at the collar. The coat. The plain way Elias stood in the yard. Two or three seconds, no more — the look of a man confirming a valuation he had already made.

He looked back at Murphy.

"I wonder," he said, "whether private matters brought to the yard of Fort Farwell remain private."

Murphy said nothing.

"A man makes a claim against a resident of this settlement," Solomon said, "he makes a claim this settlement has to consider." He turned his horse a quarter step, not toward Murphy, not away. The small reorientation of a man settling in. "T.C. Power is a significant operation. I have always respected Mr. Power's arrangements." A pause. "I would be sorry to see those arrangements complicated by a claim that can't be made to stand."

The yard was quiet.

Murphy looked at his men. He looked at Farwell. He looked at Solomon's two men at the gap in the fence.

He looked at Elias last.

The look said what it said.

Then he turned and pulled himself back onto his horse. His men mounted behind him. The wagon came around with the long creak of cold axles. They went out through the gap and turned south.

The yard went quiet.

* * *

Elias looked at Farwell.

"Thank you," he said.

Farwell received this. He looked at Elias in the way he had always looked at him, measuring something that did not have a column in any ledger.

Then he turned to Dunn. "See they ride out. Then stay on the ridge an hour."

Dunn nodded. Turned.

"Reverend," Farwell said. "Moses."

The trading post door closed behind him.

* * *

Solomon had not moved from the edge of the yard. He sat his horse with his two men behind him, and he looked at something past the trading post — the coulee, or the hills beyond it, or the middle distance where a man's eyes go when his attention has already moved to the next thing.

"Thank you," Elias said.

Solomon let a breath go. Small. Through the nose.

"You'll come by," he said.

He did not look at Elias when he said it. He turned his horse and rode east through the gap and did not look back.

.

Elias walked home.

The spitting rain had stopped for good. The clouds had thinned in the west and the hills showed through them in long grey shapes, worn down and patient. The creek ran brown and fast below the ford. He crossed the lower yard and came up to the door and went in.

Bella was at the table. Heather beside her with her slate, working at something with the focused quiet of a child who has not yet learned to perform her concentration.

Bella looked at him. She did not ask.

He took off his coat and his hat and set them on the hook. He reached up and unfastened the collar and set it on the shelf beside the door.

He sat down at the table.

The blank page was where he had left it. The pen beside it. The ruling he owed two men who had sat across from him with their legitimate grievance and their embarrassment and their need for the matter to be decided.

He picked up the pen.

Outside, the wind came down through the coulee and found the house and passed on south toward the line.

He sat there a long time before he wrote anything.

Thirty-Seven

Dunn came before the lamp was lit.

He came the way he always came, without preamble, the door barely opened before his presence had already communicated what his words would confirm. He stood in the frame and looked at Elias and said Murphy had not gone.

Elias listened. He did not speak.

"He's in the bluff. South of the road."

His message delivered, Dunn went his way.

Elias stood at the house's south window, coffee cup in hand. The country beyond it was still dark, the bluff invisible at this hour but present, the way a thing is present when you know it is there.

He had come in on that road. The south approach through the poplar stand, the ground rising then falling into the settlement, the path worn smooth by men who had been coming and going before either fort existed. He had come through it with the collar wet against him and his boot heel gone and the wound speaking with every breath.

The Wilson residence sat on the south side of the fort, east side near the creek. If you stood at the bluff line and looked north you could make out the smoke from its chimney.

He stood at the glass until the cold from it had reached his hands.

Bella appeared beside him.

"What did Dunn want," she said.

He turned from the window and looked at her.

"Farwell wants the land ruling."

Days past, two men had come to him with their dispute — a fence line, thirty yards of pasture that each man had worked as though it were common ground until the previous Christmas, when one husband had said something in front of neighbours that the other man's wife had not forgotten. He had listened to both of them and understood the difficulty: you could not rule cleanly for either man without punishing him for an arrangement both had chosen. He had said he needed to put it in writing. The ruling sat on the table where he had left it. The date entered at the top in his hand. The rest of it blank.

She looked at it. She said nothing about it.

"You were up early," she said.

"Couldn't sleep."

She turned the cup between her palms. Not looking at the window. Looking at him.

"You're waiting for something."

"No," he said.

She looked at him a moment. Then she turned to the stove.

A horse at the bluff line. One rider.

Not moving.

The ruling sat untouched on the table.

* * *

Farwell's trading post held its morning smell: dry goods, last night's fire, the ledger already open on the counter. Farwell stood near the shelves with his hands in his pockets, looking at the room the way a man looks at something he has been adding up.

He looked up when Elias appeared and set his pen down.

"He went to the ridge," Elias said. "Not south."

"Yes."

"My house is right beneath them. A man was watching it this morning."

Farwell shifted his hat.

"Murphy didn't draw a weapon," he said.

"He's made a camp. South of my fence."

Farwell looked at him. "A man has a right to camp."

Elias held the anger where it was. He kept his face even.

"I have a wife," he said. "A child."

Farwell's expression did not change in any way that was readable, which meant something was moving behind it.

"I know that," he said. He put both hands on the ledger and looked at it without reading it.

"T.C. Power moves a third of what comes through this fort." He let that stand a moment. "Without Fort Benton I have no supply chain." He stopped. He didn't need to finish it. "Murphy speaks for a man I can't afford to offend."

"The claim is false."

"That may well be," Farwell said. "And the way to prove it false is to demonstrate who you are."

Elias waited.

"Where'd you serve before this?"

He had known the question was coming.

"Fort Benton," he said. "Circuit work, mostly, along the river settlements."

Farwell looked at him.

"I didn't know there was an Anglican church in Fort Benton."

"There isn't," Elias said. "Methodist. It was what was available."

He said it plainly.

Farwell held him with those eyes for a moment. Considering.

"Then write to them," he said. "The minister. Whoever knew you there. Get a letter that says Reverend Elias Jonathan Wilson of the Methodist mission worked out of Fort Benton and was vouched for as a man of standing." He straightened. "That letter goes a long way toward making Murphy's claim look like what it is."

"And in the meantime."

Farwell looked at him.

"In the meantime, Murphy is camped on open ground south of the road. He has made no move. He drew no weapon in my yard."

The fire ticked.

"I'll send a letter," Elias said.

Farwell nodded once. As though something practical had been resolved.

"Dunn will keep eyes on the bluff," he said.

Elias put on his hat and went out.

* * *

He returned to the house. Went in and hung the collar on the peg.

Heather was awake at the table with her slate. She looked up when he came through the door.

He sat.

The ruling in front of him. He looked at the two names written at the top — the men and their fence line, the ordinary small weight of a thing requiring decision. He picked up the pen, held it a moment, set it down.

Bella came in from the yard later and moved past him without speaking and he did not call after her.

Heather worked at her sums with the focused quiet she brought to things she had decided mattered.

The wind found the eaves. He sat with it and felt the cold coming off the south wall and he did not move to the window, though the pull of it was there. His shoulders had been tight since morning. He had not eaten.

When the light had shifted he went to the window.

The bluff sat where it had always sat. The rider was still there — or another was; the light had moved and the shape read differently — but it was a man on a horse and it was not moving and that was what it had been since first light.

"Elias."

Bella's voice was calm and quiet.

He turned.

"Who's that on the hill," she said.

"I don't know."

"You been watching."

"I have."

She waited.

"A man can speak to his wife," she said. Her voice still calm and quiet.

He knew that.

"Whiskey traders came into town and they've not moved on."

She waited.

"And I don't like it."

Heather looked up from her sums.

"Why?"

Elias did not look at the child. He looked at the mother.

"I can't rightly say."

Bella did not move.

"Best you did," she said.

He held her look.

He felt the weight of the window behind him. The line of sight to the bluff. The man on the horse who had not moved since morning.

"A man came up from Benton," he said. "Claims he knows me."

Heather's pencil had stopped.

Bella's eyes did not leave his.

"And does he."

Elias held her there.

He could say the name. Say what was claimed. Say what kind of man waits on a ridge and watches a house before he comes down to it.

He did not.

"He's mistaken," he said.

The words sat between them.

Bella watched him a moment longer.

Then she nodded once.

Placement.

Heather bent back to her slate.

Elias turned to the window.

The rider had not moved.

Thirty-Eight

The voices came before the light.

Not shouts. The lower continuous sound of men who had been drinking since the previous afternoon and had not yet decided what they wanted from the night. It moved through the settlement the way sound moves when there is no wind to carry it off — staying low, finding the walls, coming through them.

Elias lay still a moment.

Bella was already awake.

He could tell by the quality of her breathing. The way a person holds it level when they are listening and do not want to announce it.

He rose and went to the north window.

Three men on the road through town. Coming from the trading post past the saloon, heading down to where the path cut through the ford and then turned south toward the camp. Walking with the unsteadiness of men walking somewhere they had not agreed to go. One of them said something and the others laughed and then it was over and they went on.

He stood at the glass and watched them move through the town.

Behind him, Bella did not speak.

The unwritten ruling sat on the table where he had left it.

* * *

Inihan Kinyen came in the last week of April.

He came at the head of perhaps eighty people — men, women, children — in the early morning before the settlement was fully awake. They came from the northwest, following the creek, and those who were up to see it watched from the high ground as the line of them came out of the coulee and moved south to where Little Soldier's camp already sat in the bend below the forts.

Elias stood at the trading post window with Farwell.

"How many now," Elias said.

Farwell looked at the page in his hand without reading it.

"More than the spring can hold," he said.

Inihan Kinyen rode at the front of them on a grey horse that moved through the ford with a weariness that could not be undone, head down, ribs showing where flesh should be. The man himself sat straight. He did not look toward the forts. He looked at the camp ahead, and the open ground beyond it.

The line of them passed.

The ford went quiet.

Farwell folded the paper.

"The firewater men are already across," he said.

* * *

The trade went hard.

Rivers set up east of Solomon's with a wagon and two barrels and a man to watch the horses. Hammond worked the creek bank south of the ford at a distance that might have been deliberate. From Fort Solomon the trade was less visible but more organised: the girls carried, the men stayed back, and the transactions happened in the coulee's shadow where neither fort's yard could see directly. At Fort Farwell the trade spirits moved across the same counter as the flour and the tobacco, in the same hours, recorded in the same hand.

Elias went to Farwell.

Farwell said he was not going to war with his supply chain over what a man chose to do with his wages on the far side of the water.

Elias went to Solomon.

He was not received.

* * *

In the second week of May he found the man in the coulee.

Solomon's man came to the house in the early afternoon. He knocked once and waited.

Elias put on his coat. He did not ask what it was.

* * *

They crossed the ford together, Solomon and Elias, with Solomon's man a step behind. Solomon walked without hurry. He did not speak on the crossing. He went into the coulee along the east bank and stopped where the willows opened onto a flat of mud above the waterline.

The body lay there.

Face down. One arm out.

Elias crouched. Turned the face.

He knew him. The particular stillness of the man's face, even now — the same economy that had been there when he stood outside his lodge and said: Go away.

He looked once at the wound. That was enough.

He stood.

Solomon regarded the body with the same attention he gave a ledger.

"Drunk Indians," he said. "A quarrel in the night." A breath. "This is the second this spring."

Elias said nothing.

"The camp is not managing itself," Solomon said. "The disorder is becoming a material problem."

The creek moved below them.

"I'll speak to them," Elias said.

"Of course."

Solomon turned back toward the ford.

Elias remained a moment longer.

Then he followed.

* * *

He came out of the coulee and turned south along the bank.

The ground rose slightly before it fell again toward the bend where the camp sat.

He slowed there.

Across the creek, his house stood where it always had. The window catching what light there was. Nothing moving around it.

His eyes lifted.

The bluff above the road.

A man there.

Horse beneath him.

Still.

Too far to make out a face, but near enough to know he was being looked at.

Elias held it a moment.

Then he went on.

* * *

He crossed south into the camp.

The change was immediate.

Not in what could be named. In what could be felt. The dogs louder. Men sitting in the open ground at midday with no work in their hands. A fire burning that did not serve a purpose Elias could see. Two of Kinyen's men near the picket line watched him come in without moving.

He asked for Gabriel.

Gabriel was not there.

He was told to wait.

He stood where he had been told.

Time passed without measure.

Men moved around him without including him in their movement. A boy came once, looked at him, and left again without speaking.

When he was brought forward, it was not to Little Soldier's lodge.

It was to a larger one set slightly apart.

* * *

They were both there.

Little Soldier sat to one side.

Inihan Kinyen sat opposite.

Two others stood behind him.

Elias remained standing.

No one asked him to sit.

He waited.

No one spoke.

He said it himself.

"There's a man dead in the coulee."

The young man near the entrance translated.

Kinyen did not look at Elias. He spoke to the man beside him. A short exchange. Then silence again.

Elias continued.

"He was killed in the night. There's a story being told in the forts. I've come to understand what happened."

The words were carried into the room.

Kinyen spoke again. Longer this time. The tone even. Unhurried.

The young man at the entrance translated.

"He says the man is dead."

Elias waited.

"And who killed him."

The question moved through the room.

No one answered it.

Kinyen spoke again, this time looking past Elias, as if placing the words somewhere behind him.

The translation came slower.

"He says men die in the spring. He says this is not new."

Elias held where he stood.

"I'm here to prevent what comes next," he said.

Kinyen said something short.

The translator did not translate it.

Elias looked at him.

"What did he say."

The young man shook his head.

"He says nothing for you."

A quiet entered the space.

Elias turned slightly toward Little Soldier.

"I was told this is not the first," he said. "If there are men responsible—"

Little Soldier did not look at him.

He spoke.

The words came without hurry.

The translator took longer with them.

"He says they do not bring these things to him. He hears them. He cannot act on what he hears."

Elias waited.

Little Soldier spoke again. One line.

The translator looked at Elias.

"He says you should go. Before the spring is done."

Elias stood in the space that followed.

No one addressed him.

No one asked anything further.

The room had moved on from him without moving.

He put on his hat.

He left.

.

He came back through the camp.

At the north edge, near the willows, he found Marguerite.

She was washing something in a bucket. The same motion repeated — in, wring, in again — the hands doing what they had learned to do while the mind went elsewhere. Luc beside her, carrying. She looked up when he came and what crossed her face was not relief. It was calculation.

"Madame Bouchard."

"Reverend."

Luc watched him.

"How are the children."

"Claire is well. Anne's arm still gives her trouble." Her hands went back to the bucket without pausing. "The girls stay close."

"Is there anything you need."

She looked at him.

"What I need," she said, "is for the men who come into this camp with their whiskey to stop deciding by morning whose fault the night was." She held his eyes. "My daughters are here."

"I'm working on the matter."

She received this without comment.

Then she turned back to her washing.

He went on.

* * *

He went north through the willows.

He did not return to the house.

At the edge of the ford he stopped.

The water ran high with the melt, brown and fast between the stones.

Across the creek, the settlement lay quiet in the afternoon light.

Beyond it, Fort Solomon.

He looked at it.

Then his eyes went south.

The bluff above the road.

He had come to expect the shape of a man there.

There was none.

The ground lay open.

Then he saw it.

The bluff was no longer a place a man sat.

It had been used.

He did not go up to see.

He stood where he was.

Behind him, the sound carried again from the bend — voices, laughter breaking and reforming.

A man dead.

He could feel the shape of it settling into place without him.

No account. No witness.

No man to answer for what had been done.

The water moved at his feet.

After a moment, he turned Northeast, followed the coulee's edge up towards Fort Solomon.

Thirty-Nine

Fort Solomon received him as it always had. The gate standing. Two men in the yard who looked and looked away. The sound of the place coming through the walls before he reached the door.

The room was full for the hour. A man at the bar with his head down, not sleeping, not quite anything. Two girls moving through the tables with the practised unhurry of women who had learned to read a room from across it. The piano was shut. The smell was the same it had been since October — whiskey, smoke, old perfume, and under all of it something older that the boards had taken in and would not give back.

The girl with the tray caught his eye. She set it down and crossed toward him without being asked. 'He's in the back,' she said.

He followed her through the narrow passage where the sound fell away behind him and the air grew closer. She knocked once at the frame and stepped aside.

* * *

The room was as it had been. Smaller than Farwell's office. Cleaner. The table. Two chairs. The bed against the far wall with the cover drawn straight. Basin on a stand. Solomon's coat on its peg.

Solomon stood at the window. He turned when Elias entered, as he always turned — without hurry, without the appearance of having waited.

"Reverend."

He indicated the chair.

Elias sat.

Solomon looked at him. Not up and down. Not measuring. Simply looking, as a man looks at a figure he expects to balance.

"You've been to the camp," he said.

"Yes."

"And."

Elias held a moment.

"There's no clarity," he said. "No one claims it. No one will name a man. They say it's nothing new. Men die in the spring."

Solomon inclined his head slightly, as if acknowledging a statement entered.

"And your ruling."

"I haven't made one."

"No."

A small silence.

"I can't make one," Elias said. "There's no evidence to ground it."

"You've written nothing," he said.

Elias did not answer.

"In the absence of a written thing," Solomon went on, "men write their own." He turned one cufflink. Straightened it. "They write it in the coulee. In the night. In what they take from one another when no one is watching."

Elias sat where he was.

"The trade has increased," Solomon said. "You've seen it."

"Yes."

"More men. More movement. Less restraint." A breath. "And now a second body."

Elias said nothing.

Solomon looked at him.

"A place where men die without record is not neutral ground."

Elias felt the words settle.

"The coulee agreement was for passage," he said. "Not for—"

"—not for ownership," Solomon said. "No."

He looked at Elias.

"And now we what that makes."

A pause.

"Unwritten ground becomes claimed ground," he said. "Not by principle. By use."

Elias kept his voice level. "That isn't law."

"No," Solomon said. "It's what happens in the absence of it."

A longer silence.

The creek could be heard somewhere beyond the walls, moving under its own authority.

Solomon moved to the window overlooking the coulee. His back to Elias.

"There was a man," he said, "by the name of Doyle Hardwick. Called you John."

Elias did not answer.

"You remember him."

"Yes."

"I do as well."

"You came to me that night."

Elias said nothing.

"I delivered him," Solomon said.

Elias held.

"You took him south."

The evening light fell through the window and lay on the floor in a way that removed the colour from things.

"You wrote in the book," Solomon said, without turning, "circumstances unknown."

The words remained where they had been set.

Elias looked at the table.

The window held the coulee. The trees along the edge showed the changing season, leaves budding, swelling.

A sound from the main room, brief, and then absorbed.

"This spring," Solomon said, "a man named Murphy rode up from the south." He let the name stand in the room a moment. "He says he recognizes the Reverend Wilson from Fort Benton. A bookkeeper. A man by the name of John Heath, who had a gift with ledgers." A pause.

"Whose gift, as Murphy tells it, was in making figures land where he wanted them rather than where they belonged."

Solomon looked at the window. Then turned back to the room.

"Murphy is camped on the bluff," he said. "South of the road."

He did not say what was below the bluff.

He did not need to.

The room held its quiet. The basin. The coat on the peg. The cover drawn straight on the bed. Outside, the creek moved.

"I have no interest in a man named John Heath," he said.

Elias lifted his eyes.

Solomon met them.

"That is not my concern. My concern is order."

He rested his hand on his cuffs.

"And in knowing which book records it."

The room narrowed.

"What are you asking," he said.

Solomon received the question without expression.

"The coulee," he said. "As it stands, it belongs to no one."

"It belongs to all."

"Yes," Solomon said. "Which is to say: it belongs to whoever takes it."

He turned.

"That is not sustainable."

Elias held his ground.

"The agreement—"

"—is insufficient," Solomon said.

Not sharply. Not loudly. Simply placed.

"There is movement. There is trade. There is death." A breath. "And there is no line."

The words did not press. They accumulated.

"Set it," Solomon said.

Elias did not speak.

"East bank to my side," Solomon said. "West to Farwell's."

The room was very still.

"In your hand," Solomon said. "In the book. As law."

Elias felt the weight of it before he answered.

"You're asking me to write what isn't true."

Solomon regarded him.

"I'm asking you to write what holds."

The words sat between them.

Elias said nothing.

"A place without a line," Solomon said, "is a place where men decide for themselves." He gestured once, lightly, toward the door, the settlement beyond it. "You've seen what that looks like."

Elias held.

"And while it remains unwritten," Solomon said, "a man sits above your house asking questions I have no answer for."

The sentence was placed without emphasis.

It did not require it.

Elias felt it land.

"My house is not your concern," he said.

"No," Solomon said. "It is yours."

A pause.

"And you are the man who has chosen to live in it."

The quiet returned.

Elias stood with it.

"You're asking me to bind the settlement to you," he said.

"I'm asking you to bind it to a line," Solomon said.

A slight movement of the head.

"The rest follows."

Elias looked at him.

"And if I don't."

Solomon did not answer at once.

"In that case," he said, "nothing is written. And matters continue as they have been."

Elias felt the narrowing.

"I need time," he said.

Solomon studied him. Something moved across the surface of his attention, brief and controlled.

"A dead man in the coulee unresolved. Inihan Kinyen's people camped alongside Little Soldier's. Firewater men working the creek bank in plain view of both forts. A quick decision serves everyone's interest."

"Including yours," Elias said.

"Including mine," Solomon said. He said it without apology, the way he said most things — not concealing what was true, only declining to be troubled by it.

He sat with his hands flat on the table and waited with the patience of a man who had already finished the argument and was simply allowing the other man to reach the end of it.

"You may go home," he said.

"You may think."

He rested his hand flat.

"But the man on the bluff will still be there when you return."

Elias stood. He took his hat from the table. He went to the door and through it. The passage closed the sound of the room behind him and then gave it back as he came out into it.

The girl with the tray looked at him once.

He did not look at her.

He went out through the gate and down the bank to the ford.

The air met him clean.

He crossed the ford without looking to the bluff.

He did not need to.

He knew it was there.

Forty

The door stood open.

Not forced. The latch was intact. It stood at the angle a door stands when the last person through it had their hands occupied and did not pull it behind them.

He crossed the threshold.

The fire was low but had not gone out. Bella's mending sat on the chair — needle still in the cloth, the cloth folded over the arm as though she had stepped away for a moment and would return. On the floor near the bed, one of Heather's boots. The other foot was shod, wherever she was.

He did not move through the room. He stood and read what it held.

The chair at the table had been pulled out at an angle that served no purpose in this house. The water bucket was where it always sat. The tin cups. The small things of a morning that had gone on as mornings went on, until they stopped.

He looked at the bluff through the south window.

He did not go up.

He came to the table and sat down.

He opened the book to the page he had not completed — the fence dispute he had promised to resolve and had not.

He turned to the next page.

He picked up the pen.

* * *

The ruling occupied one side of a page. He did not pause over the writing of it. He wrote it the way a man writes what he has already decided.

East bank to Solomon. West bank to Farwell. The coulee and the wooded ground along the creek, Solomon's side. He named the ford. He wrote the date.

He signed it below.

He looked at it once.

He closed the book.

.

He went out through the door and across the ford and northeast along the bank toward Fort Solomon.

* * *

The gate was standing. A man in the yard saw him come and went inside without being spoken to. No sound followed. The yard held only the usual things — a horse at the rail, tack hung on the fence, the lamp above the gate moving slightly in the evening air.

Solomon came out himself.

He looked at Elias. He looked at the book under his arm.

"They've taken my wife and child," he said. He handed the book to Solomon.

Solomon opened it. He found the page and read it without haste, in the manner of a man going through work he expects to find in order — not searching, not hurrying, simply moving through each line in its turn.

He stopped.

His finger rested on the page.

"The crossing," he said.

Elias took the book back. He added three words to the ruling's final line and set the pen down.

Solomon read the correction.

He read it twice.

He closed the book.

He nodded once.

He went to the door and through it. His voice moved into the main room at an ordinary volume, unhurried, carrying the tone of instructions that did not need to be given more than once.

The sound of the room changed.

Chairs. Movement. The particular register of men's voices when a purpose has been handed to them and they have set other things aside.

Elias went into the yard.

He stood at the fence.

The horses came out from the back lot in the dark, tack already on them, riders up before they had fully settled. Five men. Six. Solomon's foreman last, who looked once at Elias in the way he might look at a document he had signed — noting it, and moving on.

Solomon rode up beside him.

"Walk from your house to the bluff. In plain sight." He looked at the road ahead. "Engage the man. Keep him there. Keep his attention." He did not look back at Elias. "We will come from the south."

Elias nodded.

They went out through the gate and west to the ford, then up into the hills.

The lamp above the gate swayed and held.

Elias stood until the sound of horses was gone.

Then he turned and walked down to the ford.

Forty-One

The bullets were kept in the locked cabinet in the bedroom. Safe from children's fingers. He used the key and loaded the gun. Closed the cartridge. Put six extra in his back pocket. Locked the cabinet. Put the gun in his jacket pocket.

He came out the back.

The sun was dropping behind the western hills, orange and flat, pulling long shadows east across the yard. Fort Farwell lay half consumed by them. Across the creek, the light still caught the upper walls of Fort Solomon. Below the bend, the first fires of the camp were beginning to show.

He crossed the yard without looking up toward the bluff.

Anderson's grave was where it had always been. The mound had settled through the winter into the ground around it, losing its definition, becoming simply a place where the earth had been disturbed and was returning to itself. Bella had set a stone at the head of it in the fall. It was still there.

Beyond the grave, her garden.

The soil had been turned within the last week. Four rows, maybe five. A line of small green shoots that had not been there when he last looked at this part of the yard with full attention. He had repaired the fence last month — two rails split and the post leaning — and she had planted behind it, inside the perimeter he had made. He had not known she was going to do that.

He opened the gate and went through.

He latched it behind him.

He moved south around the yard's edge, keeping the house between himself and the bluff as long as the angle allowed. When the angle ran out he walked into the open.

He did not hurry.

He did not slow.

The rise was above him still. A figure on the track where it bent upward turned without apparent urgency and went over the crest and out of sight.

He walked on.

* * *

The track rose through broken ground and then opened onto the flat of the bluff. The sun had gone to a red rim at the edge of the hills by the time he reached the top.

Murphy's camp stood fifty paces south. Four horses on a picket line. A fire with a pot over it, cold. Two bedrolls folded. A wagon at the back of the flat with the canvas tied down.

Murphy stood in the centre of it.

He was not a large man. The kind of size that gets mistaken for patience. Coat on despite the evening warmth, hat worn without thinking about it. His right hand was forward and empty. The other rested near his belt.

Bella was there.

She was standing to the left with Heather in front of her, Heather's back against her legs, Bella's hands on the girl's shoulders. Heather's face had gone still the way a child's face goes still when the adults have become unreadable.

Two men at the wagon. One at the side with a rifle at waist height. The man who had come down the track, standing near the horses with his hand already at his gun.

Murphy looked at him the way a man looks at something he has been waiting a long time to see and wants to take a moment to confirm.

"That's far enough."

He stopped.

"Hands where I can see them."

He raised them.

The man from the wagon came forward and took the gun from his belt. Then the knife from his boot. He stepped back.

Murphy looked at his man.

"Tie them."

The rope went on quickly — wrists crossed behind, a double loop, pulled firm. He did not move while it was done.

Murphy studied him.

"John," he said.

He looked at Murphy.

"John Heath."

"What is it you want," he said.

"I want the ledger."

"There's no ledger."

"The book. What was taken and where it landed." Murphy looked at him. "The one that shows what you did to my name when you were done with the money."

He held.

"I don't know what book you mean."

"Yes you do."

The air moved through the grass at the bluff's edge. The settlement lay below them, going dark in the shadow of the hills. He could see his house from here. The yard. The fence. The garden inside it.

He looked at Bella.

She was looking at him the way she had not looked at him before. Not with the attention she gave him in the house. With something that had been held back and was no longer.

Murphy watched him look at her.

"She didn't believe me," he said. There was something in it that was not quite satisfaction. Closer to vindication. "Told me I had the wrong man. Told me Reverend Wilson had come through this country since the winter before last. She was very firm on the matter."

"She's right," he said.

"She is not." Murphy said it without heat, the way a man states something he has already verified. "A man can wear a collar and have his wife believe it and that doesn't make him what the collar says he is."

The rope was taut behind him. He was aware of it the way he was aware of the drop at the bluff's edge — not because he was looking at it, but because it was in the calculation of everything he did.

Keep him here.

"You rode a long way," he said.

"I did."

"For a ledger that doesn't exist."

"For the man who made it not exist," Murphy said. "There's a difference." He studied him. "Fort Benton. The spring of seventy-two. A man who skimmed three different accounts over eight months without any of the principals noticing because he kept the totals right and moved the interior figures." He looked at him. "The kind of work you don't forget."

"And yet you can't place his face."

"I can place it fine." Murphy held him in his attention the way a man holds a figure against a column before he marks it down. "I placed it in the trading post in September. I just needed to hear the name."

He said nothing.

"Say it," Murphy said.

Stillness in the camp. The grass at the bluff's edge. The creek south of them moving where it bent. The horses at the picket line breathing and settling.

He let the moment sit.

"John," he said.

Something moved across Murphy's face and was controlled.

"Heath," Murphy said.

He looked at him.

"John Heath." Murphy said it again, the way a man reads a name back from a document to confirm the entry.

"What you're looking for doesn't change what's in front of you," John said. "A man with his hands behind his back." He nodded toward Bella and Heather. "A woman and a child who have nothing to do with what you came here for."

"What I'm looking for changes what happens to them," Murphy said. He said it as a fact that had no feeling in it, and for that reason was worse than if it had.

Bella's hands had gone flat against Heather's shoulders.

"She goes," John said.

Murphy looked at him.

"Bella and the girl. Whatever you have with me, it's with me."

Murphy looked at them both. Some calculation made and set aside.

Then: "I have no argument with her."

John looked at Bella.

"Go," he said. "Take Heather and go down."

Heather began to turn. Bella's hands held a moment longer. Then they released.

Bella looked at him.

What was in her face was not the anger he might have borne. It was something else. The look a person gives when they are trying to locate what it was they were seeing, all the months they were seeing it. She did not find it.

She turned and took Heather's hand and went to the track.

Murphy watched without comment.

"The accounts," John said. "You want me to confess to accounts that—"

"I want what was taken," Murphy said. "Which I suspect you no longer have. In lieu of the money, I want the name and the record. A man has a right to his own name and I lost mine to a figure in a ledger who didn't have the patience to run a fraud that only hurt its principals." His voice did not change. "You made it my problem. I'd like it to stop."

"I can't give you—"

"You skimmed it," Murphy said. "Say that."

Below the bluff the sound of their steps had gone quiet. John did not look toward the edge.

"I kept the books for T.C. Power and Company," he said. "There were discrepancies."

"There were."

"I left before they were resolved."

"After they were resolved," Murphy said. "In your favour. And the name that resolved them in the debit column was not John Heath."

John held.

He said nothing.

Murphy looked at him with the attention of a man who has arrived at a thing after considerable travel and is taking his measure of it. Then he turned toward the wagon.

"The cart will take us to the Missouri," he said over his shoulder. "From there I have a letter that names you in terms the Fort Benton magistrate will find informative." He did not pause in his work at the canvas. "This doesn't have to be uncomfortable."

John said nothing.

He let himself look toward the edge once. The slope below was empty.

He looked back at Murphy.

Murphy had turned from the canvas.

He was still speaking when the first shot came.

* * *

It came from the south face of the bluff without warning and the sound of it was enormous in the open air — a flat crack that crossed the distance before the mind could place it. Then the second. The third and fourth together, so close they blurred.

One of Murphy's men went down at the wagon. He made a sound first and then did not.

The man with the rifle spun south and got two rounds off before a shot took him in the chest and he sat down against the wagon wheel and stayed there.

The man by the horses was running and then he was not running.

The horse nearest him shied hard against the picket line and the line held and the horse kept trying.

Murphy was moving before John had located him — low and fast for the wagon's far side, his gun already out.

John threw himself sideways. He got his right wrist turned against the rope and worked it forward. The loop was cinched but practical — the kind of tie that holds a man not trying to leave — and the friction took skin from the back of his wrist and then it gave.

He was moving before he was fully on his feet.

His gun was on the ground near the dead man from the wagon. He went for it. As he came up a shot came from Murphy's side of the wagon and he felt it cross above his head — a sound like cloth tearing, close enough that he dropped flat before he had decided to.

He pressed himself against the wagon's side.

Shots still coming from the south face. Solomon's men, working up.

Murphy was on the far side of the wagon bed. John could hear him — his breathing, the shift of his boots in the grass, the particular sound of a man orienting himself.

He moved around the wagon's end low and fast.

Murphy heard him coming and turned.

The gun was coming up.

John fired.

Murphy's body jerked once. He held where he was a moment longer, as though the shot had not yet reached him.

Again.

A third time.

Murphy went back against the wagon board and stayed there. His gun discharged as he fell, the shot going wide into the evening sky, and the sound of it was still in the air when everything went quiet.

The horse at the picket line had stopped pulling.

The creek ran.

John stood where he was with the gun in his hand and the smoke rising from it. Murphy lay with his head against the wheel and one arm out at the angle of a man reaching for something he did not reach.

He looked at his gun.

He lowered it.

He had been in the act of turning when he heard it. The man by the horses — not dead, it turned out, or not yet. On one knee in the grass fifteen paces back with his gun raised.

The shot hit him in the left side above the hip and knocked him a step sideways. He kept his feet.

He turned and fired twice.

The man went down in the grass and did not get up.

The silence that followed was complete.

* * *

He stood in it.

The pain had not arrived yet. There was heat at his side and the sense of a thing that had happened, not yet fully declared. He pressed his hand against it. His hand came away wet.

His gun was still in his hand.

He did not put it down.

Below the bluff's south face, boots in loose rock. Then a man's head above the lip. Then Solomon's foreman, coming over at an angle, taking in the camp the way he'd take in a room. He looked at Murphy. At the man in the grass. At John.

He did not speak.

Two more men came up behind him. They went to the wagon and started working the canvas loose without being told.

* * *

He heard her before he saw her.

Bella's voice from below the track, calling Heather's name, and then her steps coming fast up the rise. Heather's voice answering from somewhere south on the slope, frightened and whole.

He turned away from the wagon.

She came over the crest at a run and stopped.

What she saw: the wagon. Solomon's men at it, working without haste. Murphy against the wheel. The man in the grass. The camp that had, minutes ago, contained her husband alive and someone else's men alive and a conversation she had arrived too late to witness the end of.

She saw him.

He was standing with his hand at his side and the blood coming through his fingers.

She crossed the ground to him without hesitation. She said nothing. She moved his hand and opened his coat and looked at the wound and then she pressed his hand back against it with her own over the top of it. The pressure was firm and unhesitating.

He stood.

She was looking at the wound, not at him.

"Bella."

She did not look up.

"I need to know if Heather is safe."

"She's below," he said. "She didn't come up."

She said nothing to that.

Her hand was still over his.

He looked at the top of her head and at her hand on his hand and at Murphy by the wheel and the man in the grass and Solomon's men going through the wagon. The red had gone fully out of the sky. The hills to the west were dark now, one shade above the colour of the creek below.

She had not moved her hand.

He did not know what to make of it. Or rather: he knew, and could not hold it.

"He said," she began.

She stopped.

He waited.

She did not continue. Whatever it was, she had arrived at it and found she could not say it and could not yet turn back. Her hand remained where it was, and the blood moved through both their hands together, and neither of them spoke.

Heather's voice called from the bottom of the track.

Bella lifted her head.

"Stay there," she called back. Her voice was steady in the way that costs something.

She looked at him then.

He looked back at her.

There was a long moment in which nothing was decided and nothing was forgiven and she had not moved her hand.

Forty-Two

She sat him in the chair by the table. She took his coat off his shoulders without asking and opened his shirt where the blood had dried to it and looked at the wound in the lamp's light. She did not speak while she looked. She went to the cabinet for the cloth and the basin and came back and did what needed doing with the same attention she gave everything — not gentle exactly, not rough, simply thorough. He sat still under her hands.

Heather was in the doorway. Bella looked up at her once. "Go to bed," she said.

"Is he—"

"Go to bed."

The girl went.

She finished with the wound and dressed it and tied it off and sat back. She looked at it. Not at him.

He told her. He did not begin with the name — she had the name already, had heard it on the bluff from a man who carried it south from Fort Benton — so he began with what she did not have. The bookkeeping. T.C. Power and Company. Eight months of it and the particular patience the work had required, the figures moved in increments small enough that no single month declared itself. He told her about Murphy. What he had done to Murphy's name in the ledger, how the debit column had landed, and that he had not stayed to see it resolved because by then there was nothing to stay for. He told her about the road north. About the man he had found there. He said the name plainly — Elias Jonathan Wilson, Methodist minister — and what the man's condition had been, and what he had taken from him, and why. He said that by the time he reached Farwell's he had already been Reverend Wilson for three days and there was no clean way back through it.

He said he loved her.

He said he loved Heather.

She was looking at the window while he spoke. Not at anything beyond it — the glass was dark, the night against it — but away from him, in the way a person looks away when they are hearing something and do not want the speaker to read their face while they hear it.

When he had finished she did not speak at once. She picked up the cloth and folded it. Set it on the edge of the basin.

A long moment.

"I should have told you," he said.

She received this without answer.

He waited. He wanted something from her — not forgiveness, he knew better than to name it that — but some acknowledgement that what had been real was real. That the winter was real. That what had been built in this house was built. He sat with wanting it and did not say so.

Then she spoke: “I don’t have that man in this house.”

She stood.

Went to the hook by the door and took down his hat. Set it on the table in front of him. She moved past him to the other room. The lamp in there was low and she turned it up slightly and the light came through the door and fell across the floor of the kitchen in a long pale shape.

He sat looking at his hat on the table.

After a time he put it on. He picked up his coat from the chair. He stood there a moment.

"Bella."

The light from the other room. No answer.

He went out.

* * *

He did not go to Farwell's that night. He went to the church. The night had fallen, and the wound pulled, and his bad foot found the places where the ground changed without warning. Ten minutes north at his pace.

The work had begun in May. The frame was up. He did not make a fire. He lay down in the dark and closed his eyes.

.

He slept badly on his side, and woke to the wound's verdict on the position, and moved, and woke again. By the time the light came through the east he was already awake.

The cold damp sat in his bones. He lay within the half-built church a long time, with his eyes not looking at it. Not looking at anything.

He stood.

The wound had stiffened and it pulled in a way that took his breath. He stood until it passed. Then he went to Farwell's.

.

Farwell came to the door himself. He had been up. He looked at John, at the coat, at the careful way he was standing.

"Come in," he said.

The trading post was empty. Farwell set the lamp on the counter and stood with his back to the shelves.

"Five men on the bluff," he said. "T.C. Power's men, some of them. Murphy." He looked at John. "Everyone in the settlement heard the guns."

"I know."

"Indians didn't do it."

"No."

Farwell held him with that steady attention. "Who did."

"Solomon's men came from the south face." He did not look away. "Murphy had my wife. And the girl."

"You were there," Farwell said.

"I was there."

Farwell did not move. He looked at the counter, at the ledger lying closed on it, and then back at John.

"My name is John Heath. I kept books for T.C. Power. There were irregularities. I left before they were resolved."

The fire ticked.

"The man in the collar," Farwell said.

"I found him on the road."

A pause.

“He was dead when I found him.”

Farwell exhaled through his nose. The sound a man makes when a thing he suspected comes in confirmed and he is deciding what it changes.

"The collar gets left in this house," he said.

John looked at him.

"If you're in my fort, you're not wearing it." His voice was flat.

"Whatever you are here, you're not that."

"Alright."

John reached up an undid the collar. It was cold and wet in his hand.

He put it by the ledger.

“I got no place to stay.”

The words sat in the room.

Farwell received them. Looked at the ledger. Turned his hat slow.

He reached under the counter and set a key down. "The room at the back of the saloon. The one facing east." He put his hand flat on the key. "I haven't made a decision. I'm making one." He looked at John. "In the meantime."

John took the key.

“The coulee,” he said. “Solomon had been asking for a ruling. East bank to his side, west to yours, the ford common.” A pause. “Last night, when I found my wife and child taken — I wrote it. I delivered it to him before I went to the bluff.”

He held Farwell’s eyes. “It’s in writing. Signed.”

Farwell looked at him for a long moment. He did not move.

"I’ll send Mary to tend the wound," he said.

John went.

* * *

There was no declaration, no scene of public naming. But the priest’s shirt without its collar is a spoken thing. A man not living in his home is a thing folk remark. He felt it — the way a man at the forge found something to attend to when he looked up, the way Nora passed him near the water barrel with her eyes already elsewhere. Not hostility. The cooler attention that follows when a thing that was assumed has been reconsidered. He did not stop to test it. He walked through it and went on.

* * *

He found Gabriel at the south end of the ford, mending tack in the afternoon light. Gabriel looked up when he came. He did not look away.

"A ruling's been entered," John said.

Gabriel set the tack across his knee and waited.

"East bank to Solomon. West to Farwell. The ford shared." He kept his voice level. "Given the deaths this spring, the trade situation, the — disorder. The camp needs to know. Little Soldier. Kinyen both."

Gabriel looked at the tack in his hands. A long moment.

"You want me to tell them," he said.

"Yes."

Gabriel did not speak. He ran his thumb along the stitching where it had come loose. He held the leather up to see it better.

"I'll tell them," he said.

John turned to go.

"What they say back," Gabriel said, "I will also tell you."

John nodded once and went on.

* * *

What the camp said back was nothing. Or rather: Gabriel came the following morning and stood in the saloon doorway and reported with the economy of a man repeating what he was told precisely. Little Soldier had listened. Kinyen had not received Gabriel himself. The men who received him for Kinyen had listened and spoken together in low voices for a time and then one of them had said, in English, that he understood. He said nothing further.

* * *

The horses went the night after.

Eleven from the line behind Fort Solomon, three from Farwell's south corral. No noise, or none that reached the sleepers in time to mean anything. Hoofprints south in the mud by the ford, then lost in the grass beyond the bend. Dunn came into the saloon at first light and said it plainly: horses gone. Farwell stood in the yard looking at the cut line and the empty ground and said nothing for a long moment. The horses had been good ones. That was the nature of the answer.

.

Thomas Hardwick came in on the last day of May. He came with a dozen men, riding from the southeast along the high ground above the creek, and he came with the settled manner of a man who had spent the journey deciding what he wanted and had arrived at it. He stopped on the rise above the settlement and looked down at it — both forts, the houses along the road, the bend in the creek where the camp sat beyond the willows — and took his measure of it in silence. Then he brought his horse forward and the men came behind him down the slope.

Forty-Three

The knock came when the light had just begun to find the east window.

He had taken the room Farwell had given him and lain down in it without undressing. Not sleeping. Not much. The cot against the wall. The table. The glass intact in the window. Not his old room. He had not asked which room. Farwell had given him the key and he had found it.

The knock came again.

He sat up. The wound pulled. He waited for it to pass and crossed to the door and opened it.

Mary stood there with her bag in her hand.

She looked at him and said:

"John."

Not Reverend. Not Reverend Wilson.

She stepped past him into the room. Set the bag on the table beside the gun and pulled the chair to the cot and sat. He closed the door and came back and opened his shirt where Bella had dressed the wound.

Mary looked at it the way she had looked at the wound beneath his ribs in the first days at Farwell's. Without sentiment. Without hesitation. The way she looked at everything that required her hands.

She worked in silence. Removed the dressing. Cleaned what needed cleaning. The light from the east window crossed the table and reached the far wall and moved. Outside the settlement came awake in pieces. A horse. A door. The sound of the ford running low.

She tied off the fresh dressing and sat back and looked at what she had done.

Then she looked at the work that had been there before. At the clean tight wrapping and the knot placed where a careful hand had placed it.

"You could live with this," she said.

He did not answer.

She put her things back in the bag and stood. At the door she paused. Her hand on the frame.

Then she went out.

He sat on the edge of the cot with his shirt open and the room quiet around him. The gun on the table. The east light. The sound of the ford.

.

He did not go out until midday.

Nora was behind the bar. She looked at him when he came through and looked away and kept working. Two men at a corner table he did not know by name. A Métis freighter eating alone near the door. The usual smell of the place — smoke and sawdust and the sourness of a room that had been full of men the night before and would be again tonight.

He took a stool at the far end of the bar. Nora set a cup in front of him without asking.

'Farwell's been in,' she said.

'And.'

'Said to tell you the bluff is clear.'

He held the cup.

The bluff was clear because the men who had been on it were in the ground. The bluff was clear and Bella's house sat beneath it with Bella in it and the child, and that distance was not a distance that the clearing of the bluff had changed.

Nora moved to the other end of the bar. He drank the coffee and looked at the room.

* * *

They heard them before they saw them.

The sound came from the south road in the last of the afternoon — horses first, then voices, the lower continuous sound of men who had been a long time on the trail and had arrived somewhere and not yet decided what they wanted from it. It came through the walls the way sound comes when the air is still. Nora stopped wiping the bar. The freighter near the door turned his head.

John looked at the window.

A dozen horses on the road. Men still mounted, looking at the settlement the way men look when they have been riding toward something and are now measuring what it is against what they expected. Lean men, trail-dirty, the horses rough-coated and ribby from a long chase that had come to nothing. The man at the front was broad through the chest with a beard gone reddish-grey and a hat pulled against the last of the light. He turned in the saddle and said something and two of the men broke off toward the hitching post.

Nora came up beside him.

'You know them.' She did not say it as a question.

'No.'

She looked at them a moment. At the horses and the rifles and the particular way the men carried themselves, that specific looseness that is not ease but its imitation.

She went back behind the bar.

* * *

They came in without ceremony. The door opened and they were simply there — eight of them, the rest staying with the horses — and the room changed the way a room changes when its available space has been taken by bodies that have not asked permission to take it.

The broad man came in last. He looked at the room the same way he had looked at the settlement from the saddle — with the measuring attention of a man who has been disappointed enough times that he no longer announces his expectations. He took a table near the centre and sat with his back to the wall and his hat still on.

The men drank. Nora poured and kept her face even and her movements unhurried. One of them said something to the girl carrying the tray and the girl moved past him without looking at him and set her tray down at the next table and did not go back his way again. Nora noted it. She refilled cups and said nothing.

No one paid.

John sat at the end of the bar. He did not move. He had no collar and no instrument and the room knew both. The freighter near the door had finished eating and had not left and was working very hard at appearing to have no interest in the proceedings.

The broad man had been watching him since he sat down.

* * *

He came to the bar with his cup. He set it down and looked at John without the preliminary of a man uncertain of his ground.

'You the lawman here.'

'No.'

'What are you.'

John looked at him. 'I keep the settlement's records.'

The man studied him with the patience of someone who has asked questions a long time in a territory where direct answers were rarely the first thing offered.

'Thomas Hardwick,' he said.

He said it the way a man says his name when he believes it will be recognised. When he believes the name has arrived ahead of him.

'I've not heard it,' John said.

Something moved through Hardwick's expression and was controlled. He turned the cup once.

'I'm looking for my brother,' he said. 'Doyle Hardwick. Last known heading north through this country in the fall.'

The room had grown quiet in the way a room grows quiet when the men in it have decided to listen without appearing to.

John held his cup.

'I knew a man by that name,' he said.

Hardwick went very still. 'Knew.'

'He came through in the fall. He'd been drinking at Solomon's. He went south.'

'He didn't come home.'

'No.'

Hardwick looked at him. The thing in his face was not grief exactly. Grief had been in it once and this was what had taken its place — something harder and more directional, a feeling that had found its shape.

'What happened to him.'

John looked at the bar. At the cup in his hand. He thought of Doyle Hardwick on the south road in the dark with the whiskey in him and Solomon's men behind him and the camp below the bend. He thought of what he had written in the settlement's book.

Circumstances unknown.

He could send this man south.

'The Assiniboine camp,' he said. 'South of the curve in Battle Creek. Your brother went that direction the night he left.'

He said it evenly. He said it the way a man states a fact that exists without his having made it.

Hardwick received it. He did not speak for a moment. Around them the room held its quiet.

'Assiniboine.'

'Yes.'

'How many in that camp.'

'Three hundred. Perhaps more. Little Soldier's band and Inihan Kinyen's people both.'

Hardwick looked at him.

'Much obliged,' he said.

He went back to his table.

* * *

The light went out of the room and the lamps came up and they were still there.

They drank through the evening. The whiskey came from Solomon's — one of the men had crossed the ford in the last of the afternoon and come back with a case of it and set it on the bar without asking and Nora had said nothing because there was nothing to say. They drank it the way men drink when they are drinking toward something rather than away from it.

John did not leave.

His bad foot and the wound together made the idea of the back room feel like retreat and retreat felt like abandonment and so he stayed at the end of the bar and kept his cup in his hand and watched the room. Nora moved through it with the practised attention of a woman who had spent years reading the temperature of men's drinking. She did not rush. She did not slow. She kept herself in the room's sight lines and out of the reach of hands.

One of the men stood and crossed to the bar and leaned over it and said something to the girl with the tray. The girl stepped back.

John stood up from the stool.

The man looked at him once.

Nora moved between them from the side. She set a bottle down in front of the man with a small clean sound and looked at him without expression.

'On the house,' she said.

He looked at her. At the bottle. Then once more at John. He took it and went back to his table.

John sat down.

Hardwick had not moved from his chair. He sat with his back to the wall and his cup and watched the room the way he had watched it all evening — not with the attention of a man enjoying himself, but of a man accounting for what was his and what was not. He had not spoken again. He looked at John once, across the room, and John held it, and then Hardwick looked away.

The camp was south of the curve in Battle Creek.

Three hundred people.

John turned his cup in his hands and did not think about it.

·

Farwell came in with Dunn at his shoulder and two more men behind.

He did not raise his voice. He stood in the doorway and looked at the room and then at Hardwick and said:

'I'll ask you to take your men across to Solomon's for the night.'

Hardwick looked at him.

'We've not finished,' he said.

'You've finished here,' Farwell said.

He said it with the weight of a man who has decided and is not announcing a decision so much as confirming one already made. Dunn stood at his left with his arms at his sides. The two men behind filled the door.

Hardwick looked at Farwell. He looked at Dunn. He made his accounting.

He stood. He pulled his coat from the back of the chair.

'Boys,' he said.

They went out without incident. Not in submission. With the specific economy of men who have identified the better ground and are moving toward it.

* * *

John stood at the window.

The settlement had gone dark. Farwell's fort across the road, the windows lit from within. The creek beyond it catching the last of the sky. South of the ford the coulee ran east to west the way it always had, a darkness within the dark, and beyond it the plain where the camp sat in the bend below both forts.

He watched the men cross the ford. Hardwick and his riders, single file through the shallow water, the horses picking their steps. The torches at Solomon's gate were lit. The gate stood open. The men went through it one by one and the light from inside fell across them as they passed and then they were inside and the gate swung closed behind the last of them.

The ford went quiet.

The coulee lay between the forts and the camp the way it had always lain. The church site stood empty on the high ground to the north, its frame holding the dark between the uprights, open to the sky.

Nora came up beside him. She looked at what he was looking at.

She did not speak. After a time she went to the bar and began to close up the room.

He stood at the window a moment longer.

Then he went to the back room and closed the door and sat on the edge of the cot in the dark.

Forty-Four

The first day of June came in clear.

He lay on the cot and watched the east window go from black to grey to the particular flat blue of a morning that had decided to be fine. No wind. The settlement was quiet in the way it was quiet on Sundays, which was not silence but the absence of the sounds that meant work was beginning. A horse. The creek. Somewhere a door.

He rose carefully. The wound had stiffened through the night and the first movement said so plainly. He stood until it passed. He crossed to the window and looked out.

Solomon's fort on the far bank, the gate standing open. Smoke from cook fires in the yard where Hardwick's men had made their camp the night before. Figures moving in that smoke, unhurried, the particular movement of men who had been drinking since the previous evening and had not yet decided whether morning required something different from them. South of the ford the creek bent away through trees and low ground, and beyond that bend, out of sight from this window, the joined camp sat where Little Soldier's people and Inihan Kinyen's people had made their uneasy spring together.

Three hundred people in the bend.

He put on his coat. He sat down again on the edge of the cot.

* * *

Farwell came before the saloon had opened.

He came through the back and knocked once and put his head in the door. He looked at John on the cot. He looked at the coat already on him.

"Come," he said.

John stood. He took the gun from the table and put it in his belt. Farwell watched him do it and said nothing about it.

They went out through the saloon into the morning. The air was cool and clean and the sky above the western hills had the quality of a sky that intended to hold all day. Farwell moved at his usual pace. John kept it. His bad foot found the soft ground near the ford and he adjusted without pausing.

"You've been to the camp before," Farwell said. He did not say it as a question.

"Yes."

"Little Soldier knows you."

"He knew the collar," John said.

Farwell looked at the creek.

"He knows what a man does," he said. "Not what he wears."

He went into the ford without waiting for an answer. John followed him in.

* * *

The water was low for the season. It reached John's knees at the centre and ran clear over the stones. The cold of it entered through his boots at once.

They came out on Solomon's side and turned south at once, keeping the creek to their right and the willow growth to their left where the bank widened and then narrowed again. The fort fell behind them. The ground here was softer than the crossing, broken by old horse tracks and the runnels left by spring water now mostly gone. Ahead, the creek curved east around the wooded bend that hid the camp from the forts and the forts from the camp. A person could stand at the ford and think the country open. It was not. It folded. It kept things from one another until they were nearly upon them.

They went around the bend.

The camp opened gradually. First the smoke. Then the upper poles of the lodges through the trees. Then the low ground itself with its spread of people, horses, hides, children, movement.

Marguerite Bouchard was at the water's edge on the northern side of it, just above where the bank gave way to the camp's open ground. She was crouched over the creek with a cloth in her hands. Her youngest was on her back in a cradleboard, asleep or nearly. The older two were behind her on the bank, the boy sitting and the girl standing with her arms out for balance on a rock, watching the water move around it. The sun had not yet reached this part of the bank and the four of them were in the cool shade of the trees.

She looked up when they came out from the bend. She looked at John and then at Farwell. She rose from her crouch without speaking and gathered the children with a word and a movement and went back toward the lodges.

Farwell watched her go.

Then he kept walking.

* * *

The camp had a different quality than John had known it. Not the wrong kind of busy, not yet. But altered. The particular attention of a place that had heard something in the night and had not resolved it.

Two women were pulling the pegs of a lodge on the southern edge. A man John did not know was moving horses from the far picket line toward the creek, three animals at once, not rushing but not stopping. The dogs that had always watched the camp's edges were not in their usual places.

Little Soldier came out to meet them.

He was dressed. His face had the quality it always had — the ground that had been under weather long enough to stop reacting to it. He looked at Farwell and then at John and what he made of John's collarless coat and the gun at his belt he did not say. He spoke briefly in Assiniboine. A younger man appeared from behind the nearest lodge and stood at his left.

"He says he has heard the men at the north fort are moving," the interpreter said.

"We've come to ask him to move his people farther south," Farwell said. "Back from the open ground. Into the trees if he can."

Translation. Little Soldier listened. He answered at length.

"He says he has already asked this," the interpreter said. "His people are ready. Some have gone already." A pause. "He says Inihan Kinyen's people will not move."

From the far end of the camp, voices. Not argument exactly. The sound of men testing the weight of a decision that had not yet been made.

Little Soldier looked toward the sound. His face did not change. He said something short and quiet.

"He says the young men have been drinking since last night," the interpreter said. "He says fear and whiskey make the same sound."

John looked toward the sound. He could see them from here — twenty, maybe more, Inihan Kinyen's men and some of Little Soldier's younger warriors together at the north end of the camp. Inihan Kinyen stood at the centre of them. He was a big man, straight-backed, and he was listening to something a younger man was saying with his arms open and his chin raised, the posture of a man inviting disagreement. Inihan Kinyen's face was turned away and John could not read it.

Farwell said, "Can he bring them south."

Translation. A longer exchange. The interpreter paused before he turned back.

"He says he cannot move another chief's men," the interpreter said. "He can only move his own. He is doing that."

Little Soldier looked at John then. The full attention, the way it had always been — not hostile, not warm. The attention of a man reading something he had read before and was checking his translation against the original.

John said, in the Cree he had, "Tell your people to go south. Into the trees. By the water."

He heard the words go wrong as he spoke them. The grammar incomplete. The Cree of the trade routes, not the camp. Little Soldier heard it. He heard the gap between the words and the man saying them, the same gap he had heard in the fall of '72 and had not named.

He answered in Cree. Slowly. Clearly. The way you speak to a man who is trying.

"He says he knows," the interpreter said.

Little Soldier turned away. He called once toward the women at the southern lodge. Then he moved toward the north end of the camp, toward the sound of Inihan Kinyen's men, with the steady unhurried walk of a man who had decided what he would attempt and was not expecting it to work.

* * *

Inihan Kinyen did not take long to read.

He listened to Little Soldier. His face was still. The younger man beside him — Wincanahe, the one who had been speaking with his arms open — said something without waiting for the exchange to finish. The men around him laughed. Not all of them. But enough. Inihan Kinyen looked at Wincanahe a long moment. Then he looked north, toward the bend, toward the hidden line of creek and trees that ran back toward the ford and the forts.

He did not move his people.

Little Soldier came back. He did not speak. He looked at Farwell once and then walked past him toward his own lodge, where a woman was waiting with a child on her hip and a bundle in her arms.

* * *

The sound came from the north around midday.

A man's voice, carrying. Cursing in two languages, the French and English running together the way they do when a man is too angry to choose. Then other voices underneath it, lower, the sound of men agreeing.

Farwell lifted his head.

John looked back the way they had come, toward the bend and the hidden ford beyond it. The noise was not from the camp. It was from up the creek, nearer the forts.

Farwell started north at once. John went with him.

They did not run. The ground would not take it and neither of them was a man for wasted motion. They came back around the bend with the camp behind them now and the line of the creek opening north again. The ford came into view. Beyond it, on Solomon's side, Hammond was in the yard outside the fort with his arms out, turning in a circle the way a drunk man turns when he is trying to point at everything at once.

His horse, he was shouting. His horse again. The Indians had taken it again and a man could not leave anything in this country without some red son of a bitch deciding it was his.

Hardwick was there too. Not in the centre of it. Off to one side near the cook fires, watching Hammond the way a man watches weather that may yet prove useful.

The men at the fires had stopped what they were doing.

They were listening the way men listen when something gives them permission.

Farwell said, "Stay south of the water."

He crossed the ford alone.

John stopped on the camp side where the bank rose a little above the crossing. From there he could see both directions: north to Solomon's yard and south around the bend toward the camp. He stayed where Farwell had left him.

Farwell went to Hammond and spoke to him. Hammond gestured south. Farwell put a hand on his arm. Hammond pulled it back. Farwell looked once at Hardwick and his men and then back at Hammond and spoke again.

Hardwick did not move.

In the camp behind John, Little Soldier's women were moving faster now.

* * *

Farwell came back across the ford with Hammond behind him and two of Hardwick's men behind Hammond.

He came to John first.

"The horse wandered," he said quietly. "It's not stolen. Labombarde's looking for it now." He looked south around the bend where the camp lay out of sight. "It doesn't matter."

He went past John toward the wider ground on the camp side of the ford where Hardwick had now crossed with four of his men. Hammond came too, still talking. Still swearing. Still making the same claim as though its repetition improved it.

Hardwick stopped on the north edge of the camp side open ground, just below the bend and above the trees that screened the lodges from the ford. This was not the camp itself. This was the stretch of bare bank and trampled grass between the crossing and the first lodges south around the curve. Creek on one side. Scrub and timber on the other. A place where men could stand and look into the bend.

Farwell stopped in front of him.

John could not hear the words from where he stood. He could hear the register — Farwell's voice level and direct, the voice of a man making an offer he considered reasonable. An open hand. Two horses from the camp, held at the fort until Hammond's animal could be located. A surety. A way of letting the day end without the shape it was taking.

Hardwick looked at him. He looked past him too, south into the bend where the tops of the lodges showed beyond the scrub and the first movement of women could be seen between them. His face gave nothing back.

Then he said something brief.

He did not look at Hammond when he said it.

Farwell stood a moment longer. Then he nodded once and turned back toward the camp.

Hammond called after him:

"You go get me those two horses then."

He called it the way a man calls to a servant. Not asking. Sending.

The men around him laughed.

Farwell did not break his pace. He went south around the bend toward the lodges. Going for the horses, or believing there was still time to go for the horses because the alternative was to stand in the open and admit what he was looking at. He did not look back at the men gathering along the north bank.

John watched him go.

Then Hardwick turned to his own men.

He said something John could not hear.

They began to move at once.

Not down into the camp. Outward. Sideways. Into position.

Two went east into the scrub line above the bend where the trees overlooked the first lodges. One stayed near the bank above the ford with a clear line south. Another moved west along the creek and knelt where the ground fell away enough to give him cover. Hammond hung back nearer the crossing, still talking, but lower now. Unnecessary now.

No one shouted.

No one hurried.

Rifles came up into hands in the same quiet way tools come up into a workday.

John stepped off the bank and went toward Hardwick.

Hardwick saw him coming and did not stop what he was watching.

"These people have done nothing to you," John said.

That brought Hardwick's eyes to him.

The look was not anger. It was worse than anger. It was the look of a man for whom the question had already been answered elsewhere.

"Where is my brother Doyle."

John had no answer for that.

"Get out of the way," he said. "Unless you want to be one of them."

From the bend below them came the sight of a woman running between two lodges with a bundle in her arms. Not running blindly. Running with purpose. A child behind her. A dog crossing the open ground low and fast. Life still trying to remain itself.

John said, "There's three hundred of them a dozen of you. Do you think this will end well."

Hardwick's gaze did not change.

"It will end," he said.

One of the men in the trees worked the lever on his rifle and settled in behind it.

Hardwick looked past John to the camp. To the open ground in the bend. To the men who had not moved south when they had been told. To Wincanahe, visible now at the north edge of the lodges with three others near him and no cover worth the name.

"Move," Hardwick said.

John did not move.

Hardwick drew his pistol just enough for the metal to show clear at his coat and said, "You've had your say."

That was enough.

John stepped back.

Not toward the camp. Not into the line. North and west, away from the muzzles, until he stood on the shoulder of ground above the ford where he could see both the men in the trees and the first lodges in the bend and was of no use to either.

Below him, the creek ran low and clear over the stones.

South in the bend, Little Soldier's women were pulling children toward the trees by the water. Inihan Kinyen's men were still too far north, still too open, still not believing or not willing to look like men who believed.

Farwell was somewhere among the lodges looking for two horses that no longer mattered.

Wincanahe shouted something from the camp's north edge — contemptuous, loud, the sound of a young man refusing the shape of the day even as it closed around him.

No one answered him.

The men along the bank had finished spacing themselves now. One above the ford. One kneeling by the creek. Two in the scrub line where the branches screened their bodies and left the barrels clear. Hardwick standing slightly back from them all, where he could see into the whole bend.

Between the rifles to the north and the camp below, the open ground lay empty in the flat clear light of the first day of June.

Forty-Five

The shot came from the scrub line.

Then the others.

The camp went from stillness to motion at once. Women running south between the lodges. Children caught up mid-step. Dogs going low and fast toward the creek bank. Inihan Kinyen's men at the camp's north edge went down or scattered or stood where they were.

Little Soldier's people were already moving. He had done that much. They went south through the gaps between the lodges toward the trees along the water, the women with bundles and children ahead of the men, the old ones helped or hurrying. He moved among them without haste, directing, steady, the way a man moves through work he has done before and knows how to finish.

John stood on the shoulder above the ford.

He could see the whole bend from there. The scrub line where the shots were coming from and the open ground below it and the camp beneath the willows and between them the stretch of bare ground that had no cover.

Marguerite was running along the near bank with the youngest on her back in the cradleboard. The older two ahead of her. The open ground between her and the trees was fifty yards. Perhaps less.

She did not make the trees.

The shooting did not stop.

* * *

Across the ford, figures appeared at Farwell's gate. The sound of the rifles carried clean in the still air and there was no preventing the sound from going where it went.

Nora had her hand flat against the gatepost. Bella was beside her. Mary stood behind them both.

On the western rise, Farwell appeared with two horses. He stood with Dunn at the gate of Fort Farwell. Stood with his hand on the beast beside him, looking southwest, past the ford, at the puffs of smoke rising from the repeating Winchesters.

On the rise northeast of the ford, above Solomon's gate, two horsemen sat against the sky. Solomon and one of his men. Not moving. Watching the smoke rise from the bend below the way men watch a fire from the right side of the water.

* * *

The shooting continued through the middle part of the day. Not without pause. There were stretches where it thinned to single shots and the camp below went quiet in the way that is not emptiness but things drawing still. Then it would resume.

Some of Inihan Kinyen's men had rifles. The exchange lasted longer than Hardwick had planned for. Inihan Kinyen himself took a wound — his left side — before he and his warriors withdrew.

* * *

The creek bottom was full of people moving south through the willows. The sound of the rifles was behind them and growing smaller.

John had come off the shoulder and into the creek bottom while the shooting was still going on. He kept the bank between himself and the open ground and moved south through the willows with the water cold through his boots.

He found them where the bank overhung the water — a woman and three children pressed into the overhang out of sight of the open ground, the woman with one hand over the mouth of the smallest, the other two children held against her sides. She looked at him when he crouched at the bank's edge. The look was not relief. It was the look of a person measuring whether the new thing is the same as the last thing.

He did not speak. He held out his hand.

She looked at it.

He waited.

She gave him the smallest child and took the hands of the other two and they went south through the water under the bank, John first with the child against his chest, the woman behind him with the other two. The water was low and cold and the stones turned underfoot. He did not draw his gun. He went forward and the woman went with him and the children did not make a sound.

He brought them out at the south curve where the willows thickened and Little Soldier's people were gathered in the trees. A woman came forward and took the smallest from him without speaking.

He straightened.

John stood at the tree line with the creek at his back and the smoke above the bend and the woman he had brought out sitting with the others along the bank. Not looking at him. Looking at each other.

He looked north through the gap in the willows where the creek came around the bend. The smoke above the open ground. The light on the upper poles of the lodges still standing.

He knew where Marguerite had fallen.

The ground between was open.

He did not go.

John stood in the trees. He did not go back up

* * *

When the last of his people had passed him, Little Soldier stopped.

He turned and walked north. Toward the scrub line. Toward the rifles. Toward the open ground between them and everything that had come down through it.

He spoke.

His voice carried in the still air.

The words were his own language. John could not catch them. He heard the cadence of them — long, unhurried, the sound of a man who has said what needed saying and is now saying what is true.

One phrase in it was clear.

"White men."

The rest was not their language.

The shot came before the last of it had settled.

He went down in the same ground where he had stood.

* * *

The shooting had stopped by the time the sun had moved off the centre of the sky.

Hardwick's men came down from the scrub line and into the camp. Rifles inverted in hands. The dead moved and moved again.

By late afternoon the heads of the dead were on the poles at the camp's north edge.

Farwell cross the ford. He went to Hardwick directly.

John could hear the register of it from where he stood. Farwell's voice even — the horse had been found, it was in the yard, it had never been taken. The thing that had started the day was settled.

Hardwick looked east. The Indians who had not been killed had gone into the trees.

Farwell said it again.

Hardwick said something short to his men.

They went east.

* * *

Paul Rivers had gone in ahead of them or beside them — no one could afterward say with certainty where he had stood in relation to what happened. The shot came from inside the timber before the men had gone twenty paces. Then a second. Rivers went down and did not get up.

The men at the treeline stopped. They looked at the trees. The trees gave nothing back.

They came back.

* * *

Some of Hardwick's men came north through the ford in the last of the afternoon. Not all of them. Enough. They came with the taut movement of men who had been sent back and were not yet done. Four women came with them. Not bound. They did not need to be. They moved the way people move when the available choices have been reduced to one.

One of them was carrying a child's moccasin. She still had it in her hand when they took her through the gate. She did not appear to know she was holding it.

Hardwick's men took them through Solomon's gate.

The sound from inside the fort had been ordinary through the day — the particular flatness of a place where men wait.

Solomon turned his horse and said something to the man beside him and they went back through the gate.

When the gate closed behind them it changed. Rose. The sound of men making good what the trees had cost them.

The gate closed.

* * *

The fires had caught the lodges by then and the smoke was a single column rising straight in the still air. The ground in the bend was quiet in the way ground is quiet when there is nothing left in it.

When John came back through the ford in the last of the afternoon, the settlement was quiet.

Nora was still at the gate.

She had her hand on the post the way she had had it when the first shots came. She was looking south, toward the ford and the bend and the smoke still rising above the trees in the last of the light.

She did not look at John when he came through the gate.

She did not look away from the south.

He went past her into the yard.

The light went out of the sky and she was still there.

Forty-Six

Hardwick's men broke camp at first light.

John watched from the edge of the willows as they loaded their horses and rode out through Solomon's gate onto the south track. Hardwick came last. He did not look at the bend as he passed it. He rode south and the settlement absorbed his going without ceremony, without comment.

The sound of the horses faded.

* * *

He went into the camp at sunrise.

The lodges had burned to their frames in the night. The poles had fallen inward and the ash was soft underfoot where it had been deepest. Smoke still moved in places, close to the ground.

A child lay near the line where the grass had been worn down to earth. The small shape of it. The head turned away.

He stood until standing did not change anything.

* * *

Fort Solomon stood as it had stood the day before.

Two of Hardwick's men were at the edge of the yard near the coulee, working. John came around the fence line and saw it before they saw him — a length of canvas, a shallow trench, the particular labour of men doing a thing they had not planned to do and were doing badly. Rivers lay where they had set him down. One boot off. The other still on.

One of the men looked up.

He took in the collarless coat. The gun. He looked a moment longer and then said it anyway.

"You're a priest, aren't you."

John held his eyes.

"Say something over him," the man said. "He deserves that much."

The other man had stopped digging. He was watching.

John looked at Rivers in the dirt. At the canvas. At the trench not yet deep enough for the man it was meant to hold.

"No," he said.

The first man straightened.

"He was a man same as any," he said. "Whatever happened here."

"No," John said again.

He held the man's look until the man looked away.

Then he turned.

* * *

He went down to the ford and crossed where the stones showed. At the centre of it he stopped. The current moved around his legs.

It did not slow.

He crossed.

* * *

Farwell's place was awake. The door open. Dunn at the rail with a cup in his hand. He looked at John when he came up from the creek and then looked away again.

Farwell stood in the doorway. He had his hat on. He did not speak.

The four women from Solomon's fort were in the near yard. Mary was with them. She did not look up when John passed.

John went past without stopping. Through the window he could see the counter and the lamp still burning on it and the collar where he had set it two days before.

He kept on.

* * *

Nora was at the gate with her shawl around her shoulders. She looked at him when he came level. At his coat. At the absence of the collar. At the gun. At his face.

She stepped aside.

* * *

He went north along the upper track to the church.

The frame stood as it had stood since May — the uprights and crossbeams, the morning sky between them where the walls would have gone. He went inside it and stood where he had stood when he spoke.

The words did not come.

He waited.

He went out.

* * *

He took the northwest track.

It rose through the low ground and then out of it. The settlement fell behind him — first the voices, then the work sounds, then the quality of air above a place where men live.

At the rise he stopped and turned.

The settlement lay in the valley below. Both forts. The land falling away between them into the dark of the coulee. The ford catching the light. The church frame on the rise above Farwell's side.

The smoke below the river bend now thin, nearly gone.

The Wilson house sat where it always had below the bluff and near to the creek.

The fence ran along three sides of the yard. It was his work and it showed.

No smoke from the chimney.

The door closed. The window reflecting only the morning.

He looked at it until he had seen it.

Then he turned north and went on. His bad foot found the ground the way it always found it. The hills rose before him, the trail pale in the early light, the sky above the western hills a blue that remained indifferent.

He did not look back again.

A Historical Note

Part I — The Transfer of Rupert's Land and the Creation of the Northwest Territories

The Royal Charter of 1670 granted the Hudson's Bay Company proprietorship over all lands whose rivers drained into Hudson Bay. The territory, known as Rupert's Land, was commonly estimated at 7 to 8 million square kilometres. In practice, the Company exercised this claim through a network of trading posts and commercial relationships with Indigenous peoples. Its administrative presence was limited. Governance, in any formal sense, extended little beyond the immediate environs of its posts. The overwhelming majority of those living within Rupert's Land were Indigenous, Métis, or of mixed fur-trade ancestry.

The Confederation of Canada in 1867 brought an immediate ambition of westward expansion. In 1869, the Dominion negotiated the transfer of Rupert's Land from the Company for £300,000, together with provisions granting the Company one-twentieth of the arable land in the so-called "fertile belt." The transfer took formal effect on July 15, 1870. Rupert's Land and the North-Western Territory were thereafter constituted as the Northwest Territories under federal jurisdiction.

The legal transformation was abrupt. What had been a commercial jurisdiction became, formally, a political one. The Dominion now claimed sovereignty over a vast region extending from the boundary of Ontario to the Rocky Mountains and from the forty-ninth parallel to the Arctic. That claim, however, was largely nominal. At the time of transfer, the Canadian government had no meaningful administrative presence in the region: no established courts, no policing authority, no developed transportation infrastructure, and no effective mechanisms of governance. Laws applicable to the territory existed in a formal sense, but there was little or no institutional capacity to enforce them.

Part II — The Indigenous Nations of the Northwestern Plains

The peoples of the northwestern plains did not experience the transfer of 1870 as a change in governance. No new administrative authority arrived with it. Political, legal, and social order in the region continued to be structured by Indigenous systems of governance that had developed over generations.

Among the most prominent were the nations of the Blackfoot Confederacy — the Siksika, Kainai (Blood), and Piikani (Peigan) — whose territory extended across the western plains and foothills. To the east and northeast, the Plains Cree and Assiniboine occupied overlapping and shifting territories, their movements governed by the migration patterns of the bison herds. Further north, Nakoda and Saulteaux bands moved between ecological zones, maintaining trade, kinship, and diplomatic relationships across a broad range. Interwoven with all of these nations were the Métis, a distinct people whose freighting networks, provisioning systems, and intermediary roles were integral to both Indigenous economies and the operations of the independent traders moving through the region.

The Cypress Hills, rising above the surrounding plains along what is now the Saskatchewan–Alberta boundary, formed an ecological enclave of reliable water, timber, and game. They attracted a range of peoples for hunting, wintering, and temporary settlement. They were not the exclusive territory of any single nation, nor neutral ground in any formal sense. They were used, contested, and shared over time, access shaped by shifting alliances, seasonal need, and local power.

By the spring of 1873, several Assiniboine bands had gathered in the creek valleys of the Cypress Hills. One group, under Chief Inihan Kinyen, had come in what appears to have been the normal course of winter movement. Another band, under Chief Manitupotis — known to the traders as Little Soldier — had reached the Hills by a different route. Driven from an intended winter camp on the Battle River by starvation, they had crossed approximately three hundred kilometres of frozen prairie to reach the relative shelter and resources of the Hills. Thirty people did not survive the journey. A third group, under a leader known as Minashenayen, had lost all of its horses. Together, these bands — perhaps forty or more lodges, several hundred people in total — were in conditions of significant privation at the time of their encampment near the trading posts on Battle Creek.

Their presence that spring was not a continuation of established seasonal patterns. For at least two of the bands, it was the consequence of a winter severe enough to push people to the edge of survival, and of the broader pressures produced by the accelerating decline of the bison herds.

Part III — The Unguarded Border and the Whiskey Trade

The international boundary along the forty-ninth parallel, established by the Anglo-American Convention of 1818, existed for much of the nineteenth century as a legal abstraction rather than a controlled frontier. It was unpoliced. Traders, hunters, and others crossed it with little constraint. By the early 1870s, the southern portion of the newly constituted Northwest Territories functioned, in many respects, as an extension of the northern Montana frontier — commercially, culturally, and in terms of the forms of violence associated with that economy.

Fort Benton, on the Missouri River in Montana Territory, was the head of navigation for steamboat traffic moving north from St. Louis, and it served as the principal supply hub for trade extending into the Canadian plains. Among the goods moving north, alcohol proved the most commercially significant. American law prohibited the sale of liquor to Indigenous peoples within United States jurisdiction, and enforcement in Montana Territory, however uneven, was sufficient to create real legal risk for traders operating south of the border. Traders crossing north found the same legal prohibition on the books — but no one authorised or willing to enforce it.

The consequences for Indigenous communities were significant and, in many cases, devastating. The trade was not simply an economic transaction conducted on unfavourable terms. Observers at the time understood it to be destructive of the social and political structures on which communities depended — corroding the authority of leaders, generating internal conflict, and accelerating the depletion of the bison herds through the exchange of robes for alcohol rather than for goods that sustained life. Contemporary accounts describe the whiskey itself as a diluted alcohol base mixed with substances including ginger, red pepper, molasses, and chewing tobacco — widely understood, even then, to be a crude and often harmful substitute for distilled spirits.

By the early 1870s, Ottawa was aware in general terms of conditions in the Northwest Territories. Legislation creating the North-West Mounted Police was enacted on May 23, 1873. The force would not be deployed to the region until 1874. In the interim, the conditions that had sustained the whiskey trade — the absence of enforcement, the cross-border mobility, the practical impunity — remained in place.

Part IV — The Whiskey Trade Network: Fort Benton, Fort Whoop-Up, and the Posts on Battle Creek

In December 1869, traders John J. Healy and Alfred B. Hamilton established a post near the confluence of the St. Mary and Oldman rivers in what is now southern Alberta. Destroyed by fire within a year, it was rebuilt in more substantial form and became known as Fort Whoop-Up. The profits it generated attracted further traders, and a supply route developed between Fort Benton and the northern posts. By 1872 the network had reached the Cypress Hills.

The commercial infrastructure sustaining this expansion was concentrated in Fort Benton. The T.C. Power Company, among the most prominent wholesale concerns there, supplied goods on credit to independent traders operating across the region. Both Abel Farwell and Moses Solomon were Power Company customers — competitors in the field who drew their supplies from the same source and operated within the same commercial system.

The posts at Battle Creek — Fort Farwell on the west bank and Fort Solomon on the east — were modest log structures rather than fortified installations. They were seasonal operations. Their function was largely transactional: to exchange remaining trade goods for robes and pelts before the end of the season and prepare those goods for transport south.

Farwell was an experienced trader who had operated out of Fort Benton for several years. His interpreter was an aging Métis named Alexis Lebombard, who had worked previously for Solomon before joining Farwell in the autumn of 1872. Farwell's common-law partner, a Crow woman named Mary, was also present at the fort. She would later receive the Assiniboine women taken captive after June 1 and give testimony in the proceedings that followed. Moses Solomon was a more recent arrival to the region — described in some sources as a New Yorker of Polish-Jewish descent — who had previously operated at Fort Standoff within the Whoop-Up network. A part share in his business was held by George Bell, a former United States infantryman.

In the final days of May 1873, Farwell had ridden out to a temporary settlement of Métis winterers camped roughly twenty-five miles from the posts and hired enough men and carts to carry his season's returns south to Fort Benton. Several of this party — among them Baptiste

Champagne, Joseph Laverdure, and Joseph Vital Turcotte — arrived at Fort Farwell on the morning of June 1. Their presence that day was incidental to the violence that followed. Several of them later gave testimony at the proceedings that attempted, and failed, to produce a conviction.

Relations between the traders and the Assiniboine were strained going into that spring. The dynamics of the whiskey trade — disputes over the fairness of exchanges, the destabilising effects of alcohol, accumulated grievances — had produced escalating tension. There were reports of shots fired into Solomon's post and of threats exchanged in the days before June 1. By late May, the situation in the valley was volatile. No external authority was present to mediate or impose order.

Part V — The Events of June 1, 1873

The event has been reconstructed many times, and the reconstructions do not agree. The witnesses had interests. The courts had politics. What survives is a convergence of partial and sometimes incompatible accounts, each reliable in the direction it pointed and uncertain in much else.

A general shape of events can be made out.

The events culminating in the violence at Battle Creek began approximately two weeks earlier in Montana Territory. On or about May 17, a group of wolfers — hunters who harvested wolf pelts, typically using strychnine rather than traps — were camped near the Teton River, south of Fort Benton, when a raiding party rode off with approximately forty of their horses. Most accounts attribute the theft to a passing band of Cree, though the identification was disputed at the time.

After returning to Fort Benton and receiving no assistance from the local military garrison, the wolfers organised their own expedition to recover the animals. The party, approximately a dozen men, was led by Thomas Hardwick and John Evans. All carried Henry and Winchester repeating rifles.

The party followed the trail north for approximately two weeks before losing it in the Cypress Hills. By the evening of May 31, they had located the trading posts on Battle Creek and established a camp near Fort Farwell. Hardwick and Evans approached Farwell to ask whether the nearby Assiniboine camp might be harbouring their stolen horses. Farwell was cool in his reception. He told them the camp held only five or six horses and had not taken theirs. He extended hospitality nonetheless, inviting the party to return for breakfast the following morning.

The morning was marked by heavy drinking among the traders, wolfers, and others at the posts, continuing from the previous evening.

On the east bank, the situation in the Assiniboine camp was already unsettled. Chief Inihan Kinyen had been warned by a trader that the new arrivals were dangerous and gave instructions to break camp and move. A man in the camp named Wincanahe dismissed the warning, challenged the chief's assessment, and persuaded others to remain. In the hours that followed, some members of the camp turned to alcohol. By midday, accounts suggest a number of people were significantly intoxicated.

Around midday, George Hammond raised an alarm that his horse had been stolen by the Assiniboine. The claim was almost certainly mistaken, but it carried weight given the animal's recent history. It was one of three stolen from Fort Farwell by Stonies in April. It had been returned to Hammond only the previous day, with the Indian who returned it receiving two gallons of whisky, a blanket, and tobacco in exchange. The horse had walked out through an unlatched gate and was grazing undisturbed in the brush a few hundred yards away.

Whether Hammond knew this at the time is not established by the record.

What the record does establish is that Hammond moved through the post calling on the Benton men to take the Indians' horses in return. They were already primed on the subject of stolen horses. Most of them went. Farwell attempted to slow it down, pointing out that the same people had returned the horse willingly the day before. Hammond was not persuaded. As the party crossed to the east bank, Lebombard spotted the horse being led quietly back into the fort and shouted after Hammond in French. Hammond glanced back and did not stop.

Farwell had already gone ahead into the Assiniboine camp.

Two Métis from Farwell's freighting party saw the armed men moving on the camp and ran ahead to warn the Assiniboine. They told the Indians they might not live to see nightfall and urged them to take cover. Women ran for the surrounding brush with their children. Men took up their weapons and scattered after them. This movement was read by the whites gathering in the coulee as confirmation that the camp was preparing to fight.

What Farwell was doing in the camp at this moment is contested, and the contention matters. Farwell would later testify that he had reached an agreement with the chief — that horses would be held as a token of good faith until Hammond's claim could be checked. Lebombard, his interpreter, would testify that Farwell and the Assiniboine shared almost no common language beyond a few words of trade.

At some point an Assiniboine man raised a gun toward Farwell. A woman intervened, pushed the weapon down, and steered the man away. When Farwell returned to the coulee he reported the arrangement, offered to fetch Lebombard to confirm it, and asked the men to hold their fire.

The men in the coulee did not wait.

Positions had been taken along the coulee's edge overlooking the camp below. Those in the coulee were partially concealed and held clear ground. The Assiniboine camp lay exposed on the slope. Who fired first was the central question in every legal proceeding that followed. It was never resolved. Farwell maintained that Hammond fired without provocation. Several of the Métis freighters testified that shots came from the camp first, or that a warning volley from the whites was answered as a challenge. The courts reached no consistent finding on this point.

What followed was sustained and one-sided. Those along the coulee carried repeating rifles capable of rapid and continuous fire. The Assiniboine were equipped primarily with muzzle-loading firearms and bows. Volleys were fired into the camp from positions of partial cover. People attempting to flee or take shelter were shot. Additional fire came from individuals associated with Fort Solomon, shooting from the roof and from in front of the post.

Estimates of casualties vary across the accounts. A commonly cited figure is approximately twenty Assiniboine killed, though some sources suggest the number was higher. The attacking party suffered one fatality — Ed Legrace, shot during a later phase of the confrontation.

Hardwick took a smaller group across the creek to continue firing on survivors who had taken cover beyond the main camp. During this pursuit, Farwell confronted Hardwick directly with the fact that Hammond's horse had already been found safe in the fort. Hardwick's reported reply was that the attack would continue regardless. Indians concealed on the hillside above the fort drove the group back toward the creek. It was in this exchange that Legrace was killed.

Chief Little Soldier — Manitupotis — was found in the final stage of the violence. His wife found him incapacitated and tried to move him from the camp. He would not go. Accounts record that he addressed those nearest him, saying that white men would know what they had done, and that a Cypress Hills Assiniboine had never harmed a white man. He was shot by a member of the Benton party.

After the main violence subsided, the camp was looted and the lodges heaped and burned. An elderly man named Wankantu was killed with a hatchet. His severed head was raised on a lodge-pole.

Four Assiniboine women, one with a small child, were taken into custody and held overnight at Fort Solomon before being handed into Mary Farwell's care the following morning. Testimony given later by one of the women forms part of the legal record and documents further violence committed against the captive women during the night.

The dead were not buried. Ed Legrace, the single fatality among the attacking party, was interred beneath the floor of Solomon's cellar. The forts were subsequently burned — a common practice in the region, as departing traders knew that deserted posts were typically fired by those who came after in any case. The broken remnants of the Assiniboine camps dispersed and were eventually taken in by sympathetic Métis. The valley held their remains for years afterward.

Part VI — Aftermath: The Creation of the North-West Mounted Police and the Failure of Justice

Participants in the violence returned south to Fort Benton within days. Reports reaching Canadian authorities took considerably longer. Accounts arrived in Ottawa in late August 1873 through two channels: reports made by Farwell to authorities in Montana Territory and relayed through American officials, and accounts carried east by Métis who had assisted the surviving members of the Assiniboine camps.

Some early reports placed the killings south of the international boundary. Once it was established that the events had occurred on Canadian soil, responsibility fell to Ottawa. Lieutenant Governor Alexander Morris warned the government on more than one occasion that the massacre represented a turning point in the Dominion's relationship with the western nations, and that credibility in the treaty negotiations ahead depended on how it was handled. If Americans could kill Indigenous people on Canadian territory and return home without consequence, he argued, the government would soon find itself facing difficulties of a far graver kind.

Public reaction in eastern Canada was sharp. The fact that American nationals had participated in violence on Canadian soil reinforced broader concerns about the absence of effective sovereignty in the Northwest Territories — though it was also understood that individuals present in the region, including some associated with the trading posts, had taken part.

Legislation establishing the North-West Mounted Police had been enacted on May 23, 1873, before the events at Cypress Hills. The creation of a mounted police force had been under consideration for several years, driven by concern over the whiskey trade and the absence of effective legal authority in the region. The events of June 1 did not give rise to the policy. They reinforced its urgency.

An Order-in-Council dated August 30, 1873, authorised recruitment. The NWMP was conceived as a small, mobile force capable of asserting Canadian authority across a vast territory — a response to the whiskey trade, to perceived American encroachment, and to the conditions that had allowed both to persist unchecked. The force would not reach the Cypress Hills until 1875, when Fort Walsh was established on Battle Creek approximately two miles from the site of the massacre.

In September 1873, cabinet resolved to pursue extradition proceedings against the participants in the violence. Sir John A. Macdonald, then minister of justice and beset by political difficulties of his own, commissioned Gilbert McMicken in Winnipeg to move against the wanted men before they could return north for the winter hunting season. Warrants were issued for Hardwick, Hale, Devereaux, Harper, Vincent, and others. The season was already too advanced. The matter remained in McMicken's hands until May 1874, when it was transferred to the newly commissioned North-West Mounted Police.

For the better part of two years following the massacre, the principal participants had gone entirely unmolested. In the spring of 1875, Assistant Commissioner James Macleod was appointed a special agent to proceed to Fort Benton. On June 21, 1875, Macleod and Inspector Irvine, working alongside United States marshals, found seven of the wanted men at Fort Benton and took them into custody. Two escaped almost immediately. The remaining five — Hardwick, Hale, Evans, Harper, and Devereaux — were transferred to Helena for extradition proceedings.

The hearing opened in Helena on July 7, 1875, before United States Commissioner W.E. Cullen. It was conducted in a charged atmosphere. The prisoners were represented by lawyers closely aligned with the Democratic party and the anti-British sentiment running strongly in territorial Montana. The hearing became, in part, a proceeding about something other than what had happened at Battle Creek.

Farwell was the prosecution's principal witness. His account — that Hammond had fired first and without provocation, and that he himself had reached an agreement with the chief before the men in the coulee disregarded it — was the foundation of the Canadian case. The foundation proved unstable. Lebombard testified that Farwell and the Assiniboine had shared almost no common language; the supposed agreement could not have occurred as Farwell described it. The defence brought witnesses to attack Farwell's character and consistency, with substantial effect.

Commissioner Cullen discharged all five prisoners. His findings were, in their way, a precise statement of what the evidence showed and what the law would not allow him to do with it. The weight of testimony pointed to the Indians having fired first, he concluded — but they had been provoked into doing so by an armed party advancing on their camp. The defendants' conduct had been reckless and unjustifiable. The evidence, however, did not meet the standard required to commit them for trial on a charge of murder. Cullen was clear that moral responsibility existed. The legal mechanism available to him did not allow him to act on that view.

Helena celebrated openly when the verdict was announced. The men returned to Fort Benton to a hero's reception. The Fort Benton Record described the participants in the massacre as defenders of the frontier — men at the advance of civilisation rather than in violation of its principles. The gap between that view and the one held by Canadian authorities was not a legal disagreement about the sufficiency of evidence. It was a difference about whether an Indigenous life counted equally before the law.

The extradition failure did not end the proceedings. Philander Vogle and James Hughes were discovered living openly in the vicinity of Fort Macleod and were arrested by Macleod, sitting as a stipendiary magistrate, and dispatched to Winnipeg for trial. George Bell was found in the Cypress Hills and added to the party. In June 1876, Bell, Hughes, and Vogle stood trial for murder before Chief Justice Edmund Burke Wood at the Winnipeg assizes.

The prosecution's case rested again on Farwell. His central account — that Hammond had fired first — withstood cross-examination, but Lebombard again undermined the question of the supposed agreement with the chief, and with it the broader reliability of Farwell's testimony. The Métis freighters called by the defence proved the more decisive factor. Several testified that the Indians had fired before the main exchange, or that a warning volley from the whites had been taken as a challenge. Their apparent independence as witnesses carried weight that the prosecution's contested testimony could not match. Bell and Vogle testified on behalf of each other, each placing the other inside Fort Solomon when the fighting began. Hughes offered no direct evidence in his own defence.

All three were acquitted.

A Note on Sources

This account draws on Robert S. Allen's *A Witness to Murder: The Cypress Hills Massacre and the Conflict of Attitudes towards the Native People of the Canadian and American West during the 1870s* (Parks Canada, National Historic Parks and Sites Branch), the most detailed reconstruction of the trial testimony surrounding the events of June 1, 1873, along with the Canadian Encyclopedia and Indigenous Saskatchewan Encyclopedia (University of Saskatchewan) entries on the massacre, the Royal Canadian Mounted Police's own historical record of the force's founding, the Galt Museum & Archives' history of Fort Whoop-Up and the whiskey trade, and supplementary reference material from Wikipedia. Where these sources disagree — as they often do, on casualty figures, the sequence of events, and the reliability of individual witnesses — this note has tried to represent the uncertainty rather than resolve it by fiat.

The Characters

Rev. Elias Wilson

Abel Farwell

Moses Solomon

Bella Hawthorne

Heather Hawthorne

Dunnard McTavish

Mary Farwell

Chief Manitupotis

(Little Soldier)

Gabriel Lavallee

Nora Cardinal

Author's Note

What Was Written began as an inkling to write a Canadian Western.

The novel is set in the Cypress Hills in 1873, during a brief and unstable moment in Canadian history. After Confederation and the transfer of Rupert's Land to the Dominion, the Northwest Territories existed without effective law enforcement. South of the border, American authorities were beginning to enforce laws prohibiting the sale of alcohol to Indigenous peoples. North of the forty-ninth parallel, no such authority yet existed. Traders, whiskey runners, and opportunists moved into that gap. Order, where it appeared, was improvised and temporary.

This absence is the ground of the book.

The mythology of the American West often rests on the idea that a single man—with a gun, or a badge—can impose law and bring order. This novel resists that idea. Elias Wilson does, in a sense, become the law. He writes it, speaks it, and enforces it. But what he creates does not hold. Law without structure, authority, and continuity is not law at all. It is performance, persuasion, and, at times, self-interest.

The events of June 1, 1873—the Cypress Hills Massacre—stand at the centre of that failure. I have taken liberties in the telling, but I have tried to remain faithful to the conditions that made such violence possible: the absence of enforcement, the presence of alcohol, and the unequal and often devastating contact between settlers and Indigenous peoples, particularly the Assiniboine.

The title reflects the novel's concern with the written word—law, agreements, records—and their limits. What is written carries authority. It shapes memory, justifies action, and claims truth. But writing does not guarantee justice, and it does not prevent harm. The distance between what is written and what occurs is where this story lives.

I hope you found something in this story worth staying with. If you did, and would like to explore more of my work, you can visit me at www.harwoodjones.com.

Troy

Promotion

I'm an independent author. I love building worlds, characters, and stories — and sharing them with readers like you. For an independent author, the hardest part isn't writing the book. It's reaching people who might enjoy it. If you liked this one, a rating — or a short review, even just a line or two — genuinely helps other readers find it.

Scan to leave a rating or review for
What Was Written

Thank you for reading.

www.ingramcontent.com/pod-product-compliance
Lightning Source LLC
LaVergne TN
LVHW020654110826
845149LV00012B/2002

9781997984030